THE
FOREIGNER'S
CONFESSION

THE FOREIGNER'S CONFESSION

LYA BADGLEY

LURE  PRESS

Published by Lure Press, Snohomish, Washington
www.lyabadgley.com

Edited and designed by Girl Friday Productions
www.girlfridayproductions.com

Cover design: Emily Weigel
Book development editor: Sara Spees Addicott
Image credits: cover © Shutterstock/Nataliia Kucherenko; Shutterstock/SantaLiza; Shutterstock/Luciano Mortula - LGM

ISBN (paperback): 978-1-7378265-0-7
ISBN (ebook): 978-1-7378265-1-4

Library of Congress Control Number: 2021920639

This book is dedicated to Aleksandar Babić, who challenges and supports me every day. He first told me the tale of Natasha Garmatjuk, the Belgrade socialite who became the initial seed of the story. And, of course, to Izabel Babić, the best thing we ever did.

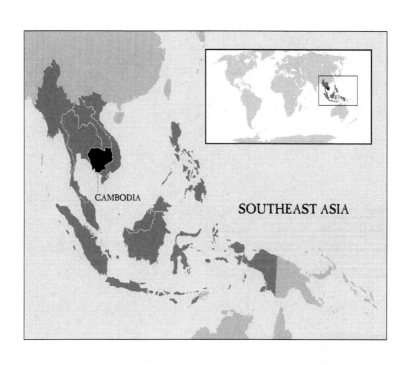

CAMBODIA

SOUTHEAST ASIA

AUTHOR'S NOTE

Born in Yangon, Myanmar, I lived many years in Southeast Asia, moving to Phnom Penh, Cambodia, in 1992, where I worked as director of the Cornell University Archival Project at Tuol Sleng Museum of Genocide. The goal was to film, preserve, and catalog all extant materials of the former Khmer Rouge prison.

I worked every day beside dedicated Cambodian colleagues microfilming salvaged propaganda booklets, training manuals, and of course, the prisoner confessions. I touched and held the actual documents—typed folders and smudged notebooks and boxes of crumbling photographic negatives—as they shared their personal stories of incredible loss and pain.

The experience took me by the heels and shook me upside down, changing everything forever. Bearing witness to the humanity, as well as the evil, of which human beings are capable was more than profound. I learned each of us holds the potential to do unimaginable things given the right set of circumstances. My story is an effort to reconcile that understanding.

I'm immensely proud that those reels of microfilm shot under difficult conditions became evidence in the crimes-against-humanity trials of prominent Khmer Rouge leaders and will remain preserved and available for posterity.

This novel is a work of fiction inspired by historical events. Please excuse the timeline liberties taken with the 1993 Cambodian general elections and the Pchum Ben holiday in order to enhance the plot. Actual people inspired some characters, but everything within the story comes from my own imagination, and any mistakes are mine alone.

In this era of cultural-appropriation awareness, it's critically important to be sensitive and respectful of the voices that inhabit our stories. We must strive to tell our tales from a foundation of authenticity and truth. I did my best to represent the grandeur and despair I witnessed. Part of me will always remain in Cambodia.

Though I don't have an amputation, I was diagnosed with multiple sclerosis in 1987 and live with the challenges related to that disease. I've tried to be true to the daily obstacles associated with "disability." Choosing to survive and thrive without fear is a difficult but exhilarating choice.

PART ONE

CHAPTER ONE

EMILY 1993

Pochentong International Airport
Phnom Penh, Cambodia

Emily Mclean exited the Air France Airbus A320 and balanced precariously at the top of the narrow boarding stair. Fierce tropical heat slammed against her. Welcome to Cambodia, indeed.

Positioning her body sideways, with one hand on the sizzling aluminum railing and the other clutching the handle of a heavy case, she began to clump down the steep staircase one slow step at a time. Swing, set, balance. Repeat. She disregarded the impatient passengers behind her, concentrating instead on not plunging down the steps. Emily was accustomed to such glares and, as a rule, ignored them. She was exhausted and in more pain than usual.

The stream of travelers headed toward a small building in the distance. Emily limped along, struggling to keep up. Could she make it that far? The tarmac shimmered in the sun, and she felt her shoes stick. She passed through an entry flanked by two armed soldiers cradling machine guns. Slouched in the shade, they resembled teenagers in their baggy dark-green uniforms. In both French and Khmer, a faded sign announced *Immigration*. The line for foreigners was long, and when she finally reached the counter, the official, an unsmiling chunk of a man, muttered something unintelligible.

"I don't understand. Do you speak English?"

"Visa no good," he said gruffly, dismissing her with a wave.

"What do you mean? I got it in Bangkok at the Cambodian embassy; they assured me everything was in order!"

"Slip him some money," hissed a French businessman waiting behind her.

"Really?" She pivoted to face the man.

"Cost of doing business in Asia." He shrugged his shoulders.

Shaking her head, Emily opened her purse, pulled out a twenty, and handed it to the official. He pocketed the money with a grunt and stamped her passport, barely glancing at the full-page visa within. *"Allez, allez."* He shooed her away.

An ancient-looking man, in shorts and a T-shirt, grabbed the case from her hand and took off, surprisingly spry. She hobbled after him, leg yelping. The arrivals hall was small and crowded with a scrum of jostling people. Sweat ran down her back as she pushed strangers aside, trying to keep sight of the man and her case. Relief washed through her when she spotted a young Cambodian man wearing dark-blue slacks and a crisp white dress shirt, holding a sign with her name.

"That man took my bag!" she called out. "Stop him!"

The young man put out a hand to halt the old porter. "Don't worry, he only wants to help with your luggage. Welcome to Cambodia, Madame Mclean," he said. "My name is Sovannarith, but you can call me Sonny."

"Hello, Sonny, I'm Emily," she wearily replied. "And please, tell him to be careful with that—it's valuable."

With all her baggage collected, they followed the sinewy man out to a white Toyota Land Cruiser waiting near the entrance—UNTAC printed on the side in bright blue lettering. Energy drained, Emily had trouble balancing to reach up to the high seat. Noticing her predicament, the old man held out his arm for support. Pushing down on his shoulder, she hoisted herself up, swinging her left leg into the cab, weight on her right. His eyes widened in surprise.

"*Soumsavkhum lokasrei*," he said, hands together in a prayer position. "Welcome, madame."

Once settled, Emily pulled the door shut with a satisfying thud and wiped the perspiration from her face with a corner of her blouse. Sounding the horn and using the vehicle's tank-like size as a weapon, Sonny maneuvered through the traffic and onto the highway leading to the capital. Removed from the jarring chaos of the airport and floating high above the pothole-filled road, Emily took a deep breath. The earth along the shoulder was dark red, and a chill passed through her that had nothing to do with the full-blast air-conditioning. *Like blood.* She shuddered.

"Have you been to Cambodia before?" Sonny asked.

"No, I haven't done much traveling outside the US, only to Canada and Mexico."

As she'd planned her trip, Emily never doubted her decision to come to war-torn Cambodia. The logistics of getting visas and up-to-date shots and deciding whether to take the recommended malaria medication were appreciated diversions. She enjoyed the shocked voices of her former colleagues at the law office where she'd worked before the accident. She was in control again after months of weakness during her convalescence. The most difficult part had been explaining the trip to her parents.

Gripping the steering wheel to maneuver over the uneven roadway, Sonny said, "I've been back for a while after many years in California. I love living here." He swerved abruptly to dodge a slow-moving sedan. "You will, too, I'm sure."

Dense traffic slowed their progress as they reached the outskirts of the city. A child, no older than six, shouted up at her to purchase a newspaper with flowing Khmer script. Just beyond, two women squatted in the dirt, haggling over a mound of dusty chili peppers. A motorcycle, an entire family of four piled onboard, passed on the right, narrowly missing them. Sonny sounded the horn in long bursts.

Two- and three-story structures lined the road. Ground floor businesses had iron security gates pulled open to the sidewalk, with terraced apartments above. People streamed everywhere, smiling and lively. With no apparent traffic laws, Sonny navigated through a swarming mosquito cloud of motorcycles. At an old art deco market, vendors spilled into side streets with a plethora of wares. Emily held on to the door handle with white-knuckled fingers.

"I guess Phnom Penh traffic does take some getting used to," Sonny said with a glance at Emily's tense posture. "When I first returned, I was nervous, but you become accustomed. The key is to never come to a complete stop."

"I'm not sure how reassuring that is," Emily said, silently vowing to never drive.

Leaving the busy commercial district, they passed into a lovely residential area of mature trees and wide boulevards. Two monks in dark-red robes sauntered along the median, oblivious to traffic. Gracious villas peeked from behind tall walls.

"We are near the Royal Palace. I will show you one day. At the end of this boulevard, you can see the hill of Phnom, the namesake of the city. The Tonlé Sap River is close by." He pointed to a crumbling, moss-covered pagoda on the top of a small rise. The stone structure melted into the surrounding junglelike greenery.

Sonny turned into a walled compound with a rustic barbed-wire gate pushed to the side. He stopped before a shabby two-story villa. Broken shutters dangled from rusty hinges. Magenta bougainvillea poured down the sides of the faded-yellow stucco walls, competing with ribbons of black mildew. Dark-green tamarind trees and a blossoming jacaranda shaded the bare-earth yard, where a young boy, sweeping dry leaves and purple flowers, stopped to gawk at their arrival. A tiny concrete box of a building stood to the left, a hand-painted wooden sign above the door—Survivors Assistance Foundation Headquarters.

Stiff from the long ride, Emily swung out of the Land Cruiser, leg zinging. She took in the decrepit house, the wire barricade, and the garagelike office of the agency. *This can't be it?*

"It's not much," Sonny said, registering her disappointment. "But, as you know, Cambodia is still in recovery from decades of war. There's a shortage of modern commercial amenities; we do what we can with a limited budget. Please come this way. My aunt will bring us something cool to drink."

Sharp shards of multicolored broken bottles, embedded in the top of the wall, flashed in the sun, both pretty and vicious. "Why is glass on the walls?" Emily asked.

"It's to keep thieves away." Sonny unlocked the door of the garage. "The poor are desperate here."

A pair of small dogs ran out of the front door, then barked and nipped at Emily's ankles.

"Mais non, mauvais toutous! Arretez d'aboyer!" shouted a stout Khmer woman as she struggled down the veranda steps after them. She wore a traditional ankle-length skirt with a billowing floral print top, her graying hair pulled into a knot at her neck. Scooping up a dog under each arm, she said, "Je suis désolée pour les chiens, madame. Bienvenue au Cambodge."

"My aunt apologizes for the dogs and welcomes you," Sonny translated.

"No problem, I can't feel it," Emily said, adding, "*merci beaucoup*," in her rusty high school French.

The SAF office had a single window filled with a wheezing air conditioner. An antique mahogany desk with a modern computer took up most of the room. Two folding chairs and a battered metal filing cabinet occupied the remaining space.

"Please sit, Miss Emily."

She could see Sonny more clearly now. He'd given a youthful impression at the airport, but he now appeared older, with deep worry lines furrowing his forehead. His wavy black hair was swept back, tamed with a glossy pomade. He looked like a man who had forgotten how to smile.

Emily perched on a shaky chair. Outside the door, terracotta pots with pink flowers lined the whitewashed wall. *Hibiscus?* Taking what seemed like her second deep breath since landing, she felt a wave of euphoric exhaustion pour through her limbs, washing away the anxiety of the journey. *Too reckless,* the doctors had advised. But it's easy to be brave with nothing left to lose.

Sonny's aunt entered with a covered tray. "This is my father's sister," Sonny said, introducing her. "Her name is Boupha."

"You have a beautiful home," Emily said.

Putting her hands together, Boupha smiled and retreated to the house.

"Is that a Cambodian greeting?" Emily asked. "The porter at the airport did it, too."

"Yes, the word is *sampeah*. It shows respect." Whisking the checkered scarf off the tray like a magician, Sonny revealed glasses of cold water, a French press with dark coffee, and a plate of white meat on bamboo skewers.

Emily hadn't eaten much on the plane and was suddenly ravenous. "That smells delicious!"

"This is grilled pepper chicken. Try dipping it into the bowl of special white pepper—it is grown in the south of the country. We mix it with fresh lime juice," he said with obvious pride.

Rolling a bit into the mixture and popping the morsel into her mouth, she tasted the heat of the spice combine perfectly with the cool tartness of the citrus. "I think I'll like Cambodian cuisine."

Sonny poured out fragrant coffee. "At least a few nice things still remain. The coffee is also cultivated here." Plucking a piece of the chicken for himself, he asked, "How familiar are you with my country's past?"

"Well, before accepting the position, I researched Cambodia's recent history for an overview of the situation with regard to amputees. But, honestly, I was in high school during the Vietnam War era, and growing up in Montana, Southeast Asia seemed far away." She took a sip of the coffee and smiled again in appreciation.

"What happened here with the Khmer Rouge after the Vietnam War is unknown to most Americans." Sonny tugged at the cuffs of his white shirt. His wrists were dark and elegant in contrast to the cotton. "Our story isn't well known in America, but much of our immediate past is directly tied to the United States' strategy for the region. We still remain a pawn in the global superpower chess game."

"Why don't we know more about it?"

"Well, truthfully, I think Americans are indifferent to the world around them. You believe your politicians when they spread misinformation."

Bewildered by the tone, Emily set her coffee cup into the saucer with a clatter. "What do you mean?"

"Forty years of war ordnance is plowed deeply into our rice fields, just waiting for unlucky farmers to find. Thanks to American bombs, Cambodia has more amputees than any other country."

Stung by Sonny's anti-American sentiment, she said, "Well, I can't answer for US policies, and I may not know all the details of Cambodia's past, but I do know something about amputees." She pulled up the right leg of her jeans to reveal a prosthetic lower leg and foot.

"Apologies, Emily. I sometimes preach." Sonny poured the last of the coffee into her cup. "I didn't mean to lump you into the category of lazy Americans. The Survivors Assistance Foundation is very important to me, my chance to give back to my homeland. Though, to be honest, it's been a struggle. You're here to help and I'm grateful."

She leaned forward on the shaky chair. "What are the main issues?" She'd drafted thousands of contracts and sat through a hundred or more mediations in her career as a corporate attorney. How different could it be here? She didn't trust much about herself these days, but she wasn't afraid of this. She understood law, and what she didn't understand she knew how to learn.

Sonny stood and faced the laboring AC unit. His russet skin glistened with sweat, even in the air-conditioned office. "You must understand, Emily, though the war officially ended fourteen years ago, it still continues. Our fundamental civic infrastructure is shattered. Our people are, as well. Each person alive today in Cambodia is damaged in some way. Whether you can see it or not."

Is he warning me? she wondered.

He unlocked the metal cabinet and pulled out a file containing Emily's original SAF application, a small photograph paper-clipped to the corner, and a copy of her passport. Leaning over the beautiful old desk, they finalized the necessary work-visa paperwork for the Ministry of the Interior. When she stepped into the encompassing bear hug of Southeast Asian humidity, Emily staggered; it felt like the hot air could burn her lungs.

Before climbing back into the cruiser she glanced down at her fiberglass prosthesis and up at the wall embedded with broken pieces of glass. She remembered other glass, in another place, scattered across a nighttime highway.

She knew about damage, seen and unseen.

CHAPTER TWO

MILIJANA 1977

S21 Prison
Phnom Penh, Cambodia

Someone shrieks nearby, a long-drawn-out wail with an inhuman shrillness—impossible to determine if it is a man or a woman. The horrible noise stops. In the ominous silence that follows I hear a child crying, young, by the sound of her sobbing. Is she one of my daughters? It could be little Rachana. I'm physically ill with distress for my family, yet the rage is stronger. Is my trembling from fury or fear? How dare they bring *me* to this place?

I'm in a huge empty room, hungrier than I've ever been, sitting cross-legged on a hard floor of dirty orange and white tiles, a *cahier* school notebook propped on my lap. How do I fill its pages? What belongs in this "confession" they demand? The paper is cheap and coarse and might disintegrate with the humidity and heat. The questionnaire is in Cambodian, which I speak but can't read. The guard who brought me here, dressed in the black pajama uniform favored by most Khmer Rouge, sits on a wooden chair. I begin, but the writing is laborious. The pencil in my hand slips with sweat. I'm barely able to hold on—it's only a few centimeters long and needs to be sharpened. I write.

Name: Comrade Milijana Petrova
Date: April 9, 1977
Born: Belgrade, Serbia, 1938
Parents: Ana & Aleksandar Petrova
Marital Status: Married, Rainsey Sisowath
Children: Daevy, born 1970; Rachana, born 1975
Affiliation: COMMUNIST

The guard squats down and leans far over my shoulder to examine my words. His body odor is sharp, his breath stale and tinged with garlic. The thought of food makes my gut clench. For several days I've eaten nothing more than a thin soup made with weeds and several kernels of rice. This morning a purple petal floated in my spoon. How did a blossom survive in the massive caldron? I remember flowering magenta bougainvillea clambering up the front of our Phnom Penh villa, bright-blue sky glowing. I imagine the petal now, swimming in my stomach, dissolving into my blood. This is a terrible mistake.

He is satisfied, though I doubt he can read. He is young, like all the guards here, with the heavy square face and dark complexion of the rural Khmer. More boy than man. He moves back to his chair in the corner and barks at me to continue. I rub my palms against the rough homespun of the *sampot* sarong they gave me when we arrived. The black dye colors my skin. I must write in French. I am to confess my crimes. What crimes? Of what am I guilty, other than my own stupidity?

A high-ranking cadre officer enters the room. He brings the fragrance of imported cigarettes. His black pajamas fit him well, without the baggy slouching of the threadbare uniforms worn by most of the soldiers. His red-and-white-checked *krama* scarf is clean and neatly wrapped around his neck like a dandy's ascot. He wears black-framed eyeglasses. The young guard snaps to attention and scuttles from the room. As he leaves, the officer demands another chair. I know this man!

CHAPTER THREE

EMILY 1993

It came to Emily, as it always did, in the hours before dawn. In the dream, she wakes to find herself lying on her back, water falling on her face. It is night. There is only the sound of the rain. Suddenly, grinding pain envelops her. Wet asphalt is cold and hard under her back. *Steven?* A glittering galaxy of broken glass is strewn along the road.

She woke with a gasp, air conditioner throbbing. It took a moment to know where she was. The past's familiar weight pressed down on her chest. She struggled to move, forced herself up. A dim illumination showed under the door—someone else was already up—5:00 a.m., according to her travel clock. *Could she do this?*

Reaching for the lamp, she flooded the room with light, replacing the shiny black road. A wooden desk matched the bedside table. A cream-and-blue bedspread of hand-woven cotton in a traditional ikat pattern stretched across the bottom of the bed.

She swung her legs over the side, her right ending below her knee in a tapered tip, now smoother after the second surgery. She pulled on a socklike liner and then tugged on the silicone sleeve, working to smooth any wrinkles. After grabbing her new plastic-and-titanium prosthesis with its waterproof, slip-resistant sneaker, she slid it onto her leg, listening for the click that told her the pin was securely in the socket. Putting on the new device was as easy as putting on a boot.

White tiles covered the small bathroom with an open shower in the corner. She splashed water over her face before looking at her reflection in the mirror. Her mother said she was pretty in an old-fashioned, Doris Day kind of way, with her cornflower-blue eyes, clear complexion, and wavy blond hair. The haunted expression of recent months had faded, yet her eyes were red. *Steven!* She wanted to tear the sink from the wall.

The main room was illuminated with overhead fluorescent lights. The sterile feeling of the boxlike room contrasted with its opulent furnishings—a thick rose-colored carpet and various pieces of dark French-colonial antiques. A massive oil painting of a pastoral European landscape in an ornate gilded frame was propped against the wall adjacent to a cabinet containing a collection of glazed opium pipes and the stone head of an ancient Khmer king. The room's overall effect was that of a 1930s boudoir. The silhouette of a slim woman in a thin kimono stood motionless on the outdoor terrace. Hearing Emily, she deftly flicked her cigarette and entered the room.

"Bonjour! Did I wake you?" She spoke with a heavy French accent.

"No, I'm jet-lagged, I think," said Emily. "You must be my new housemate?"

"Where are my manners? Yes, I'm Yvette Morceau, *enchantée.*"

The woman moved close, put her fingertips on Emily's shoulders, and kissed each cheek. She looked deeply into Emily's eyes for a long moment. The scent of sandalwood and cigarette smoke swirled around them both. Emily felt a flash of uneasiness as she submitted to the stare. Yvette's long dark hair tumbled around her neck, her ivory skin tone offset by the blue silk of her kimono.

"I apologize I couldn't be here to welcome you last evening. I had a late meeting." She stepped back.

"I fell asleep early. I've never traveled so far before. It seemed like it took a week. Thank you for leaving me some supper."

"Sometimes it can seem like we're on the other side of the moon, here," Yvette said, with a bitter laugh. "Come and sit—I want to learn all about you. The maid will bring us coffee soon." She gestured to one of the green velvet armchairs.

The two overstuffed chairs faced a small garden. The sliding doors were open to the freshness of the morning and Emily heard the sound of birds waking to the humid dawn. It was pleasant after the cold air-conditioning of her bedroom. Sinking down in the musty seat, she sneezed and wondered if the fabric was moldy.

"Do you mind if I smoke?" Yvette glanced at Emily's new nonslip foot. "Sonny mentioned that you wear a prosthesis. He thinks it will help you relate to SAF's clients."

Emily shrugged. "Do you know Sonny well? He seems like a nice guy."

"Sonny and I have been friends since he arrived. His dedication to SAF is remarkable; we all envy his passion. I was close with his wife."

"He didn't mention he was married," Emily said, surprised.

"Such a sorry story." Yvette adjusted her dressing gown.

"What happened to her?"

"Perhaps it is not my place to say. I'm sure he will tell you when he's ready. There are many sad stories here." Yvette waved a hand, a jeweled ring flashing. "You will probably hear more than you can manage . . . ah, Chan. She's the maid as well as the cook. If you have any washing, leave it on the floor of your bedroom. I prefer to take my breakfast outside before it gets too warm. We'll have papaya with our croissants, shall we?"

The garden was a small patiolike area facing the wall that encircled the property. *More walls,* Emily thought. A banana tree and potted plants created a relaxing oasis. Yvette explained that the house was new, built by their landlady, Thida Noth, who was a wealthy Chinese-Khmer lady with ties to the government.

"Nepotism is the way to accomplish things in Cambodia— like all Asian countries, I suppose." Yvette flipped her hair behind a shoulder. "Thida attends high-level functions and is a personal friend of Prime Minister Hun Sen, yet she and her extended family live crushed together in a single room at the rear with the noisy generator. She is very shrewd, taking the rent money from all us foreigners. The United Nations and their mission here is making millionaires of the lucky ones. Well, I guess they deserve any luck they can find."

"Where are you from, Yvette?"

"From Paris, of course!" Smoke trailed from her newly lit cigarette. "My father is an academic at the Sorbonne. His specialty is Khmer Buddhism. He met my mother here, back in the sixties, as he wandered about Angkor Wat deciphering the stone murals and ogling the *apsaras'* round breasts. A local village girl, my mother worried that the Frenchman didn't have a sun hat, so she sold him one. She's been taking care of him ever since, though she refuses to acknowledge her roots. I didn't know I was half-Cambodian until I was a teenager. And you, Emily?"

"I'm originally from Montana. I lived in Seattle, until this," she said, indicating her leg.

"May I ask what happened?"

"Car crash."

"How horrible for you."

"What do you do here for the United Nations?" Emily changed the subject.

"Well, as you know, UNTAC, the UN's transitional authority, hopes to provide both military and civilian support for free and fair elections." Yvette's kimono slipped open as she crossed her long legs. "I work in the human rights component, the division that provides education—what *are* human rights and so forth. It is truly that basic. Very fundamental for a population traumatized by decades of civil war. Ah, at last she comes. I'm useless without my morning coffee!"

Chan appeared, setting out a French press, a plate of sliced fruit, and a basket of fresh-baked croissants.

Emily reached for a buttery pastry. "I didn't expect to be having such a continental breakfast. I thought it would be rice three times a day."

"One of the residual benefits of French imperialism?" Yvette stubbed out her cigarette on her coffee cup saucer and lit another.

After their alfresco repast and a quick shower, Emily was ready for the first official day at her new job. Wearing a flowy cotton dress, she hoped to be cooler than in her jeans.

"How lovely and fresh you look," observed Yvette. "Now, let's find you a moto. Sonny mentioned that he didn't have a car available, but the local motorbike taxi system is cheap and reliable. There's often one or two waiting on street corners, or you can just put up your hand and wave one down, like the taxis in New York. Will that work for you?" she added, with a glance at Emily's prosthesis.

"We'll find out, won't we?" Emily said, with more enthusiasm than she felt, slinging her bag across her chest.

Yvette introduced her to the watchman, an older man with a shock of white hair wearing a quasi-uniform of indigo shirt and trousers. She said he would open and lock the gate at dusk and dawn. Usually, Emily could ask him to find a ride, but for today, Yvette would show her the ropes.

The house was located in the residential southern Chamkarmon neighborhood of Phnom Penh. New concrete houses were springing up between the stately French-colonial villas, changing the ambiance of the former Garden District. Next to the house was an undeveloped field of tall grass with a small abandoned wooden hut at the center.

"That's the ghost house." Yvette pointed. "Don't walk by it alone after dark!"

Emily couldn't tell if she was serious or joking. Open drains filled with questionable water lined the unpaved road. *It's now or never,* she thought, swinging her leg and hopping across.

Yvette exclaimed in delight as a moto immediately pulled up—conjured out of thin air. Shadowed by a large floppy canvas hat, the driver's face was invisible. Yvette explained in Khmer the location of the SAF office and the price Emily would pay for the ride. The driver nodded once in acknowledgment.

"Well, that's lucky," Yvette said. "These guys bargain like crazy, especially with a foreigner. Here's some local currency—a few thousand riels will be enough."

Sensing her unease about jumping on the back of the small motorcycle in her long dress, Yvette demonstrated how to sit sidesaddle on the seat. "Don't worry! This is how all the ladies do it."

Mimicking Yvette, Emily hoisted herself up. "Is there a helmet?"

Yvette laughed. "You can grab the driver!"

With her head brushing against his hat, Emily put a hand on the man's waist, leaned against his narrow back, and lifted her feet. She was on the other side of the world, getting on a tiny motorbike with a stranger in a country with terrible hospitals, and she wasn't even wearing a helmet. She felt equal parts terror and joyful surrender.

With a jolt, the moto shot forward, and they were off, speeding down the lane. Finding her balance, she leaned as they swerved into the boulevard, weaving into the chaos of Phnom Penh's rush hour traffic. Something tight within her chest loosened and she laughed out loud. It was her first laugh in a long time.

Safely at SAF headquarters, Emily hopped off the seat and dug in her bag to pull out the notes Yvette had given her. The driver lifted his hat as she held out the money, and she saw his face. He was younger than she had expected but had the look of someone who'd had a hard life. Emily remembered Sonny's words about everyone who lived through the Khmer Rouge era having some sort of damage. *What is your damage? Were you a soldier?* The man's gaze was intense; his irises black, the whites yellow and red. *Had he been drinking?* He stared directly at her, his frowning face reminding Emily of a teak mask depicting a devil that her friend had brought back from Bali. A shiver ran through her and she took a stumbling step back. She thrust the money toward him again, but he ignored it, only continued to stare. *Does he hate me because I'm a foreigner? Will they all hate me?*

She pivoted and strode to the gate, still clutching the foreign notes. Looking back over her shoulder, she saw him unmoved, watching.

CHAPTER FOUR

MILIJANA 1977

It is my friend, Son Sen! His heavy eyeglasses are unmistakable. I'm certain he will sort out this mistake. "Comrade," I cry out. "It's you!" I look up at him, filled with hope. I saw him less than a week ago at the screening of the Yugoslav film crew's footage. Brother Number One, Pol Pot himself, had requested my presence.

Son Sen arranges two wooden chairs by the open window at the rear of the room. He politely invites me to sit with him. I relax and expect he will explain this is all an error. He will take us from this horrible place. Outside, I see papaya trees, motionless in the morning heat. The air is cooler near the window, but the humidity is still oppressive.

With his perfect French and Parisian accent, he apologizes for the crudeness of the young guard, shrugging his shoulders and implying that he and I are both somehow allied against that coarseness. The inhuman screaming starts again, but he seems not to notice the horrific sound. My heart hammers.

We sit facing one another, our knees almost touching. I set the school cahier and pencil in my lap. My eyes follow the path of several ants as they cross a cream-colored tile near my bare toes. They stop at a black smudge. A fly buzzes in anger at the interruption and then settles. I realize the smudge is a small puddle of blood and my eyes widen in shock. Son Sen is watching me. His fleshy lips are curved, but the smile doesn't reach his eyes behind the thick glasses.

"Do you understand why you are here?" he asks.

"I'm not sure where I am," I honestly reply.

"You are in S21, a prison for counterrevolutionary traitors."

With a horrifying jolt, I recall the whispers about this place.

Pointing at the notebook in my hands, he states, "You will write your confession in the format of a political biography."

I am confused and stutter a stream of questions. "What is the nature of my crime? You know me, comrade. Surely my past proves my commitment to our cause, to the revolution? Where is my husband, Rainsey? And our children? Does the king know I am here?" The howling abruptly halts. My voice fades to fearful silence in the room.

His face like a mask, he remains indifferent to my entreaties. Towering above me, he slaps me across the face and I fall from the chair.

"You must be complete and honest in confessing your counterrevolutionary crimes." His voice spits with hatred. "If you do not comply, you will receive the same treatment as the other prisoners." The sting of the slap turns to numbness as he hovers above me. "I will personally be reviewing your words. I will know if you are spreading lies. You will be punished. Your daughters were born with the same bourgeois stain as you. They are also guilty by reason of birth."

My bile rises and I think I will vomit my meager breakfast. "They're just babies!" I scream as Son Sen leaves the room without a backward glance.

The guard returns and commands me to continue with the notebook. He gestures with his foot as if he might kick me where I lie. *Where do I begin?* As long as I write, I remain alive. I decide to record more than just facts. I will relay my story. A memoir of guilt and stupidity to share with any survivors of this social experiment gone terribly wrong. I will write for my daughters, may they still live.

I will write this as a prayer to the god in whom I never believed.

CHAPTER FIVE

EMILY 1993

The driver with the floppy hat waited every morning. He now accepted payment, but there was still something odd about him. Sonny wasn't concerned. The man was normal enough, and he seemed grateful to have a regular fare. Emily chalked it up as another mystery in a mysterious land, feeling glad she didn't need to stand in the hot sun trying to flag down a ride.

The morning of her first candidate interview, she was working in the sweltering heat of the office, attempting to tame the contents of the chaotic metal cabinet. It had no consistent filing method, so trying to find anything was like digging through the mind of a madman. The generator was dead again and she was dripping with sweat when she heard a man's voice. Stepping outside, she saw a one-legged young man arrive in the compound balanced on the back of a motorbike. He held his crutch like the lance of a medieval knight.

"Bonjour! *Susaday!* Good morning! Sam come!" In his early twenties, he was handsome, with a long face, mahogany complexion, and short black hair. He wore faded khaki shorts, a T-shirt, and a tattered dark-green army jacket. His clothing was old but clean.

"Welcome, Sam." Sonny walked down the veranda steps. "Would you like a coffee? Come meet Madame Emily."

In an effort to catch a cool breeze, they sat with their drinks under the jacaranda tree. Sonny described how he'd first met Sam at Happy Herb Pizza.

"Happy Herb?" Emily asked in disbelief as she shook out her hair. It *was* cooler outside.

"Yes, indeed. *Herb* being the key ingredient to the restaurant's success."

"Marijuana?" she confirmed.

"Yes, madame," Sam said. "The people like very much. Eat too much!"

"Cambodia traditionally uses marijuana as a condiment," Sonny said. "But regardless, the pizza is excellent. I developed a taste for it during my years in the States. Though I don't go for the drug, of course. Sam stood out from the rest, and I thought he might be a suitable candidate for SAF."

Emily looked from Sam to Sonny as she sipped from her cup. "Do you work there, Sam?" She wondered how a one-legged man could wait on tables.

"Yes, I work." The young man was mesmerized by Emily's blond curls. "Much work. Five maybe six restaurant I work."

"Working is one way to describe it. He makes his living panhandling at the places frequented by expats," Sonny said.

Emily shifted in her chair and her skirt hiked up to reveal her prosthesis. "You no leg like me!" Sam said.

"That's right. I'm like you." She smiled. "Would you like a new leg like mine?"

Sam thought for a moment. "No, thank you, madame. Good leg no money. I need money." He indicated the hand-made crutch lying on the ground beside his chair. "Make people sad. Poor man no leg. More money for me and family."

She watched Sonny for clues about how to proceed. How could this young man not want to better his life?

"Let's learn more about you." Sonny opened a blank folder and pulled out an application form. "Where were you born, Sam?"

"My family farmer Takeo Province. Come Phnom Penh after I step on *krob min* play football."

"How old were you?" Emily imagined the terrible scene—a young child just wanting to have fun playing soccer and instead triggering a bomb.

"It's common for children to tread on the mines," Sonny said. Emily was beginning to be annoyed by his pontificating tone.

"Sam maybe ten?" His bright eyes glistened.

"Heartbreaking." Emily shifted again to relieve the spot where her prosthesis sleeve chafed. The climate wasn't friendly to tender skin.

"Let's just continue with the background, shall we?" Sonny clicked his pen. "Where is your home now?"

"Me, *yeay*, live near trash dump. Pa kill Pol Pot time. *Mak* sick, die here after come for leg. Hospital help me but leg gone. Now only me, *pahoun proh*, and *yeay* together." He leaned forward in his seat, putting his elbow on the part of his leg that ended high above his knee. The scarring was extensive and rough-textured.

His words evoked Emily's wrenching months of multiple surgeries and physical therapy. She had had a modern hospital and the aid of her family. Both Sam's parents were dead, and he had only his grandmother to support him and his little brother. *How did he do it, here?* She was keenly aware of the place where her own body ended and the artificial one began.

"I very sick long time. No money for doctor. Yeay get lucky money from *barang* or I die." His hands trembled as he wiped at his eyes.

"We have to help him." Emily knew the dedication it took to come back from such a traumatic injury. After her accident, she hadn't thought she had the will to do the terrible physical therapy work. She had to relearn her balance, cope with pain and depression, and perhaps the most difficult, come to terms with her new identity. In an instant, she had gone from being an acknowledged professional starting a new family with the man she loved, to being a despondent widow with a titanium leg.

"Emily." She cringed at Sonny's tone. "Many of these people share horrific stories, there's no doubt about that. But some are skilled at manipulating foreigners to get as much as they can from them. We have to be careful about investing in someone who might not commit to our protocol for rehabilitation."

"These people?" Emily repeated. "This is a man who needs our help."

Sam looked back and forth between them, not following all the meaning but understanding there was some dispute.

Sonny continued, ignoring Emily's frustration. "Where do you earn income besides outside Happy Herb?"

"I get money from barang!" Sam said with pride. "Work many restaurant, I nice with owner, give some money, so no police come to me like other, who pay bribe. I smart man. Work hard."

"Indiscriminate begging," Sonny muttered under his breath as his pen scratched the paper.

"I make good money help yeay and pahoun proh. Sometime pay for school for pahoun proh. Sometime not. Little brother work pick trash and find things sell. He very smart, too."

Emily considered Sam's words and the life he lived, so different from her own. "I think you're quite brave."

"Yes!" He understood the sentiment, if not the entirety of what she said.

A breeze arrived as dark clouds gathered at the edges of the sky and the temperature dropped a couple degrees. Several fragrant purple blossoms tumbled down. Emily took one and held it tenderly in her palm, the light fragrance making her smile. The young man mirrored her expression.

"More coffee?" she asked him.

Speaking in Khmer, Sonny explained the benefits of having a modern prosthesis and how it could change his life for the better. But Sam didn't budge, convinced that he wouldn't be able to provide for his family if he accepted help from SAF.

Sam rose to leave, using the crutch to gracefully push himself up on one leg. "*Arkoun chraen,*" he said with a deep sampeah. "Thank you, madame. Sam go now."

Shaking his hand in the Western style, Emily said, "It was a pleasure to meet you." She was disappointed they couldn't help him; his story had touched her heart. "Goodbye, Lancelot," she whispered as he rode away on the waiting moto like a jousting knight.

"I generally prefer to accept amputees from the countryside who are still working as farmers." Sonny crossed his arms. "I don't want to encourage a rural exodus to the cities, and I haven't had a chance to travel to the provinces for months. Sam looked like a potential candidate." With a sigh, he added, "I think our donors would have liked him." He slipped the form into its folder.

They lingered in the coolness as Sonny's aunt joined them with a tray of fresh lime juice. *"Merci beaucoup,"* said Emily to the old woman. "This is my favorite beverage—sweet and salty together." After a deep drink, she turned to Sonny. "I hope I'm not intruding, but Yvette mentioned that you had been married. Do you have any children?"

Sonny's face shut tight. She'd made a mistake.

"No. No children." He stared past her, clicking his pen with so much force it broke in two. Blue ink smeared his fingers. "That's enough for today. We'll start again in the morning." He retreated to his office, shutting the door.

Boupha's eyes followed him, and then she got up to take the cups and glasses back to the house. *"Au revoir, madame."*

Emily picked up the now bruised jacaranda flower lying on the table. *We've all lost pieces of ourselves,* she thought, reminding herself she didn't own the sole right to despair.

That evening, back at the apartment, Yvette noted Emily's quiet mood. "It's time to have some fun. You must experience Phnom Penh's crazy nightlife. I want to introduce you to some friends."

Emily felt a welcome sense of anticipation as they beautified themselves with summer dresses and lipstick and headed out into the night. Sitting at the wheel of her UN Land Cruiser, Yvette explained that the city had a largely ignored nighttime curfew. She carried spare cigarettes to entice any machine-gun–toting soldiers into letting them pass quickly through the checkpoints.

The first such stop was at the end of their lane. Rolled barbed wire stretched across the center of the road. Yvette reached out the window with a cigarette between her slim fingers. A young soldier in green fatigues approached the vehicle and shined a flashlight into the interior. With a grin, he called out to his friends squatting in the shadows.

"What is he saying?" Emily asked.

"Pretty barang women. He is calling us the Cambodian term for foreigners from the West. He's using it as an insult."

The man leaned into the window, his AK-47 pressed against his body. The red-and-white insignia of Angkor Wat's towers was on his shoulder. He was chewing raw garlic and the smell instantly made Emily nauseated. Two others sauntered up to Emily's side.

One grizzled man with a black-toothed smile said, "Bonsoir, mademoiselles. Où allez-vous ce soir?"

"Cigarette . . . ?" asked the leering teenager as he caressed his rifle.

"Ou de l'argent? One dollar?" Laughed the older one as he spewed his light in Emily's face.

"Chkaout!" hissed Yvette as she thrust a cigarette at the garlic-chewing soldier. "Ahoeuy yeung toweh meuh. Leah senhi!" The men jumped back as she sped forward and around the barricade.

Emily twisted to watch the men laugh and wave and fade back into the darkness. "What did you say?"

"I told them to fuck off and let us go," Yvette fumed. "It's really just a game for them."

"Fun game . . . with automatic rifles?"

"Don't worry, my friend, we will be fine. Settle in—there may be several checkpoints to get through. Managing curfew is an art form in this city."

CHAPTER SIX

MILIJANA 1977

Again I am pushed and prodded from my cell, blinded by the rancid hood. The heat is a heavy cloak. As I stumble on concrete steps, I hear frogs—the monsoon will come soon. The stifling covering is removed with a harsh tug. It is a smaller room than yesterday.

There are three *santebal* demons watching me. A trinity of secret police. One is the Interrogator. A wolf stalking his dinner. He cradles a metal rod in his arms. He kicks my stomach, causing me to retch on the tiles. He shouts doctrine from a pamphlet, his spittle spraying in the shower of words. The propaganda is familiar, though much rougher than the

Marxist-Leninist dogma I know well. I may have helped craft some of it and listen for my voice in the bulletlike fusillade of sentences. Do they know who I am?

The Guard leans in the doorway, observing me closely. He moves to grab my arm, pulling me up from the floor. "Ha! A princess feels pain like the rest of us," he says. "Look, the barang is so white." He pinches my exposed thigh, twisting and bruising the flesh.

The third man is the most terrifying. He is the Watcher. Not for me, but for the Guard and the Interrogator. *What might they do to me without his presence?*

The Interrogator intervenes by handing me a new pencil. It is sharp. "Get to work," he screams into my ear. "Confess!"

I briefly consider sinking it into his eye. He reads aloud and now I recognize my own words, come back to taunt me. *How did this all begin? How far back do I go . . . ?* I start to write.

I joined the Communist Party in 1950 . . .

I wanted to anger my parents and interest a boy at school. A young girl's way to be independent, to set herself apart, or so I thought at the time. I must have been about fourteen and naive. Ana and Aleksandar Petrova had escaped the Bolsheviks as children—fleeing Russia to Belgrade, Serbia, in what would later become Yugoslavia. They hated all things remotely communist, and loved their ancestral portraits, ornate wallpaper, and oversize furniture, all trappings of their beloved bourgeois life.

One afternoon, after finding a battered copy of *Das Kapital* in my schoolbag, my father locked me in my room for a full day while my mother wept in the sitting room.

"You've betrayed our family!" he shouted through the door.

"How dare you go through my things?" I screamed back. "You *do* know Yugoslavia *is* a communist country?" He forced me to burn the offending book in the stove, black smoke billowing from the chimney.

They decided I would follow my brother to Sorbonne University. He was studying law and I would study literature. Like most middle-class Serbs, my parents looked to France for culture and education, and they hoped the experience would help civilize my unacceptable tendencies. They were wrong.

I was already fluent in French and determined to fully exploit my new independence. Meeting the artist Jacques Morel in a left-bank café ensured that I did.

France in the 1950s was an exciting place to be; ideas swirled and flowed like a mighty ocean in which I swam. Postwar Paris was the thinking capital of the world. My girlfriends and I played at intellectualism, trying on different principles as if donning new dresses. We emptied carafes of cheap red wine as we haunted the cafés and nightclubs until daybreak. The Latin Quarter was the focal point of the modern world emerging from the ruins of World War II. We venerated Jean Paul Sartre and Albert Camus as vanguard thought generals leading the next generation of artists, writers, and musicians re-creating what it meant to be young and alive. Live jazz became our soundtrack, existentialism our dogma, and equality of the sexes our new norm.

I first met Jacques one evening after drinking far too much. He was an abstract painter, infamous for his romantic conquests. He was older than my usual group but still handsome, with his linseed-oil-soaked clothes and tattered beret. When he sat down uninvited at our table I was flattered. He commenced to challenge us about the role of women in the coming world order.

"Females are just for fucking and procreation," he said.

"What cave did you crawl out from?" I demanded.

We argued bitterly, all the way to his bed in the nearby hotel where he lived. I soon learned his beliefs were the polar opposite—as a committed communist, he accepted the equality of men and women. He knew I would only sleep with him if he engaged my mind. He took my virginity but left me the gift of philosophy and a deep desire to better the world.

I continue writing.

> *I joined to defeat the capitalist ideology of my
> class . . .*

A flash of lightning illuminates the page and the three watching men. Their scowling faces are imprinted on my retinas. I clutch my little pencil, waiting for the thunder that is sure to come. How ignorant to think I could change this world. What a dangerous fool I've been. In the dim light, I see purple bruises covering my arms and thighs like South Sea tattoos— no pretty petals in my soup today.

The Guard. The Interrogator. The Watcher.

The Interrogator is grinning as he walks toward me, spinning his metal rod.

CHAPTER SEVEN

SONNY 1993

Sonny sat in the swelter of his small office, sweat dripping into his eyes. City power out again, and there was still no cash to repair the generator. A financial spreadsheet lay before him on the scarred mahogany desk. There was no money to fix that, either. Survivors Assistance Foundation had skidded into the red. He'd hoped bringing Emily on board would placate the donors and the dollars would cascade back. But so far, the empty bank account confirmed his plan hadn't worked.

※ ※ ※

In 1978, Sonny, his mother, and his younger sister landed in Southern California like thrown-away coats. Their church sponsors had no idea how to support the grieving refugee family broken by war in a country they couldn't find on a map. Green bean and tuna casseroles, unfamiliar food cooked and donated by ladies of the church, rotted in the refrigerator.

"Rice?" Sonny managed to ask with the help of an old Khmer-English dictionary.

"Of course, sweetie," said the pastor's wife. "I'll pick up some Uncle Ben's instant for my next visit."

One night, looking down at the gelatinous substance the foreign lady insisted was rice, he announced, "I want to go home."

His mother searched his face. "What home?"

"Cambodia. Kampuchea."

"There is no Cambodia left. It has burned to the ground. Our home is here now. Enough nostalgia for the old days, my son. You are a man, and you must honor your father's legacy."

Sonny's sister tenderly placed another serving on his plate. He looked away, hiding the tears burnishing his face. "This place is a lie," he said, pushing his plate away.

Ten years later, Lisa walked past Sonny during an English composition class at Cal State University in Long Beach. She was the classic California surfer girl, blond, long-limbed, with honey-colored freckles. He now knew a lot about America and the possibilities for a brown man like him. He never understood why she chose him, and he waited every day for the punch line.

"Find a girl of your own people," his mother pleaded.

But each glorious time he entered Lisa's pale body he planted a flag on enemy soil.

Kenneth Roberts was a wealthy LA-based veteran of the Vietnam War. Like many of the donors, he carried residual guilt from the debacle of that era. Sonny met the charismatic man during a Hollywood fund-raiser for a well-known animal shelter. After a few glasses of champagne, Sonny convinced Ken his money might be better spent helping human beings torn apart by land mines rather than lonely pets. The man had an extensive network and SAF was born.

※ ※ ※

But now the donations had dried up. True to form, the easily distracted Americans had lost interest. They wanted *results*. *What were the metrics for success in a place like wounded Cambodia,* Sonny wondered. How many plastic arms and legs stuck onto damaged and defeated men and women would make a difference? How many mangos picked by an armless child? It took time and patience. And money.

Sonny stood in the door of his office. Emily sat outside under the jacaranda tree, transcribing notes from a previous interview. Her gold hair shimmered in the sunlight, and for a brief moment, he thought it was his Lisa. But his wife was gone, like all the promises made by the Americans.

Lisa was dead, murdered by an American land mine, her body blasted into pieces. Her lovely California hair had floated up and back down to land on the shattered windscreen, still attached at the scalp.

Sonny forced the Technicolor memory back into the black-and-white newsreel in which he lived. At his desk, he watched the sweat drip, forming a pattern on the useless spreadsheet. His anger churned.

CHAPTER EIGHT

MILIJANA 1977

The Interrogator with the metal rod stands over me. He taps the rusty end against my cheek—I know he could crush my skull with ease. I clutch my pencil and notebook, searching for the beginning.

I write.

> *I first met Saloth Sar in Paris during the early 1950s . . .*

Many different communist groups sprang up after the war, all determined to better the world. The Cercle Marxiste organization was created by members from Cambodia and Vietnam, both then under the dominion of France. Jacques knew one of the Cambodians and thought I should meet a dedicated adherent to the Marxist-Leninist principles I studied.

I accompanied Jacques one evening to a meeting held in the back room of a left-bank café we frequented. The owner napped at his zinc bar, sleepily waving a hand as we walked down the narrow corridor to a smoky room in the rear. I smiled at several people I recognized from the neighborhood. Three men and a woman, whom I assumed to be Cercle members, sat together. I had never associated with people of Asian descent before.

"*Bonsoir*," I said, seating myself next to a pretty, raven-haired young woman about my age.

"*Bonsoir*," she replied. "*Êtes-vous déjà venez-ici?*"

Charmed by her lovely accent, I shared that it was my first time. She leaned closer to introduce her friends. I did my best to correctly pronounce the syllables, much to everyone's delight, although I was confused by the unusual names. I prophetically promised to learn the Khmer language one day. When I introduced myself as Milijana Petrova, one of the men inquired if I came from Russia. I explained that my parents had come from Russia originally, but we made our home in Belgrade, Yugoslavia.

"*Tako sam srećan što sam vas upoznao!*" he gushed in Serbian. "I'm so happy to know you!" Introducing himself as Saloth Sar, he said he'd passed a summer with a work collective building roads outside of Zagreb. He had enjoyed it so much, he returned the following year and traveled extensively throughout Yugoslavia. He appreciated the hospitality and generous spirit of the people. Delighted to be speaking my mother tongue, I reached out to embrace the man.

An older comrade named Solange called the gathering to order by tapping loudly on her coffee cup with a spoon. We went around the room with introductions. I was warmly welcomed as someone from a homeland that already embraced communist values. Solange then presented one of the Cambodians as our speaker.

Hou Yuon was young like the others but seemed more serious. He was hunched forward in his seat, eager to share his message. His hatred for colonialism became obvious as he spoke about his family's peasant circumstances and life under the domination of the ruling power.

I smiled to myself as he began to speak, enjoying the irony that he was criticizing those same French who had paid for his tuition at the best university in Paris. But his words quickly resonated with my own beliefs, my own despair about countries conquered and overtaken. I was indignant that indigenous people had been enslaved to harvest their own natural resources, that ancient social systems had been decimated and replaced with strictures founded in racism and capitalist economic greed.

I write.

I hated colonialism to the core. I wanted a world of equity and compassion . . .

The Interrogator steps out of the room and I stop for a moment to look around at this wretched prison room so far from that Parisian café. I hope my passion, my commitment, will come through my pencil into my jailer's heart. I see the bloodstains of those who came before me. I see the tattered soldiers who are the remnants of our grand experiment gone so terribly wrong.

Was that evening the embryo of my transformation? Were seeds planted in that smoke-filled back room? I'd been surprised by Hou Yuon's thesis. Most Marxists were industrialists, advocating cooperative farm complexes and modern urbanization. But he felt Cambodia should return to the agrarian lifestyle of the peasant. I felt a deep affinity for him and all the others who believed so passionately in a new society for their home. Peasants held the truth of the land.

Coming, as I did, from a bourgeois background, I worked hard to escape the perceived flaws of my parents' middle-class convictions. I romanticized the lives of villagers, begging my parents to allow me to accompany my best friend when she spent a weekend in the countryside with her grandparents. Mealtimes there were filled with laughter and shared hearty meals made from vegetables and meat grown in their own backyards. I embraced those happy people, many of them illiterate, but knowledgeable in the seasons and the production of food.

After each visit, I would come back to my family's apartment, which was stuffed with the artifacts of our class—religious icons, books, musical instruments—but empty of love. I pretended to be a peasant from the small village I had just left.

I was deeply moved by the young Cambodians from that dingy café. Their lofty aspirations became the future framework for a new nation—Democratic Kampuchea. Saloth Sar, the man who loved my home country, Yugoslavia, became Kampuchea's leader: Pol Pot, Brother Number One.

My stomach growls. What I wouldn't give for a small bite of a ripe purple plum from my friend's fruit tree. I can clearly taste and smell something.

But no, it is sulfur. The monsoon's artillery has arrived.

CHAPTER NINE

EMILY 1993

Located on a side street just off one of the main boulevards, the Gecko Club was a popular nightspot for expats. Emily stood at the entrance of a long narrow room decorated like a Chinese restaurant, with red lanterns and black walls. Mostly male, the patrons were packed against a counter at the back, all vying for the attention of a pretty bartender. Emily remembered another crowded smoky bar from a long time before.

※ ※ ※

Emily first met Steven Wright during her second year of law school at the University of Montana in Missoula. His transfer from NYU had made him a bit of a celebrity. One Saturday night, Emily was pleasantly surprised to see him standing alone with a beer in the Top Hat Lounge.

"It's the new guy!" Emily nudged her friend.

"Go on, go talk to him."

Emily sauntered over to stand next to the good-looking man. "Hey, newbie." She leaned against the bar, brave with two pints of ale. "Missoula must be small after New York."

"Yes, it's different, but I like it here. I think I'm a cowboy at heart," Steven said.

Oh no. Another one of those? Emily met a lot of summer visitors who arrived with foolish fantasies of the Wild West. "We're a lot more than cowboys these days. Guess you need a better guidebook!"

"Perhaps I do. Do lots of people from the East come here expecting John Wayne to ride a horse down Higgins Avenue?"

"Yeah, we get quite a few dude rancheros from New York. You can see them a mile away with their new Stetsons and enormous belt buckles." She took in his preppy, handsome appearance. "You look like you're straight out of Yale or Harvard."

"That would have pleased my folks, but NYU was the right choice at the time. Eventually, Manhattan became too claustrophobic and intense."

"I've never been back East other than a high school field trip to Washington, DC."

"I understand why you wouldn't want to leave. It's beautiful here. When I heard about the program, I thought, *Why not?* Big Sky Country and all that. Are you from here originally, Emily?"

"Born and bred, though my parents are originally from Northern Ireland."

"What are you studying?" He signaled for a round of beers.

"Corporate, I think, but I'm intrigued by family. Though it does seem sad, all that fighting over who gets what." She nodded her thanks for the fresh pint.

"Corporate? I'm doing tax. I guess our paths will cross?"

"I hope so." Emily had smiled.

※ ※ ※

As Emily and Yvette stood in the doorway of the Gecko, several men waved at the Frenchwoman, anxious for her attention. Ignoring them, Yvette returned the wave of an attractive woman seated at a corner table with a burly man in a Green Beret uniform sporting a bandolier of ammunition across his broad chest.

"Beware of Colonel Kurtz," she said. "I don't think I can manage his warrior/poet philosophizing tonight. Let's go sit outside with the journalists."

Three men in the midst of a heated argument, all in filthy green fatigues, stopped talking abruptly as the women headed toward their table.

"Yvette, my beauty!" an older man said in a plummy British accent. "Come sit down if you're looking for a seat away from the lion's den. You are a sight for sore eyes."

The youngest man hopped up and pulled over two chairs. He gave Yvette a lingering kiss on her lips. "I missed you, lovely." He turned to Emily. "Are you new in town? I'm Johnny Lester, with the AP news agency. And that old Brit is Philip Jones, editor of our local English-language newspaper."

"I'm Emily Mclean. Nice to meet you." She sat down, taking in the men's feral appearance. They smelled of sweat and clothing unwashed for weeks.

"How do you do," said Philip. Emily half expected him to bow and kiss her hand; he had a formal old-school quality.

"These are my dear friends," Yvette said. "But beware, they can be very naughty."

An awkward silence ensued as the third man remained quiet, frowning at the interruption. "For fuck's sake, Nick," said Johnny. "Quit being an asshole and say hello. Emily, meet the infamously rude Nick Landrey, aka Gator, American wartime correspondent and freelance stringer. He's called Gator because he was raised in the Louisiana bayous, catching crocs and snakes for dinner, and the jungle is his happy place."

"Shut the fuck up, Johnny. You sound like goddamn bingo balls crashing around in my skull." Nick fumbled with a cigarette and Zippo lighter. "Hello, girls," he said.

"Don't mind Nick," Yvette said. "His bark is worse than his bite."

Emily imagined him wrestling a boa constrictor, and then cooking it over a fire for supper.

Philip picked up the conversation where they had left off. "I accuse you, *mon garçon*, young Johnny! What a fuckup that was. Where was our darling Khmer Rouge when we need a juicy story? You swore the intel coming from Preah Vihear was solid. We drove all that way, in that broken-down jeep of Nick's with no bloody suspension. My spine will never recover!" He waved his drink in Nick's face.

"It was straight-up intel from my best source," Johnny said.

Philip slapped the table. "The African UN peacekeepers stationed there are a complete cock-up! Just the usual pitiful corruption and smuggling. Who gives a shit! Old news! You boys had better find me a real story!"

Emily realized the men were extremely drunk and began to twist in her seat to signal Yvette they should leave. But Yvette was unperturbed, obviously well accustomed to such passionate outbursts from the group.

Nick growled, rising to push his face into Philip's. "How can you expect untrained police from the goddamn dark continent to know how to provide 'free and fair' elections? They don't even have democracy in their own asshole of the world. What the fuck is that to them? They come here, get paid obscene amounts of money in wages from the United Nations tit, and they're supposed to take it seriously? What a fucking joke." He grabbed the half-empty bottle of Stolichnaya and splashed most of it into his glass as he sat down. "This whole thing is one vast publicity stunt thought up by those idiot diplomats in their Manhattan ivory towers."

"Should we just deny what's happening here?" Johnny said. "Ignore the blood-soaked history of those bastards in the jungle? The boogeyman is fucking real, my friend! And he's all around us. Half those moto drivers waiting over there to drive your drunken ass home are Khmer Rouge, and the other half spy for the goddam government CPAF military mafia."

Philip ignored Johnny and shook his fist in Nick's face. "What a bloody racist you are! You don't think the Africans can do what the blasted Americans can?"

Yvette laughed as the men grew louder. Emily noted the bottles—one empty and the second now almost gone. *How much do these guys usually drink?* The bartender appeared with yet another bottle tucked under her arm. She also carried a box of orange juice and two glasses that she plunked down for the women.

"Now, boys!" she said in a motherly tone. "Do I have to call the police?"

"Jules, honey, come sit on my lap." Nick leered.

"No thanks, love, I learned my lesson last time." She laughed but sat on his knee anyway. "Yvette, dearie, is this your new housemate?" The woman was slim, with strawberry-blond hair and an East London accent.

"Yes, this is Emily Mclean. Emily, meet Julia Davies, owner of the Gecko. Everyone in Phnom Penh is in love with her."

"Now that's a laugh. Call me Jules, everyone does." From her perch, she poured drinks for the women and then topped up the journalists. "*Choul mouy*, everyone! I keep everyone drunk, so of course they all love me!"

"Don't sell yourself short," said Philip. "You are the most charming addition to our little *Heart of Darkness* outpost here."

"Ha!" Jules snorted. "Now, Emily, don't let these idiots ruin everything for you with their doom and gloom. They live to speculate and argue and talk, talk, talk. Boys, be nice to Emily, we want her to stay awhile." With a swipe at the table with a dirty rag, she hurried off to attend to other customers. The men ignored the women as they continued their diatribes.

Yvette quickly finished off her vodka and orange and poured another. "How are you doing, Emily?" she asked in her husky voice. "Is it getting any easier?"

Easier? Never having traveled outside the United States, Emily wasn't surprised to be surrounded by differences—the heat, the blast of tropical colors, and people of a different culture—but something much greater than a superficial otherness surrounded the city.

It seemed like a loud, unheard howl engulfed everything she saw, wherever she went. She wouldn't have been surprised if everyone walking down the street just stopped in their tracks, lifted their faces to the sky, and *wailed*. Like in an old movie where, in the middle of a scene, people break into song and dance. But there was no singing here, no dancing. The people all smiled, but there was pain behind their eyes.

Easier than what? she pondered, sitting in the dark on the other side of the world, outside a noisy bar next to drunken, war-crazed men.

A streetlight cast a glow made dim by swirling insects. A cyclo—the old-fashioned bicycle with a wide seat in the front to carry passengers—sat directly behind Yvette. The driver slept with his bare, muscular legs draped over the side. A half dozen moto drivers had parked near the entry, silently smoking and waiting for possible fares. Raucous laughter spilled out every time someone opened the door. The journalists had calmed and their voices were low murmurs.

With a gulp of her drink, Emily said, "I really don't know. Cambodia is so strange. I feel like we could be somewhere in Europe, yet there's this undercurrent I don't understand. Is it violence? Is it fear? I feel like I'm in a movie or a book and I don't know the ending."

"Yes, it is an odd place." Yvette nodded in agreement. "I search for my heritage here; I see it in the faces of the people all around us, yet I can't begin to understand what lives in their hearts. There is a wall of tragedy I can't cross." She took another long drag on her cigarette. "You know, I didn't even smoke before I came here." She pursed her lips and shrugged in that typical French fashion, a gesture that meant nothing and everything. "I hear such terrifying personal histories from the inmates we interview for my work. It's all so much—the past, the threat from the KR, the military—*c'est vraiment extrême*. We are all self-medicating, to some degree." She held up her glass. "Tell me, Emily, how did you lose your leg? You said you were in an accident?"

Emily gulped her sticky drink and then poured in straight vodka. The boxed orange juice was warm and reminded her of cough syrup, but the vodka was working its magic. An army jeep roared by, its headlights illuminating the pale-yellow blossoms of the frangipani tree on the median.

Why is it simpler to speak the truth with strangers? She massaged her residual leg where the socket sock lightly chafed. The familiar pain, the reality of flesh and bone, was a comfort.

"I was in a bad car crash. My husband died."

"Oh no!"

"And I was pregnant." The words began to tumble out as Emily attempted to explain her feelings. "It had been difficult for us—we wondered if I was too old. It took a long time. But the thing of it is, I didn't mind. Not getting pregnant, that is. I had a successful career. But Steven wanted children more than anything. We had tried and tried and then it happened. Later, the doctor worried something might be wrong with the baby. But in the ultrasound the baby was healthy. We were having a daughter. We celebrated with champagne." Emily poured more vodka, and then downed it. "It was my fault."

"*Mon dieu.* It was an accident. Surely you can't blame yourself?"

"You see, I didn't really want to have a baby." *Had she done it on purpose?* Emily had confronted herself for months.

"Oh, *ma douce*, that guilt will be your ruin. You mustn't think that way! You lived—your family did not. It is fate, or God, or karma—who knows? But you are alive and in the good place here. *Regardez* the people all around you. These poor survivors must live with this very same experience. Cambodian or European or American, most of us here are surviving with some sort of terrible secret." Lighting another cigarette, Yvette said, "That's why we drink and take the drugs."

"Drugs?" Johnny lifted his head like an eager puppy and turned to the women. "Well, it's about time someone said something intelligent!" As he stumbled to his feet, the moto drivers started their engines in the hope of a fare. "Come on, comrades, it's time to have some real fun."

"Not for me, mates," Philip said. "My wife will kick me out if I stay away another night."

"You're becoming a boring old fart," Nick said. "Yvette and New Girl, will you come for some exotic debauchery?" He slipped the remaining Stoly bottle into his jacket pocket. "Jules? Jules, where are you? Put this on my tab, my sweet," he shouted out.

"You must owe her the cost of a new jeep with that so-called tab of yours." Johnny laughed over his shoulder as he mounted a motorbike.

"Emily? Will you come with us?" Yvette asked. "I promise that you will forget whatever may be hurting."

Emily looked at the flushed faces of the men, who were clearly in a hurry. She was with interesting people, the kind of "cool kids" club anyone wants to join, but she remained uneasy. Looking out at the frangipani tree illuminated by the single streetlight, she saw the moto driver with the floppy hat waiting to take her home.

"I think I'll pass. Maybe next time." The confession had sucked the air from her lungs. She couldn't reveal the entirety of her guilt, no matter how sympathetic the listener.

CHAPTER TEN

MILIJANA 1977

I think a week has passed, through time is difficult to gauge. Thankfully, they have left me alone for several days. I spend the time in my small bricked cube of a cell envisioning my children. Their soft hair brushing against my cheek, small arms around my neck. I make lists in my mind—favorite flowers, treasured books, delicious dishes. These memories sustain me like food. I dare not think of my husband. The painful guilt of what I did lurks and then leaps to consume.

I brought him back to die. He warned me and I didn't listen. My hubris, my ridiculous commitment to an ideology I could never completely understand. My inability to recognize the signs of madness on a massive scale. Silly, stupid girl, Milijana.

I squat over the ammunition case that serves as my toilet as my bowels empty. I am becoming immune to the stench, to the moans around me. The Guard is coming with his rusty keys. This one is new to me.

"Get up, you barang whore," he shouts as he unlocks my shackles. "You have a special session."

There is no black hood today. *What does that bode?* He ties the rope around my wrists and leads me like an animal out to the walkway and down the steps. For the first time, I can see where I am. A former school, the facility contains several structures. We are in one of two three-story buildings at the bottom of a U shape. An inmate is attempting to wash blood off the stairs by sluicing a bucket of water, but it only spreads the stain. The front of the building appears to be bleeding as the water runs down.

"Hurry," bellows the Guard as I slow down to take in my surroundings.

We walk across a muddy compound where schoolchildren once laughed. A prisoner is standing by the swing where they played. The thought of my own daughters overwhelms me and I stumble. The man's arms are tied behind his back and I watch in horror as he is hoisted up, his screams inhuman as his shoulders dislocate with a horrible popping.

There is a smaller wooden building in the center of the area near the entry gate. A line of about twenty ragged men waits to be admitted. A guard is checking them off a list. One of the men is actually a child. He is crying without sound, great tears making tracks down his sweet, dirty face. Our eyes lock as I am dragged past the group and to another building. The man hanging on the swing goes silent.

The silence grows and presses against my ears as if I'm deep underwater. The Guard's mouth is moving, but I don't hear his words. This is hell. What human heart could create such a place?

I'm dragged up the steps and into a classroom, the chalkboard still on the wall. A school desk is shoved in the corner, where a tall official in a black Khmer Rouge uniform stands. His round, pale face is impassive like a mask.

"Sit!" he barks. "I am Comrade Duch. Today I will interview you personally."

I am untied and pushed into the small desk seat. Duch leans back against the blackboard like he will teach a lesson. The Guard lurks near the door—silhouetted black with daylight behind him. The rain clears and the air begins to steam. Weak from little food and dysentery, I slump in the chair. My mind follows the sun and wanders out the window to hover above the prison yard. With a slap across my face, I am returned to the room. I look down to find the notebook. I open to the place where I had stopped. Someone had taken a red pen and made annotations in the margins. Some of the paragraphs are crossed out, as if a teacher had graded an essay.

"Your confession is overly bourgeois," Duch says. "You must write how you came to join the revolution. What were your reasons? What are your strong points as well as shortcomings? You must continue in the correct manner. Do you understand?"

"I think so," I stammer, afraid I will be beaten again if I admit I don't understand at all.

"Then write properly," he said, then indicated the man in the doorway. "Comrade Touy knows Daevy and little Rachana well."

I'm shocked and begin to tremble. *My children!* I drop the pencil. Touy enters the room and picks it up with a twisted smile.

CHAPTER ELEVEN

EMILY 1993

Emily tried to remember if she had heard Yvette come home during the night. She thought she remembered the heavy crash of the metal gate, but it could have been a residue from her nightmare. She put on her prosthesis and went to listen outside her new roommate's bedroom door. Inside, the AC was running, but otherwise it was silent.

She showered and dressed, looking forward to a day of relaxation before going to Sonny's for dinner. It was time to start reading one of the history books she'd lugged in her overloaded suitcase. There was so much to learn; she wanted to understand what Sonny had said about US policies influencing Cambodia's civil war.

At lunchtime, there was still no sign of Yvette, who was usually an early riser. As Chan served Emily a light meal of noodles topped with a green curry sauce, she asked, "Yvette, *elle ça va?*—Is she okay?"

"*Oui, oui,*" Chan said, though Emily was beginning to think that was the maid's standard answer—regardless of the question.

Later, after several hours plowing through her self-imposed history lesson, Emily headed into the lane to find a ride to Sonny's. The driver with the floppy hat was squatting next to his motorbike. He'd dropped her off the night before and then ridden away without a word. How could he know she would need him today? Did he just sit out there all the time?

"What is your name? Quel est votre nom?" she asked. "Why do you always wait for me?" The man just shrugged. "All right, Mystery Man. Take me to the SAF office."

Emily tossed her curls in the breeze as they glided down busy Achar Mean Boulevard. Humidity made ringlets of her natural waves. Massive colorful advertisements offering computers or photo-processing services fronted multistory shophouses. Medieval-looking bundles of burlap-wrapped charcoal for cooking fires were piled on the street below. The twelfth and the twentieth centuries existed simultaneously.

The historic national election campaign was in full swing—bright banners promoted candidates, some with loudspeakers blaring to further assail the senses. Blue-helmeted United Nations personnel from all over the globe added a multinational dimension. The moto driver swerved around the roundabout encircling the immense, red-sandstone Independence Monument, passed the Royal Palace, and then arrived at the compound. Hopping off the back of the moto and feeling emboldened by the vitality of the city, Emily put her hand on the driver's arm. "Wait a moment." She called out, "Sonny? Would you please help me?"

Sonny strode down the steps of the villa. "Is everything okay?"

"Yes. I just want to know why this guy is always waiting for me. I don't mind the convenience, but doesn't he have other customers?"

Sonny loomed over the moto driver. The man removed his hat to answer, gripping the brim and glancing at Emily as he spoke.

"It's very peculiar," Sonny said. "I don't know what to think. He claims that his father worked as a gardener for you and your family back during the Pol Pot times. He says you are a princess married to Sisowath royalty and he once played with your daughters. He believes you are a ghost come back to haunt him."

Emily took a step back, almost stumbling in the dirt. "What?"

Sonny's face twisted as the driver began to speak again. "He says you left your leg in the land of the dead with your baby and husband as a sort of ransom. You'll be made whole again after finishing your task."

Emily's heart skipped a beat. *How could he know about Steven and the baby?* Goose bumps crawled up her arms. "Is he crazy?" she whispered.

The driver looked from Emily to Sonny and then back again. He put his hands into a sampeah and looked down at his dusty flip-flops.

"I don't think so," Sonny said. "He seems harmless enough. Perhaps shell-shocked from his experiences during the war? He's a simple man. He may not have met a blond Western woman before. And many people here believe in ghosts. It's a comfort for them to think the dead are still with us. Should

I tell him to leave you alone?" Sonny took a step closer to the man.

"No." Emily felt an unusual tingling, some sort of unidentified connection to the man. She wasn't afraid of him, only intrigued. "Could you ask him to explain? What does he mean by a task?"

Sonny asked a few questions. "He doesn't understand himself, but he promises to help you. He thinks he owes you a debt for something that happened back then. An obligation is a huge deal in our society, taken very seriously."

Though unsmiling, the driver looked at her with an intense gaze that was strangely soothing. Her initial opinion changed. The sense of connection grew, as if he peered into the bleak place within her chest, empty of everything but the now-familiar guilt. Tears filled her eyes. Emily's rehabilitation had been painful. The loss of her leg was devastating, but the death of her husband and unborn daughter had hollowed out her soul, something that could not be fixed by an artificial leg. Nothing had touched that empty place until now—until this weird stranger's words.

"What's his name?"

"Me, Arun," he said, hat clutched in his hands.

"You speak English?"

"Little, little." He held up his thumb and pointer finger to indicate a small space.

"Well, that makes things easier."

Sonny's aunt announced supper. *Mysterious tales would have to wait,* she thought.

She instructed Arun to wait and, with a nod, he squatted next to his motorbike and pulled his hat low as if to nap. Emily followed Sonny up the steps into the villa. After entering, she got a sense of how lovely the home must once have been. Cool tiles of ochre, cream, and crimson covered the floor, many cracked and stained, but the design still clear. Tall windows let in light and views of the yard. Four dark, low-slung, wood-framed chairs with rattan seats and backs sat facing each other.

"How beautiful!" Emily exclaimed. "C'est très beau, ici." She put her hands together in a sampeah.

"Merci, madame. Asseyez-vous, s'il vous plait," Boupha said.

Emily lowered herself into one of the chairs; this was the first time she had been invited into the house, and she gazed around curiously. "Sonny, do you live here, too?"

"Yes. This was my father's cousin's home before the war. After the Vietnamese invasion in '79, Boupha walked back to Phnom Penh from a labor camp on the other side of the country. She found the house abandoned and moved in—it had been used as a barn during the war. The Khmer Rouge destroyed all land titles, so it was a 'finder's keeper' for a while. She's been here since then but fears someone may come and challenge her claim. It's a prime property in the center of town. Hopefully, one of the benefits of UNTAC's mission will be establishing the rule of law."

"Do you have any other family members nearby?" Emily smiled thanks to the young woman bringing her fresh lime juice.

"The little boy you've seen in the yard is an orphan my aunt has taken under her wing. The same with this girl. I have an uncle, but he lives in the south. Most of our extended family didn't survive. *Meng* Boupha, my auntie, is all I have left here after my wife's death. Many of the overseas Cambodians who fled are returning to profit from the chaos—it's easy to be a big fish in a small pond with some money and connections, but I don't want to be like them. It's an interesting time for my people."

Emily thought Sonny's voice and stiff posture felt at odds with his words, like he was talking about someone else. She took a long sip of her drink. "Yvette mentioned she knew your wife. Did she pass away here?"

Sonny set his glass down without bringing it to his lips. "Yes. Lisa died less than a year after our arrival."

"What happened?"

"We were so excited to get SAF started; we traveled around the country making assessments. One day, we were near the Thai border and driving back to our lodgings. She urgently needed to urinate, so we stopped the car. There are so many land mines left—it will take decades to clear them all. Lisa stepped in the wrong place." Sonny's hands were clenched on the chair armrests, his fingers white with the pressure. "She was from California originally. I met her in college. She shared my desire to help with Cambodia's recovery. But her time here ended tragically."

Emily felt her own deep despair. "Oh, Sonny, what a terrible thing we have in common. I also lost my husband. You must miss her very much."

"Every moment of every day. She had no reason to come here, but she did. I continue SAF as a tribute to her memory. I can't leave now and return to Long Beach and lead a normal life . . ." His voice thickened. "Enough about my sad past. Tell me more about you, Emily, and your choice to come here."

"An old friend happens to work at the UN High Commission for Refugees in Bangkok. She heard about SAF there. I was in a tough place after my accident, and she thought that being around people like me"—Emily looked at her feet—"would help me get better. Doing some useful work would change my perspective, help me heal."

Sonny's mouth tightened into a thin line. "So the generous American has come to help herself by helping these poor people?"

"Why do you say it like that?" She was perplexed by his sarcasm. "I don't want to pity anyone. I just thought I could share my own experiences, offer my skills." She reached for her glass and drained it.

"And your experience would be similar to that of an illiterate rice farmer in the countryside?"

"Of course not!" She moved to the edge of her chair so their knees almost touched. "I've lost a limb and a loved one, so I think I know something about what that farmer might be feeling. Yes, I was lucky enough to be born into a life with more advantages, but that doesn't preclude me from empathy. Didn't your wife come here to help, too?"

"Lisa came to help—and look where that got her."

At that moment, Boupha peeked into the room and gestured for them to come eat. Relieved to change the subject, Emily pulled herself up from the deep chair and hobbled to the dining room. More than her prosthesis was pinching.

They sat at either end of an antique mahogany table that could have seated twelve. Sonny absentmindedly traced the wood grain of the tabletop. Deep gouges along one side made it look like someone had tried to hack it with a machete. "We bought this table from a neighbor," he said. "It took four men to move it in. It was probably too big to cut up for firewood."

Emily ventured, "It's lovely, even with the marks."

Sonny continued as if he hadn't heard her. "We are surrounded by mangled relics of our imperialist past. Sometimes I wish the communists had been better at purging the West with their Great Leap Forward. My father hated them, but I wonder if there wasn't truth in their contention that society should never try to remake itself in the image of the conqueror."

Startled to hear Sonny speak favorably of the Khmer Rouge, Emily looked from Sonny, in his crisp white shirt and blue trousers, to gray-haired Boupha. She wondered how much his aunt understood. The young woman brought in steaming rice and a platter of small banana-leaf cups filled with fragrant curry. Boupha began to put a heaping spoonful on Emily's plate.

"*Amok! Merci, ma tante!*" Sonny said. "This is my favorite—it is Cambodia's signature dish. Have you tasted it yet?"

Emily shook her head no. *Will talking about food soothe the antagonism in the atmosphere?* "Yvette's maid isn't the most gourmet of cooks. We have lots of fried rice and curry noodles."

"Well, you're in for a treat. *Amok* is freshwater fish smothered in coconut milk, eggs, fish sauce, and palm sugar. Then *kroeung*—a paste made from pounded spices like turmeric, kaffir lime, and lemongrass—is put on top."

"C'est très bien," Emily said to Boupha after taking a bite. "Vous êtes un bon chef."

Boupha bowed her head in acknowledgment of the compliment.

"No, she just loves food—that's why she's so fat now!" Sonny said. "During the war years, everyone starved. My aunt learned how to make soup from tree bark and insects. She was happy if she could find a snake or frog for the protein. She says she now spends a lot of time in the kitchen to recoup those years. She is happy you like Cambodian cuisine, though she has made us French madeleines for dessert."

Emily spooned a second serving. The previous tension dissipated with the food. "Sonny, tell me about your parents. Are they still alive?"

"My mother lives in Southern California with my younger sister. She was surprised when Lisa and I decided to return here. She owns a successful nail salon business. My father's story is not so happy.

"I was fifteen when we escaped. It was 1975. My father mistrusted the euphoria of a better life under the communists. He was a scholarly man and read his history books. The Russian Bolsheviks proved that revolution doesn't spring from the proletariat, but from a few obsessive individuals' intellectual egotism. He thought the Khmer Rouge illiterate children led by ego-driven tyrants educated overseas."

"Didn't Pol Pot study in Paris?"

"Yes, the so-called égalité influenced all the clever young men and women of that era. Ho Chi Minh, Pol Pot—they traveled to Paris and learned how to hate their white-faced benefactors. They wanted to be freed from the legacy of Indochine. A strange name for a place that is neither India nor China. But, unfortunately, those lofty European ideals didn't root in our moist soil." Sonny helped himself to more amok. "My father was a trader and heard all the rumors. Five days before the invasion of Phnom Penh, he arranged for my family to be smuggled into Vietnam in the bottom of a fishing boat. What's that saying? From the frying pan into the fire?"

"What do you mean?"

"After several long weeks hiding in the delta, we joined the human wave fleeing the communists in Vietnam. We stayed in a Malaysian refugee camp for two years before an American church in the Los Angeles area sponsored us. I always found it ironic that the white subjugators of America were boat people like us, escaping tyranny, but still they regard us as vermin."

"I can't begin to understand what you and your family went through, what this country experienced. To survive such tragedy."

"No. I suppose not." Sonny told Boupha to bring the dessert. "As I told you when you first arrived, many of us Khmer carry scars or the obvious injury of missing limbs. My trauma is not so evident, but just as real. My father died because there was no medicine to treat his heart condition. My family shared broken hearts in our tent of a home. America offered opportunities many dream about. The American Dream." Sonny scoffed. "Nevertheless, I hold a survivor's debt to my people."

The young woman glided in with coffee and a plate of freshly baked madeleines. Emily took a bite of the almond-flavored pastry. The delicious taste was in sharp contrast to Sonny's bitter words.

"Are your parents alive, Emily?"

"Yes, they live in Montana. I moved back in with them after my accident. They worried about my decision to come here." She sipped her black coffee, rolling it across her tongue. "As you know, I was an attorney in Seattle. My husband and I had a good life. I recognize now how happy we were. But at the time, that wasn't so clear. We lived from one day to the next. And then the crash shattered everything I knew to be true. My mother asked my best friend from high school to come visit and cheer me up. And here I am."

"Yes, here you are."

What's his problem? Emily stared at him to emphasize her point. "Sonny, I get that I'll never completely understand your past. But I'm not one of those aid workers who come to so-called developing countries and tell everyone how much better things would be if they did things their way, the Western way. I read about those 'humanitarian tourists.' I respect that SAF has a simple, straightforward mission and isn't trying to 'modernize' society. Sure, I came for personal reasons, but my intention is to support the work you've begun. I want to see Survivors Assistance Foundation succeed."

Sonny's stiff posture softened as he continued to trace the grain in the wood of the table. "We'll see how successful we will be."

As the young woman cleared the table, Emily stood to thank Boupha profusely for her hospitality and to apologize for not being able to speak better French.

"Ne t'inquiète pas, ce n'est rien," Boupha said, affectionately kissing both of Emily's cheeks.

Up close, Emily noticed scars on the older woman's arms and hand, the flesh twisted and discolored. Stepping back from the embrace with a warm smile, Boupha returned to the kitchen. Emily followed Sonny onto the veranda, where he waited, a dark silhouette in the night.

"Sonny, excuse me for asking, but what happened to your aunt? Are those burns?"

Sonny took a deep breath before replying. "In 1976 a teenage Khmer Rouge commander at her work camp accused her of stealing food. He threw a wok of hot cooking oil on her as a public punishment. She almost didn't survive, as there was no modern medicine to fight the infection."

"Oh my god, I'm so sorry," Emily said.

"Yes, you should be." And with that curious comment, he turned and went into the house.

Back home, she found Yvette liberated from her room and napping in one of the armchairs, a now-cold cup of tea beside her. As she dressed for bed, Emily replayed the dinner conversation, unsure why Sonny seemed so volatile and different now. *Yvette is right—there's no way to know what really lives in someone's heart,* she thought. As Emily fell into sleep, Arun's words glinted like a coin tossed into a wishing well.

A task?

PART TWO

CHAPTER TWELVE

EMILY 1993

Emily turned pages in her *Guide to Cambodia*. As she made a list of tourist places to see, the AC blasted against the heat. Yvette worked in her room, writing up reports. She said the monsoon would start soon, promising it would make things more bearable, though she warned about the humidity. Leather shoes were known to sprout mushrooms during the rainy season. The astonishing warmth sucked the breath out of her every time she walked outdoors.

Emily wanted to visit the temples around Angkor Wat in the north, but that would take a few days. Her list for Phnom Penh was short: the National Museum, the Royal Palace, and the Tuol Sleng Museum of Genocide. A popular activity, according to the book, was shopping at the Central Market for gems and fabrics. But she didn't like browsing, especially in a claustrophobic building shaped like an art deco pressure cooker. With her chin in her hands, she followed the hypnotic movement of the banana tree leaves in the garden.

※ ※ ※

After the crash, Emily had returned home to Missoula because everything about her Seattle life reminded her of all she needed to forget in order to survive. She put her law career on hold and fled to the care and support of her parents.

Jack and Rose Mclean had met and fallen in love as teen-agers in Belfast, Ireland. Jack's family was Protestant and Rose was a devoted Catholic. Both families were firmly entrenched in opposing factions over the issue of Irish home rule. After months of secret meetings and stolen kisses, they had a civil wedding ceremony and immigrated to America, leaving the sticky tar of sectarian prejudice and violence behind.

Jack's uncle, Ronny Mclean, worked at Heinricks Jewelry in Missoula and offered to train young Jack. Rose found work as a secretary, charming everyone with her homemade cook-ies and gentle brogue. Their new lives in America were filled with love, and Emily's arrival brought them great joy. They had named her "Emily" after the colossal concrete M on Mount Sentinel's side, whitewashed every year to honor the University of Montana. They tried their best to help Emily out of the dark-ness, but it hadn't been enough.

※ ※ ※

Memories were mosquitos buzzing in her ears, threatening to bite. Her shoulders slumped and she put her head on the table, arms cradling her empty core. *No!* She got up.

"Do you want to go be a tourist with me today?" she asked Yvette.

"*Désolée,* but I have much work to accomplish."

"I'm reading about the National Museum. It says it opened in 1920 and was designed and built by a French historian and architect—his colonial version of Khmer design. It was abandoned and looted during the Pol Pot era. Have you seen it?"

Yvette walked out to the main room and leaned over Emily's shoulder. "Oh yes, many times. It is beautiful—you must go."

"All right, National Museum it is."

Released from the AC's cold air, Emily stood panting in the fiery blast of heat. Arun squatted in the shade of the wall, the headband of his canvas hat dark with sweat.

"Susaday," Emily said, trying out the slang for hello. "National Museum?" After Arun's curt nod, they headed out, speeding down the broad boulevards. Sapphire sky competed with fiery red and magenta bougainvillea plants tumbling over the medians. At a stoplight, a young child smiled and shyly waved from the back of her father's moto.

At the entrance to the stately terra-cotta–colored sandstone building, Emily pushed futilely against a towering wooden door. An old man sweeping the walkway with a straw broom hobbled over. "Le musée est fermé aujourd'hui, madame—today, close."

Disappointed, she settled herself on the step just below a huge carved lion. With dismay she pondered the option of shopping.

"Hey, you!" A tall, attractive man came around the corner of the building with a camera slung around his neck. "No loitering allowed." It was Nick, the rude journalist from the Gecko.

"I wanted to see the museum, but it's closed today." Emily was relieved to see someone she knew. "What are *you* doing here?"

"Just taking a few exterior shots for a magazine piece. I have a private session scheduled for this evening if you want to come back with me. I'm going to shoot the bats." Nick wore fatigues, his oversize cargo pockets bulging. A faded Rolling Stones concert T-shirt, red tongue lolling, covered his chest. He had a floppy hat similar to Arun's.

"Shoot the bats?"

"Yeah, a colony established itself when this place was empty, and they never left. It's the most amazing sight when they head out to feed. There's nothing like it, watching them swirl up like black smoke, pouring around all the headless statues." Nick took off his hat and used it to fan himself.

"Headless statues?"

Nick laughed. "I think you're having some kind of stroke. Let's get you out of this heat and find a cold glass of beer."

"But it's before noon."

"Exactly! That's my ride over there; it's an authentic Willys jeep. I bought it off a destitute ARVN colonel in Saigon. Is that your moto driver?" In rapid Khmer, Nick shooed Arun away.

Emily had no desire to return to her empty room and watch Yvette write her report. An hour with the man might be interesting. She hoisted herself up into the open seat of the jeep. "You're a lot friendlier than the other night."

"Maybe *you're* just prettier in the daylight." As she fumbled to find the right response and the seatbelt, the journalist stopped her hand. "Sorry, mademoiselle, no safety measures here." He grinned at her surprise and started the jeep's engine with a roar.

Emily grabbed the door for balance as he swerved onto the boulevard. Taken aback by his words, she found herself smiling in reply. She smelled a woody aftershave that reminded her of fir trees back home. He gripped the wheel with his left hand as he crushed the reluctant gearshift with his right, the muscles in his arms standing out. Her initial impression of him as arrogant hadn't changed, but his appeal was also more obvious in the sunshine.

As if reading her thoughts, he grinned again as he wove the jeep around the Wat Phnom roundabout. Out of nowhere, an elephant stepped into the traffic before them. Nick came to a hard stop and raised his fist at the mahout following the lumbering beast, prodding him with a small stick. A bamboo seat, strapped on the elephant's back, held two men wearing bright-blue turbans.

"Isn't Phnom Penh the greatest?" he shouted, swerving past the enormous creature. Emily turned just as the elephant daintily crossed over a concrete traffic barrier, the two Sikhs shouting in delight as they careened sideways.

Nick took Emily to the nearby Le Royale Hotel. Stopping under the French-colonial hotel's portico, he came around to help her down from the high seat. A man dressed in a white jacket and traditional Khmer trousers, wrapped up between the legs, walked down the steps to greet them.

"Bienvenue, Monsieur Nick," he said with a sampeah. "It has been a while."

"Yes, it has, *mon ami*. I've been in the jungle too long." He led Emily into the coolness of the foyer and pointed to a large framed black-and-white photograph. "Jackie Onassis stayed here when she visited."

Emily took in the lovely space of natural teak wood with deep mustard-hued walls and a cool tile floor. Fragrant fresh flowers decorated a marble-topped table.

"This way to the bar."

The bartender greeted Nick like a long-lost friend and guided them to a small table near a window. Nick ordered them both draft beers and pushed back, stretching his long legs. When the beers arrived, he drank his in one long swallow, and then signaled for another. "God, that's good."

"Do you always take charge like that?" Emily smiled, sipping at her glass, feeling the air-conditioning's welcome chill begin to dry her sweaty back. Outside, somnolent bodies lay around the pool, sunburned and glistening in the sun like rotisserie chickens, leaving the bar empty of guests.

"What do you mean? Order you a beer?"

"Yes, I guess. I suddenly find myself in a fancy, expensive hotel. All spontaneous and unplanned."

"Do you normally plan out everything?"

"I probably do."

Nick raised his arms up to cradle his head. Dark-blue tattoos inscribed the white insides in Khmer script. The hidden skin looked soft and tender. She wondered about the meaning, but it seemed too intimate to ask. It must have been painful.

"Have you been here a long time, Nick? Or should I say 'Gator'? I heard you speaking Khmer to my driver."

"Long enough to get into some trouble, I guess. And you can call me whatever you want." Yet again, he flashed his grin, teeth white against his deeply tanned face.

"Are you ever serious?" Emily shook her head at the barman's questioning look at her half-finished glass as he set down Nick's second drink and a dish of spiced peanuts.

"Serious as a bullet, most of the time. But the R & R times are different. Like a bit of fun with a cute girl." Tossing nuts in the air, he caught them in his mouth as he made silly faces.

Emily couldn't help but laugh, charmed in spite of herself. "Happy to oblige. How did a Louisiana boy end up here?"

"I had a good friend and mentor who made his photojournalist career showing American readers the truth behind the lies about the Vietnam War. He's the one who inspired me to come to Southeast Asia."

"Wasn't that a while ago?"

"I used to work out of Bangkok, freelancing for any stories I could sell. Mostly about drugs and trafficking. I'm sure you know—the signing of the 1991 Paris Peace Agreements ended the Cambodian-Vietnamese war. With the UN's deployment as Cambodia's interim government, I knew I'd found my story. Familiarity with the climate and speaking some of the local languages help, especially when I'm out in the mountains where no one speaks French."

"I learned that the Khmer Rouge are still active in parts of the countryside. Is it very dangerous?"

"A big white guy is conspicuous, but usually they leave journalists alone. Their army is reduced to teenage peasants, their guns as tall as they are. I worry more about some crazy colonel trying to kidnap me for the ransom, or all the land mines," he said with a pointed glance at her leg.

"Oh no. I lost my lower leg due to a bad car accident back home in Seattle."

"Tough luck."

"Yeah, it was." She rubbed the place where her wedding ring had been. She'd given it to her mother for safekeeping the day she left. "I also lost my husband," she said, surprising herself and wondering why she mentioned Steven.

They were both quiet as a New Zealand army major in uniform and an attractive young Khmer woman in a short dress entered the room and sat at the bar. The bartender's face was unreadable as he took their order.

Nick drained his second beer. "I really did grow up in the bayous like Johnny said. My grandpapa's house wasn't that much different from the ones out in the boonies around here— rough, creosote-soaked, up on stilts. I used to catch live crocodiles for extra cash when I was a kid. I'd sell them to a nasty

old swamp rat. Not sure what he did with them. I played football in high school—that's where the Gator nickname started.
Johnny likes to pull my chain with it. Cambodia, Vietnam, the
delta region, all remind me a little of home. I can find my way
around better than most barangs."

"I've never met a Cajun before. Do you like zydeco music?"

Nick stretched like a cat. "Well, *cher*, I guess that I do.
Let me bring out my fiddle, and some spicy gumbo, too." His
mocking voice had taken on a strong Louisiana accent.

Emily grimaced. "Apologies. That was kind of tasteless. I
actually love zydeco—my husband and I went dancing when-
ever a particular band played. I loved it . . ." Emily's throat
tightened.

Nick signaled for the check. "Let's scram. How about you
come with *Papa* Nick to see some of the city with me today? I
have to finish a few errands while I'm in town, and you could
tag along. Those bats are incredible."

"That sounds like a great plan." She surprised herself for
the second time that day.

CHAPTER THIRTEEN

MILIJANA 1977

I am starving. My body, my mind.

I continue to make long lists of the things I love. Food, of course, and colors, and poems, and song titles, and flowers. Orchids, the small yellow ones with the fragrance of honey. Pink bougainvillea tumbling down the yellow wall of our home. Our home—is it abandoned and forsaken like all of us in this place? And roses, even the spindly red rose plant my mother carefully tended on our balcony in Belgrade. I believe she loved that plant more than her own children. Children. I mustn't go there. I imagine violets instead, the lovely harbinger of spring. The woman in the next cell is weeping. *May love flourish,* I repeat to myself as the guard prods me up.

I'm taken to a room and shoved into a chair. A camera waits, and a man who won't meet my eyes takes my photograph.

CHAPTER FOURTEEN

SONNY 1993

Did he deceive her? Is omission a lie? The power whimpered off and the ceiling fan turned one last time. Black night was wrapped around his body, smothering, stifling, too hot to light a candle. High ceilings captured some of the heat. He imagined the stagnant air as a burning shadow looking for escape, sliding down the walls to hover over his bed.

As a refugee, Sonny soon realized life in the United States was based on a false premise. In the church that sponsored his family, with his schoolteachers, even with his fellow Cambodian immigrants, the unspoken message was that Sonny must be grateful. He was one of the lucky ones. Be humble, they taught, be filled with gratitude. The mighty West had rescued them from probable death.

That assumption of righteousness dominated his upbringing; America's supposed democratic principles were the fairest, the highest standard, and the most valued worldwide. The American Dream ruled the world. He was promised that anyone might win the lottery.

Ha! Even marrying a white girl from California hadn't changed anything. The Dream ruined him, bulldozed his beloved culture into the blood-soaked ground with media and corrupt politics and an ambitious desire for *more*. A young fugitive, thrown into the deep end of the Dream, he'd lost that most crucial thing—his Khmer soul. He wouldn't allow it to happen again.

A generator roared to life nearby. Rolling on his side, he could discern a sliver of illumination outside the window. So what if Kenneth and the SAF board of directors had cut his funding? He didn't need them anymore. He would use the American to raise his own blood money.

CHAPTER FIFTEEN

EMILY 1993

A massive boom woke Emily from a deep sleep. The electricity shut off, leaving a deafening silence without the white noise of the air conditioner. Hopping on one leg into the main room, she found Yvette sitting in the darkness, lit by the glow of a single candle. A fork of light arced, the banana trees captured for a moment like an imprint on the back of her retinas. Another louder explosion shook the house.

"Is it the Khmer Rouge?"

Yvette got up and helped Emily to sit. "No, no, nothing like that. The monsoon is starting."

Emily sank into a chair, shivering from the cool outside air. Ozone permeated everything as another lightning flash sizzled, instantly followed by a monstrous crack like the entire sky had broken open. A roaring waterfall pummeled the garden, replacing the sulfur smell with the perfume of wet earth. The wind blew out the candle, leaving them in complete darkness. "The storm's right over us, isn't it?"

"I will never tire of this," Yvette murmured.

They watched the light display, each within her own thoughts, each stirred by nature's violent grandeur. As the rain lessened, the barrage of lightning moved away, dragging the thunder with it on an iron chain.

Emily debated going back to bed, but she realized that sitting in the dark and watching the storm had created a unique cocoon of intimacy. "Yvette, I had a disturbing experience with Sonny at dinner last night."

"What happened?"

"Well, it wasn't so much what happened as what he said. His sentiment, I guess. I know he lived in the States for years, and his wife was from California. Hell, SAF funding is primarily from Los Angeles. He hired me knowing who I am, my background. But during dinner, he questioned my motives for coming. It was like he distrusted anything to do with America. He attacked himself and his connection to the US by attacking me. Why did he even hire me if he felt that way?"

A flash illuminated Yvette as she reached for her cigarettes. Flame lit her face with the sharp click of her lighter. "I don't know, Emily. I thought I knew him, but he changed with Lisa's death. He became more broken, somehow. She was my cherished friend. You see, for a large city, Phnom Penh is only a small community. The few nonaligned expats, the ones who aren't with an established nongovernmental or UN agency, generally belong to radical religious groups." She took a deep drag and then blew smoke out in a dragon-like plume. "There aren't many women here, other than the locals, of course. And it is impossible to get close to them. Good families are protective of their daughters. Khmer society remains very conservative."

Outside, the rain slowed from a waterfall to a drizzle. *The sun will come up soon,* Emily thought as she strained to see Yvette better in the darkness.

"Lisa was different from the others—we became friends quickly. It's easy to feel the connection here in our little vacuum, to put aside the boundaries one might have back home. Sonny was always a bit stiff, but he was happy to see her getting comfortable here. Then she had the accident."

Yvette's cigarette flared as she inhaled and again as she tapped ash on a saucer.

"It was horrible. She stopped to take a piss by the side of the road—she knew the area was mined—we all know to be careful along the highways. She was unlucky." Yvette angrily stubbed out her half-smoked cigarette.

"What happened then?"

"I'm sorry to say I didn't meet Sonny after that. It was as if Lisa had never been real. She was just gone, *disparu.* I think she was the only reason he had any friends at all. He was so dedicated to getting his agency going, even after the tragedy. I regret I didn't reach out to him after she died, but he walled himself off in that villa of his aunt's. I was surprised when he asked me if I needed a roommate."

The thunder was far away now, the monsoon heading over the Mekong River and southeast to terrorize Vietnam. Emily counted seconds between flashes and sound before speaking again. "It must have been terrible for you both. I know grief affects people in different ways. I wonder if he associates me with her. But I still don't have a clue what is happening and how I'm supposed to do any work. I expect things will get smoother with time." Emily hoped that was true. Somehow, she and Sonny would have to reconcile any misunderstanding if she was to remain. And she wanted to stay, she realized. Emily's core tightened as she pulled herself up to stand. "Hey, did I tell you? I ran into Nick. Did you know you can purchase a kilo of marijuana and an AK-47 in the same place?"

"Yes, the Russian Market is quite entertaining."

"We also went to the National Museum. Nick filmed the bats as they swarmed out for their evening feeding. I've never seen anything like it. He also explained why so many of the statues are headless. He said antiquities looting is a bad problem here."

"The Khmer Rouge have made the good industry beheading temple artifacts and selling on the black market."

The generator roared to life and the lights surged on. Emily glanced over at the head of the ancient king in Yvette's cabinet.

"Don't worry; he's a knockoff for tourists. There's an art school where the students are trained to make them. I will take you one day. Did Nick take you to Tuol Sleng, the genocide museum?"

"No, but it's on my list."

"*Écoutez*, I'm not working today. There's a new manager for the archival project sponsored by Cornell University. I think she's American, too. Would you care to go?"

A chill ran through Emily that had nothing to do with the rain. The word *genocide* was evocative, and images from past newsreel clips flashed through her mind—World War II–era black-and-white photographs of tumbled sticklike bodies. *Museum* and *genocide* shouldn't belong in the same sentence.

"Sure, I'd appreciate going with someone who speaks the language."

After breakfast, they headed out to Yvette's Land Cruiser. Arun waited by the gate with his floppy hat. "Madame," he said with a nod.

"Arun." Emily continued to be startled every time she found him waiting. "Yvette will be driving me this morning. You can go home."

He stared at Emily with his intense gaze and walked away.

"You're lucky to have a regular driver, especially as the rains have started. It is a bother to stand in the wet trying to flag a ride," Yvette said.

As they drove down the lane, Emily noticed Arun was following them. Was he her driver or her watcher? Passing by the hut in the field, Emily turned to Yvette. "Didn't you tell me that was a ghost house?"

Yvette looked over at the rough structure. "Thida, our landlady, warned me not to go near it after dark. A poor family had been squatting there, and people gossiped that the mother was a witch. They had a baby who died or disappeared mysteriously. The police came and made them leave. Thida claims she sometimes hears weeping in the night coming from there. Who knows—there are many ghosts, n'est-ce pas? We are now going to the place where many ghosts were made."

"Arun thinks I'm a ghost," Emily muttered. But Yvette didn't hear as she shouted out the window for a man pushing a bicycle overloaded with whisk brooms to get out of the way.

They stopped outside the entry to the museum. Several people squatted or leaned against the wall, waiting for visitors, including a young legless girl seated in an improvised wheelchair made from a rattan dining chair and bicycle wheels. As they approached the gate Emily recognized a familiar face.

"Sam!" She was delighted to see the young man.

"Madame Emily!" He hobbled toward her, wooden crutches swinging as he dodged the mud puddles. Others clustered around, some with palms out. One man had a small bucket hanging from his handless forearm, which he pushed at Emily, causing her to stumble. "Toey!" Sam yelled. "Get back. She *my* friend!"

"Yvette, this is Sam, the guy I interviewed recently."

"Bonjour, mesdames," Sam said with a sampeah and his charming smile.

Yvette told the group she would give each of them a donation when they came out. Mollified by the offer, they went back to their posts along the wall and allowed the women to enter.

"I'll see you later, Sam," Emily promised.

Slipping through the rusted gates, they entered the grounds of the Tuol Sleng Museum of Genocide, or S21 during the Pol Pot era. The compound consisted of four three-story buildings in a U shape. Walkways crisscrossed the sizable grassy space; a smaller, open-sided building was directly before them in the center. A sign informed them they must purchase entry tickets, but the place appeared deserted.

"*Allô?*" Yvette called out. A crow complained in a nearby tree. Otherwise, an eerie silence greeted them. "Well, let's go ahead and look around," she said, pulling her long hair into a knot. "I'm sure someone will be happy to sell us a ticket at some point."

The women walked along a path leading to a three-story building on their left. "This was a lycée before it was a prison." Yvette spoke in a hushed voice. Though they were outdoors, there was an odd deadness to the air. Sounds were muted and words seemed to fall to the ground, only half-heard. "They made a special facility to torture their own."

Each building's upper levels had balcony corridors with barbed-wire mesh stretched across the openings. "What is that for?" Emily said.

"To keep prisoners from jumping."

They entered a room with deep-mustard walls, discolored by dirt and streaks of mold. The floor was broken orange-and-white tiles. A small desk had been pushed against the back wall under a barred window. An iron bedstead sat in the center of the room with a steel bar and rings dangling from the frame, an ominous black stain underneath. Terrible things had happened there.

"Oh my god. What are those rings?"

"Shackles," said Yvette. Her pretty face twisted with pain. "They still use them in the prisons even now."

"And the black?"

"Bloodstain. Vietnamese soldiers discovered this place when they liberated Phnom Penh in January of 1979. They kept everything exactly as they found it. There is some controversy that the museum is a propaganda tool. But, regardless, this is an important monument to the horror of which we are capable."

"Will they keep it? Like Auschwitz?" Emily backed out of the room and stood in the doorway.

"I hope so. Cornell is working to maintain the archive. The KR were very organized—there are pages and pages of confessions. Let's see if we can learn anything more about the project."

As they wandered through the various structures, Emily felt a sense of dread physically weighing her down. By the time they reached the final building, she was wiping away tears.

The first room was filled with image after hand-painted image depicting atrocities in vivid hues: A man having his fingernails pulled out; two men carrying another, slung on a pole like a piece of meat; a man being shocked with a car battery; a man swinging an infant against a palm tree, bashing the baby's skull.

A map of Cambodia covered the wall, made entirely of human bones. Skulls outlined the country's borders and filled in much of the space. Dozens and dozens of fragile dome shapes, many showing brute-force trauma.

Buzzing, like a million bluebottle flies, filled Emily's head, and she rushed from the room to the outside walkway so she wouldn't be sick. Seating herself on the half wall, she took a few long, deep breaths. She bent down to wipe her forehead with the bottom of her skirt. Yvette joined her and reached into her purse for a cigarette. She offered one to Emily, who hesitated for only a moment before accepting. "Now I understand the smoking."

A young woman, in a colorful sampot and a white blouse, came running toward them. She appeared to be in her early twenties and was wearing bright-pink lipstick. *"Mesdames,"* she called out, *"il faut acheter les tickets!"*

"Mais oui, bien sûr! Yes, we will get the tickets." Yvette explained the entrance had been deserted when they arrived.

The guide caught her breath. "I sorry! You English lady? I want practice English."

"I'm French, and my friend is American."

"Oh!" The woman looked at Emily like she was a movie star. "Please come welcome place. Me Achariya but you say me Debbie!"

"Debbie?" Emily said in disbelief.

"Yes. I love America!"

"Okay, Debbie, let's go buy a ticket."

They began to walk across the open compound, and the noisy black crow swept overhead with a loud warning cry. Like a windup doll, the guide began her memorized speech. "Over there"—she indicated the tall frame of what had obviously been a swing set—"prisoner pull up with hand tie behind back, break shoulder." Gesturing to a man-size terra-cotta vessel nearby, she said, "Water jar, inside no breathe." Her voice sounded detached from the nightmare she depicted. She could have been describing the weather.

"Mon dieu," muttered Yvette. "I doubt she understands what she's saying."

As they walked up the steps to the small building, a stooped older man came from a back room holding a mug of tea. Seeing Yvette, he smiled and came closer. When he noticed Emily, his face turned pale with shock, and he dropped his cup, causing it to shatter.

"*Puu?*" Yvette asked, using the traditional term of respect. "Are you all right?" The man didn't speak, just continued to stare at Emily, whimpering softly as he clutched his chest.

"What's wrong with him? Can we call a doctor?" Emily said. Debbie hurried to the rear room and returned with some water. The man's hand trembled so badly he could barely hold the cup.

His name was Leap, he told Yvette in whispered Khmer. One of the few survivors of S21, he had managed to stay alive by painting portraits of the top cadre leaders, especially Pol Pot. There were hundreds to be displayed throughout the country. After liberation, they found him hiding in a nearby house. The Vietnamese put him to work recording what he had witnessed during his incarceration. Those canvases were the ones in the last building.

"He says he has something that you must see," Yvette told Emily. "It will explain his shock."

"Yes, *mesdames*, please come with me." His face was returning to its normal color.

Leap instructed Debbie to get a ring of keys from the office. They were rusty and looked to be very old. Yvette and Emily followed the old man, who leaned on Debbie as they made their way back.

Debbie said worriedly over her shoulder, "This new thing."

They trailed him through the room of skulls and scenes of torture and stopped before a small door. Carefully choosing one of the keys, Leap worked to open the lock. His fingers were gnarled and misshapen from arthritis. Hearing the mechanism release, the frail man shoved his body against the oxidized door, which opened to reveal a dark closet.

"Look," he whispered as tears filled his eyes. "Don't be afraid."

Emily and Yvette peered into the tiny space. A dangling bulb festooned with mildew and dust cast a dim light into the windowless room. Leap held something in his hands. A painting? Debbie stood back, fist pressed against her mouth.

Emily gasped.

CHAPTER SIXTEEN

MILIJANA 1977

Again, Guard Touy brings me to the former schoolroom, pulling me like a dog on a rope. There is an iron bed frame at the center of the room. I stand before the Interrogator, who is sitting at the desk, a manual typewriter before him. The Watcher slouches outside the window.

"When did you become CIA spy?" the Interrogator asks as he peers at some papers beside the typewriter.

"I don't understand," I say. "I'm not a spy."

They tell me to lie on the bed; a small device I hadn't noticed is nearby. It is a car battery. They attach cables to my toes and crank the battery—electricity courses through my body, a blinding white-hot pain. The handle is turned until I soil myself.

"I am not a spy," I scream with a voice I don't recognize.

They give me my notebook. My toes are burned crisp like *ćevapčići* sausages from home. I sit in my filth and take the pencil with shaking hands.

"How did you meet your husband?" the man shouts. The questions come fast, with no apparent reason or logic. "Write it all down!"

What is it they want of me, I wonder, *besides dates and names? How can I speak of love in this sordid place?*

I met Rainsey Sisowath in Belgrade, Serbia . . .

After my years at school, I returned home, and my father found me a secretarial position at the Cambodian embassy. I had picked up a few words of Khmer from my friends in Paris and I was eager to learn more about the culture. It was disappointing to take such employment with my degree from the Sorbonne, but I needed a job.

That's where I met my future husband. Though an official member of the royal family—first cousin to King Norodom Sihanouk—Rainsey was the cultural attaché at the Cambodian embassy. Cambodia and Yugoslavia shared strong ties. Our leader, Josip Tito, and Norodom Sihanouk became close friends and allies. Sihanouk respected Tito's nonaligned stance during that Cold War era. The king's entourage visited Tito on his private island for extended stays. Their wives, Monique and Jovanka, became good friends.

Rainsey was very handsome and made me laugh with his gentle teasing about my Cambodian accent. I often found reasons to linger in his office. He invited me to their island soirees, where endless champagne flowed against the backdrop of the blue Adriatic. Nothing could have been more romantic.

I set aside my egalitarian ideological misgivings and allowed myself to relax and enjoy falling in love with a royal.

The first time Rainsey kissed me, I knew he was my future. The handsome diplomat from the exotic east was an intoxicating cocktail. In addition, my former Cercle Marxiste friends' desire to create a better society for Cambodia remained in the back of my mind. The chance to implement our Marxist theories in the newly independent country was a powerful dream. Young and naive, I was seduced by the heady combination of principles and power.

I respected King Sihanouk, who had shown he was an astute leader as he guided his people out from the shadow of French rule. Rainsey and I often argued over our differing philosophies, but those debates became the backbone of our mutual love and respect. My parents loved the thought of their "red" daughter becoming a princess. We married in a civil ceremony in downtown Belgrade, then promptly traveled to Phnom Penh, which distressed them greatly. They feared the war simmering in the region.

In 1970, events in my adopted land brought things to a crisis point. The conflagration of the Vietnam War raged next door. Though Sihanouk tried to keep Cambodia neutral, he eventually chose sides by supporting the communists against the American-backed coup d'état led by Lon Nol. America retaliated by carpet-bombing the country. Razed villages caused thousands of refugees to flood the cities looking for safety. Many of those villagers turned to the Khmer Rouge; how could they not choose their own people over the American bombs?

A few of the KR leaders were those same Cercle Marxiste idealists I befriended during my Paris days. My heart bled for their cause, but my husband feared Sihanouk might not keep us safe if conflict exploded within our own country. When our first child, Daevy, was born, we fled the Cambodian civil war now burning around us and returned to Yugoslavia.

But the pull of revolution was irresistible.

CHAPTER SEVENTEEN

EMILY 1993

Emily rushed from the building in a daze, stunned to silence by the sight of the portrait from Leap's secret closet. The woman in the painting looked just like her. After pulling it from the dark cave of the small space, Leap had gently wiped off the cobwebs and dust and then cradled the mildewed picture with heartbreaking tenderness. Emily's arms prickled with goose bumps. It was like a nightmare where you discover you're not who you think you are. Leap began to speak about the woman. Milijana Petrova, executed in 1977. Emily couldn't breathe and rushed from the room.

Yvette followed Emily outside the building. "Let's go home," she said, taking Emily's hand. "Nous reviendrons," she called over her shoulder to the old man as she led Emily to the gate.

At the entrance, the small crowd of beggars swarmed. "Madame Emily!" Sam pushed to the front as the girl in the improvised wheelchair waved.

Emily fumbled in her purse and gave him and the little girl each a ten-dollar bill. Tears filled her eyes. The children were so vulnerable and brave. Yvette gave each of the others a one-thousand-riel note.

During the short drive home, the women were quiet and subdued. Yvette finally broke the silence. "Mon dieu, my friend. What does it mean?"

"I have no idea," Emily whispered back as if, by keeping their voices low, they wouldn't draw the attention of whatever monstrous rend in reality had occurred in that dark closet. The picture represented an alternative truth—one in which a pretty, blond-haired, blue-eyed American woman could find herself an inmate in a communist prison from the past.

Back at the apartment, they sat down to another lunch of Chan's noodles. Emily sighed and set aside her fork. She had no appetite, and her lost leg burned white-hot. How could something long gone still remain so excruciating? The doctors had warned her that phantom pain was a common experience for people with amputations. But this was the first time she had experienced it so acutely. Had it been triggered by the shock of the portrait? She wondered if the little girl suffered such pain.

She wiped her eyes with the napkin. "What will happen to the girl in the wheelchair? She can't be more than ten years old. Who takes care of her?"

Yvette took a sip of water. "I don't know, *ma chère*. If her parents aren't alive, some kind of extended family."

"Do you think she's supporting herself the way Sam is? She's so young."

"It is very sad."

Deep in Emily's gut, the true place where the soul resides, an idea began to sprout. As the thought gained shape, she saw the face of the woman in the painting urging her on. *Hurry up,* she seemed to say, *time's running out.* Emily leaned forward. "What about adoption? Is there any kind of program to get these street kids adopted into local families?"

"I'll ask around at work. There's a UN agency for everything," Yvette said. "But, Emily, you haven't said a word about what was in the closet."

"I don't know what to think. It was like looking in a mirror at a version of myself from the past or another lifetime. Leap said she'd been executed. I don't think he told us everything. How could he have created something so detailed from memory?" With a start, Emily remembered her passport photo clipped to the SAF application in her file. "And it was hidden away in that locked room? He painted it with *affection.*"

Yvette gathered the plates. "He must know more about her story. Perhaps we can track down someone who has access to the archive. We didn't find the American managing the archival project. She might know more. If the woman in the painting was indeed a prisoner at Tuol Sleng, there must be a record of her imprisonment, *non?*"

"Great idea," said Emily, her plan now blossoming. Returning to her room, she said over her shoulder, "But for now, I have to go back to work. Sonny's probably wondering where I am."

Emily decided to take a quick shower before leaving, wanting to wash away the grisly Tuol Sleng air. She was nervous, unsure of Sonny's reception after the uncomfortable conversation at dinner. Standing naked, with cool water sluicing down her body, she felt a stirring, like the flutter of an embryo under her rib.

Emily pulled hard on the SAF office door, but it didn't budge. The villa shutters were all tightly closed, the compound deserted. She called out, but no one responded. Arun parked his moto and walked to the back. He returned, shrugging his shoulders.

Where were they? Emily stood under the jacaranda tree among the scattered purple blossoms. The faded color was similar to the delicate blue of tattooed skin under Nick's arms.

"Arun, take me to the *Phnom Penh Post* office."

CHAPTER EIGHTEEN

MILIJANA 1977

The Guard. The Interrogator. The Watcher.

The room reels with heat and my wretchedness as I continue in the little notebook. Blood drips and smudges the word *order*. I will be punished.

> *We returned to Cambodia in 1976 . . . We wanted to bring our skills and talents to forge a new world order.*

Back in my cell, I gingerly touch my mouth. This beating was the worst yet—violence for the sake of it. I hope my now-missing teeth shredded Touy's fists. Bruises bloom across my skeleton of a body. Once I was a beautiful woman. Now I smell the festering of my burnt toes. I sit on the floor and remember the past to forget this present.

Food. Love. Conviction. Life back in Belgrade was simple after our five years in Cambodia. I focused on Daevy and my husband. Having a child helped thaw the relationship with my parents, though they were still outraged by my sympathies for the communists. Rainsey resumed his duties as cultural attaché at the embassy; we passed time with Sihanouk when he visited, seeking support from the international community. His tightrope walk between the West and the East continued to impress me. But the conflagration had begun and I worried I was losing the chance to join.

Revolution was a heady concept, thousands of miles away, in the safety of our cozy Belgrade apartment. Rainsey and I spent many late evenings over slivovitz and cigarettes discussing "the cause." I told him stories of my summers with the grandparents of my childhood friend Mira, picking *sliva* plums and eating grilled *ćevapčići* smothered in *kajmak*. I explained to him the deep and powerful connection between peasants and the land. And ever so slowly, my royal husband began to accept and understand my passion.

While we hosted countless dinner parties with other expat Cambodians, the Khmer Rouge poured from the Cambodian jungle in a triumphant tide to fight Lon Nol's CIA-backed regime. With the liberation of Phnom Penh in 1975, we began making our plans to return. I wanted to be part of the rebuilding, to live in the world of my dreams.

I envisioned using my language talents to spread our communist message throughout the globe. I learned that the old friends from Paris now formed the leaders' inner circle. Very little information came out of the country due to the civil war's chaos, but I was determined to help my comrades.

I hope my commitment to our cause shines through in my words when I slave over those notebooks. Will the reader with the red pen realize that I stayed loyal to the movement during all those months in the ghost city? That I was never a traitor?

I can only pray for my darling daughters. For Rainsey, my love. I am so sorry. My only excuse is naivety.

I didn't know then that history is only written by the victorious.

CHAPTER NINETEEN

EMILY 1993

Emily marched up the stairs to the office of the *Phnom Penh Post*. Journalists trained at retrieving facts seemed like excellent sources for answers. She hoped Nick or Philip would help with her mystery.

She knocked on the door at the top of the narrow stairway, where a small sign indicated she was in the right place. After several silent moments, she pushed open the door. Three desks were scattered about the room, one with a modern computer terminal. The room reeked of stale cigarettes and unwashed bodies. A man lay on a battered couch with his face pressed into a pillow. She jumped in surprise when he started snoring.

She heard a toilet flush somewhere, and Philip soon appeared, wiping his wet hands on his khaki pants.

"Oh! Hello!" he said with his BBC accent. "Can I help you?"

"I hope so. Do you remember me? We met at the Gecko; I was with Yvette Morceau."

"Of course. How delightful to see you again. How is Mademoiselle Morceau?" Philip flopped down heavily into an armchair. "Please excuse me, but it was a very late night. Have a seat."

She sat on a chair near the sleeping man's feet. They regarded each other with the snuffling man between them. The man rolled to his back and raised his arm to protect his eyes from the light filtering through the dirty window, revealing dark-blue tattoos. "Oh! Nick's here?"

Nick opened one bleary eye. "I didn't do it," he mumbled and started to cough—the sound deep and phlegmy. Sitting up, he reached for a crushed pack of cigarettes, lit one with his Zippo, and leaned back, the fit subsiding. "That's better."

Noting Emily's disgusted expression, Philip laughed and picked up a half-empty bottle of beer. "Here, mate, this will make it better." Nick took a deep swig. "Excuse us boys, Emily, we're a bit rough sometimes. Now, how can we help you?"

Emily looked back and forth at the men. *Would they take her seriously?* "It's a strange request."

"We love strange around here," Philip said. "Right, Nick, boyo?"

Nick didn't respond, busy finishing the beer.

"I was at Tuol Sleng yesterday," Emily said. "There was something disturbing there."

"Everything at Tuol Sleng is disturbing." Nick shook his head as if to clear his mind. "That's the point of it."

Emily squirmed on her hard chair. "Can I have one of those?" She pointed at Nick's cigarettes. He tossed her the pack and lighter. She lit one and took a hesitant drag. "I saw a painting of me."

"What did you say?" Philip craned forward.

"You know all those creepy, horrific paintings done by one of the former inmates? One of them looks a lot like me." Emily couldn't believe she was saying the bizarre words aloud. "I thought the paper could find out more about it, maybe do a story?"

Nick swung his legs around and sat up, tugging the smiley-face graphic tee over his flat belly.

"That *is* odd," Philip said. "An actual painting, you're sure? Not some fool-the-tourist trick?"

"The painter was terrified the moment he saw me. Yvette and I were worried he'd had a stroke. Then he took us to a back room and unlocked a closet that obviously hadn't been opened in years. He wept as he dragged it out, covered in cobwebs."

"Not sure that's my kind of thing," Nick said, his eyes scanning her body. He reached down to adjust himself.

He was different from the last time she'd seen him. He didn't even seem to recognize her. Emily stared until he pulled his hand out from his pants.

"It *is* pretty weird," he said to Philip. "I'm in town for a few days; I could check with a couple of people . . ."

Philip looked at Nick and then at Emily for a long, calculating moment. "Okay, have a quick look, but I still need you in Sisophon next week for that voter fraud story. And, mate, please, take a shower first?"

Nick stood up. "Okay, let's go. Better now than never."

As they walked down the stairs to the street below, Emily was hyperaware of the man behind her. She found him simultaneously disgusting and compelling.

The afternoon Nick had taken Emily to Le Royale had been pleasant—he took his role as a tour guide seriously. But something had shifted when they'd stood side by side within the empty museum, surrounded by broken relics of the ancient Khmer Empire.

She'd felt an intense tug of desire as his fingers casually brushed against her hip and then settled at the small of her back. They had craned their necks watching the astounding sight of millions of bats as they swirled and filled the evening sky like velvet smoke. But all Emily registered was the warmth of his hand. He'd moved away from her side, crouching and swiveling, recording the black cloud on his camera. Before she had time to register her regret at his hand's absence, he was back, with his camera's long lens in her face, adjusting his focus, capturing her naked relief at his return.

"No!" She'd trembled with rage, mortified he'd exposed her like that. It was too soon.

The hungover journalist in the newspaper office bore little resemblance to the man who'd taken that photograph. She determinedly ignored him as she stepped carefully down the steps. Arun waited, his moto up on the sidewalk near the entry. "Where are we going?" she asked.

"My place isn't far. I'll grab a ride, too. You can follow me." He lifted an arm and a passing driver immediately halted.

Arun wove through the traffic, narrowly missing a street vendor grilling marinated pork on bamboo sticks over a barrel of glowing charcoal. They stopped at a shophouse with Nick's jeep parked in front.

"Mr. Nick," called a man lounging in a chair just inside the entrance.

"Hey, Hok, what's shaking?"

"Not much, my man, not much."

Nick pulled a key from one of his deep pockets and opened the metal grill covering a dark doorway. He slid the gate open and said, with a flourish, "Entréz, mademoiselle."

Emily wondered if he was watching her ass or her prosthesis as they climbed the stairs. She tried to lift her foot instead of swing it. *Why do all these apartments have such high stair-wells?* she groused inwardly. Three flights had never seemed so far.

She entered a surprisingly airy room, completely different from the frat-boy atmosphere of the newspaper office. The tiled floor had a floral design, and a teak ceiling fan kept the room cool. An antique wooden settee was softened with colorful silk cushions. Birds chirped from cages on the veranda, where pot-ted plants softened the bright sun.

"This is beautiful."

"Yeah—not what you expected?" said Nick as he opened a small refrigerator hidden behind a Chinese lacquer screen. He took out a glass bottle enveloped with condensation. "I had a nice time the other day. Are you getting more settled?"

"I like it here, a lot. Except for the heat, of course. I didn't know what to expect before I came." Realizing she was ram-bling, she went still.

He walked toward her. She knew how a deer might feel in a hunter's sight. He took the cold water bottle and placed it gen-tly against her face, rolling it down her cheek. Wetness dripped from her chin and dotted her blouse.

"You're lovely."

Emily hadn't had any intimate relationships after Steven's death. She didn't want anyone to see her body as it was now. But feeling the attraction, the tugging pull from the museum, she was tempted to lean against him. It would be a relief to be with someone stronger, to allow herself to be weak. To be seen. His eyes were dark green with shimmering spots of gold, like the murky water of a secret bayou. She took a step back.

"Where do we find out more about the picture?"

Disappointment flashed briefly in his eyes. "I need a shower before anything; I can smell myself." He turned and walked to the bathroom door, where he stopped to peel off his T-shirt, revealing the broad chest and muscled stomach she'd glimpsed earlier. Tossing the shirt aside, he unbuttoned his fatigues and let them drop to the floor. He stood naked before her. With a smile, he inclined his head.

CHAPTER TWENTY

MILIJANA 1977

"Confess!" shouts the Interrogator.

Surely he must tire of his constant refrain, like a priest entreating his congregants. I have little strength now. The guards drag me to my sessions; my feet make tracks in the red mud. The prison fills with sounds from hell.

I write.

> *In January of 1976, one hundred expat Khmer chartered a plane to return to Cambodia to join the cause, trusting the revolution with the lives of their families . . .*

We were a naive yet doomed group of intellectuals—accountants, urban planners, architects, university professors—mothers and children and husbands. My own little family—Rainsey, who set aside any misgivings to willingly follow me into the unknown, and our dear daughters: six-year-old Daevy, and baby Rachana, still in diapers. I had gambled with their lives.

We spent the long hours of the plane journey singing revolutionary peasant songs and pumping our fists into the air with patriotic zeal. Burying my nose in the dark curls of Rachana's head, I was the happiest I had ever been. We were on the way to change the world.

After arriving at Pochentong International Airport, we deplaned down a ladderlike stair to the burning tarmac. Heat and humidity enveloped us. Large craters littered the runway. It was a miracle the pilot had landed safely.

A dozen young Khmer Rouge soldiers greeted us, dressed in ragged black cotton tunics and pants, with red-and-white krama scarves tied loosely around their necks. I pulled my daughters close when I saw that the teenagers all carried machine guns. One soldier stepped forward and began a loud verbal tirade. His accent and grammar were from the countryside, so I couldn't understand much of what he was saying, but I saw unease washing over the others. They separated us into lines beside two school buses—men in one and women and children in another. They said our luggage would be brought to us later.

Just before we boarded the bus, a black car screeched to a halt, and the driver shouted Rainsey's name. It was surprising he didn't use the honorific for addressing members of the royal family as he shepherded us into the car. We would never see our friends again. Our minders told us they volunteered to feed our comrades growing rice in a commune.

For almost a year, I chose to believe that lie. I protected myself from bitter thoughts, from remorse. Had I misunderstood our revolution?

Now I know they were taken directly from the airport and executed.

CHAPTER TWENTY-ONE
EMILY 1993

From her vantage point on the wooden settee, Emily surveyed Nick's apartment. She picked up a small silk pillow and plucked at a loose metallic thread. The sound of the shower, amplified by regret, filled her ears. Would it have been so bad to let him see her naked? She imagined what he would think. Would he be disgusted? Would he care?

Toweling his dark hair as he came out of the bathroom, Nick interrupted her reverie. He sat down and took her hand. "What's it like?"

"What?"

"You know." He pointed at her prosthesis. "Being an amputee?"

Emily's relationship to her lost right foot and lower leg was complex, nuanced with bitterness and shame. Nick might have asked her what it was like to have blue eyes, he was so nonchalant. *Would she ever accept her new body?* She snatched her hand away. "I'd think a journalist would be better with words."

"What did I say?"

"I hate that question," she spat with a sharp voice. "You imply that I'm defined by loss. I *have* an amputation. Not 'I *am* an amputee.' It's a critical distinction."

Nick was still for a moment. "Yes, you're right. It *is* an important distinction."

She realized she'd been shrill—he was only questioning her the way she'd wished her friends and family had done back home. Without pity, only simple curiosity. "I'm sorry, Nick," she said. "I'm still coming to terms with it all."

"No, please, accept *my* apologies!" He put his hand to his heart and then his forehead with a salaam gesture.

Emily laughed. "You're kind of a goofball for such a tough war correspondent."

"My reputation rests in your hands, my lady."

She reached for his hand. "No today doesn't mean no every day."

"I'm pleased to know that, Emily."

She limped out to the terrace, putting physical space between them. She was afraid to tumble into those eyes. The air was humid and smelled of potted plants. Glossy green philodendrons tumbled and climbed over the wrought iron railing. The Royal Palace's upturned corners glinted in the sunlight a few blocks away. "What an amazing view you have."

"I got lucky with this place. I'm gone much of the time, but my landlord's wife keeps things tidy when I'm away. I don't bring many people here."

"Nick, how do we find out about that portrait?"

"I know a woman at Tuol Sleng who might help us."

"Of course you do." She laughed.

Traveling at Nick's customary high speed, they arrived before the museum closed. Late in the afternoon, most of the beggars had left, off to their happy hour haunts. Only the young girl in the wheelchair lingered.

"*Soksaby*," Emily said.

"Hello, madame." The girl had a heart-shaped face, with eyes that knew too much for a child. "You come again?"

"Yes. I want to learn about someone who was here before." The girl shuddered. "No happy here."

"No, I guess not." Emily handed her some riel from her purse.

The child nodded her thanks, stashed the notes, and rolled herself away down the muddy lane. Emily stood a moment, watching her navigate the potholes.

"Do you know her?" Nick asked.

"No, I don't. But I'd like to." She imagined having a daughter to love—the most significant loss hadn't been her leg.

They pulled open the gate and then passed into the compound. Two men sat smoking and lounging on the reception bench. Emily didn't see Leap or Debbie.

"I good guide, show you everything," one man offered.

Nick explained that they were visiting the American university woman. A crow followed them across the compound with sharp cries of alarm. *There must be a nest,* Emily thought. Strange to think of baby birds here. She followed Nick into the black stairwell of a building covered with dark streaks.

"The office is this way." As they climbed, concrete echoed his words. On the second floor he strolled down the open walkway, past a chugging generator, and ducked into a room. An older Cambodian woman sat at a chipped wooden desk like a strict schoolteacher, a reminder they were in a former classroom.

Nick introduced her. "This is Madame Phang. She is the manager of Cornell University's microfilming project and Jane Bigalow's right hand."

"Bonjour," said Madame Phang, removing her glasses and reluctantly closing a magazine. Her back was stiff and straight as a board. "Jane n'est pas là aujourd hui."

"Bonjour," Emily said. "I'm sorry we missed her. I'm looking for specific information about an inmate here. Perhaps you could help us?"

"Non, non. Peut-être demain, mademoiselle. Tomorrow." She put her glasses back on and opened the magazine in an unmistakable gesture of dismissal.

Emily had the distinct impression that Madame Phang wanted nothing to do with helping them find anything. "Okay, we'll be back then."

"*Comme vous voulez,*" she said. "As you like."

Nick flashed the older woman his sassy grin, looking feral and wild. Emily chuckled as the woman looked back at him in alarm.

"We'll be back soon, madame," he said, with a sideways wink at Emily. Leaving the woman to her reading, they went out the way they had come.

"Now what?" Emily asked as they headed back to the stairwell.

"Don't worry. I expected that; she's just the gatekeeper," he told Emily. "We'll find Jane." He put his finger to his lips and pulled Emily up the stairway instead of down. "I want to show you something."

Reaching the third floor, they entered a vast open space that extended the large building's length. The walls were the ubiquitous mustard yellow streaked with slashes of mildew.

Rainwater pooled in places. Open-air windows revealed a grassy field at the rear of the museum.

At the center of the space, discarded army uniforms made an immense dark-green pile: shirts and pants and rubber-tire sandals. Uniforms from hundreds, perhaps thousands, of the dead. The decaying cloth pieces were a disturbingly intimate reminder of the people who had worn them and been brought here to be tortured and killed. The air pulsed with a horrible sense of dread.

"What the fuck!" Emily felt punched in the stomach.

"Yeah. Intense, right?" Nick kicked at something moldy near his foot. Picking up a shirt, he examined the insignia on the arm. The towers of Angkor Wat, silhouetted against a red background.

"I thought they all wore black pajamas?"

"Not all. They like the Chinese look, too." He ripped the small patch from the garment and stuffed it in one of his pockets.

"Hey, can you do that?"

"Just a souvenir, adding to my collection. Everybody does it."

A small child's pink plastic sandal peeked out, the bright color in vivid contrast to the dark green of the uniforms. "Why did you bring me here?" Emily reeled with the realization that living, breathing people had worn all the items now abandoned in a moldering, rotting heap.

"It's a part of the unofficial tour, I guess. All the expats who have been here for a while come. It's a sort of pilgrimage. I thought you'd be interested."

Emily's ears began to buzz in the dizzying heat. A woman softly wept somewhere nearby. "Do you hear that?"

"Hear what?"

The sound wavered, then trailed to silence. Emily shook her head. "Nothing. Maybe I'm hearing ghosts."

"This is the place for them," Nick said.

Emily didn't see Leap watching from the doorway of a house across the street as she got into Nick's jeep. He held the hand of a crying child.

CHAPTER TWENTY-TWO

MILIJANA 1977

As I sit in the former classroom where I am brought for inter-rogation, I observe my tormentors' faces. They are young, and I wonder where the propensity for violence comes from. How can they hate so much? I bend my head before Guard Touy notices me watching. He knows how to give the most pain with the least effort. "Write!" he shouts.

> *Comrade Driver brought us to our new living quarters . . .*

Our new life in Phnom Penh was strange from the start. We drove from the airport through the deserted city, past street after street of vacant buildings and abandoned household items in piles, everything eerie and ghostlike in its desolation. Dogs and crows were the only signs of life.

We didn't go to our villa, but to a building in the Royal Palace compound. The soldier-driver showed us to a suite of two rooms and explained that we couldn't leave the grounds without permission. One of the Brothers would meet with us soon.

"Brothers? Permission from whom?" we asked, but he only shrugged in reply.

Rainsey asked to visit his cousin, the king, but the man informed us that royals were no longer in a position to make demands. *You now work for Angkar, the organization,* he said. Pointing at me in a rude manner—a previously inconceivable way for a peasant to address a princess—he told me I would be working at the Ministry of Information and Propaganda. Rainsey would work under Comrade Ieng Sary in B1, the Ministry of Foreign Affairs. With a final disgusted look, the soldier left us alone.

"Ieng Sary—he's our friend," I said. "See? It will all be fine. He's important in the leadership circle. I'm sure this is all a misunderstanding."

Rainsey looked back at me with bleak despair. "I think we have made a terrible error."

I put my arms around my husband to infuse him with my certainty. "Please, my love, give it a chance. Surely things are confused now, and it will take a short time to straighten out. They didn't know of our arrival."

"But you wrote to them, didn't you? The embassy was in contact. This is no mistake." He pushed away from me to open the shutters to the afternoon light. The hot and muggy breeze filtered in. The electricity was not working, the air conditioner silent.

Sweat ran down my back from fear as well as heat. I calmed the tired and frightened girls by taking them out into the garden. At least that was familiar. A gardener swept fallen leaves into a pile with the soothing swish, swish of his straw broom. A little boy, no older than Daevy, gave each of the girls a handful of jacaranda blossoms. The lacy purple blooms tumbled and fell as they began a game of throwing the flowers.

It was the last time I remember hearing my daughters laugh.

CHAPTER TWENTY-THREE

EMILY 1993

Emily was weary after the unsuccessful visit to the museum. Seated in one of the armchairs at the apartment, she massaged her leg, aching from all the walking and stairs. Chan handed her a note from Sonny saying he and his aunt had been called away to Kampot for a cousin's funeral. He expected to be back in a few days and promised to bring her some of the region's famous white pepper.

"I imagine this means you'll have the holiday from work," Yvette said after Emily finished reading the letter aloud. "The *poivre du Kampot* is exceptionally delicious."

"I think I tried it when I first came," said Emily. "Sonny mixed it with lime juice and grilled chicken."

"Enough—you are making me hungry. Let's take ourselves out to a good meal tonight, yes? I can't eat another bowl of Chan's noodles. I know of a new seafood place with a decent wine list."

Emily's empty stomach growled and the women laughed.

"Ah . . ." Emily released a satisfied sigh after decimating a platter of soft-shell crabs flavored with the renowned peppercorns.

The restaurant was a plain sampan boat, moored at Sisowath Quay, with several narrow deck tables. The deep dark of the Tonlé Sap River flowed silently beneath them. The cook worked in the rear with a massive wok over a simple charcoal brazier. He chopped up their crabs with a flashing cleaver and tossed them into sizzling peanut oil. The dish arrived drenched in a flavorful spicy sauce, the peppercorns sweet and citrusy. As rumored, the wine was good.

Yvette sipped her Vouvray. "I'm delighted you enjoyed it. These floating restaurants come and go, but they always have the freshest seafood. Johnny told me about this one." She reached into her bag to pull out her cigarettes. "We wanted to come, but he's been away for a story."

"You and Johnny are close?"

"Not really; we only share some bad habits." Yvette pointed to a colonial-style building not far from where they sat. "They are making a club for the foreign journalists."

Emily twisted in her seat to look. "You *do* seem very close with the journalists."

"Oh, they are excellent fun, wouldn't *you* say?" She gazed pointedly at Emily, grinning.

"News travels fast. Did I play where I'm not supposed to?"

"There are few secrets in our town, ma chère. Everyone knows each other's business. Don't be concerned—I saw him kiss you when he dropped you off. He's a sexy man, but watch out for him; he only does what is best for Nick."

"I'll keep that in mind." Emily emptied the bottle into their glasses as the small candle wavered. *Was it the first or the second bottle?* Smoke from the mosquito coils at their feet smelled of gasoline-laced incense. "Yvette, when did you first come to Cambodia?"

Yvette took a gulp of her wine. "I was about twenty. My mother had embraced la France after marrying my father and she never returned, even when *le professeur* would come for research. She refused to speak Khmer in the home, except, of course, when they wanted to talk about me." Yvette smiled. "*Maman* became as French as she could with her dark complexion. To this day, she puts on the lotions that claim to lighten her skin, hoping to forget her village background. I never knew what she thought when she looked at me, her dusky little daughter. I always wondered about the girl in the mirror, with such black hair and eyes. What would she feel in a place where the people looked like her?"

"Women's concepts of beauty are strange." Emily slurred her words a bit. It *had* been two bottles. "I've seen advertisements for those creams. In America, women spend money to appear darker."

Yvette called out to one of the little beggar boys squatting along the quay, watching the mysterious apparitions from a different world. Tossing him some riel notes, she asked him to buy her some smokes.

"I first came on an archaeological student visa. I hoped to see Angkor Wat, and my mother's home. It was an effort to understand better my Cambodian heritage. As a Frenchwoman, I was curious about my cultural background. I studied in preparation for *la grande aventure*.

"But ten years ago, Cambodia was still reeling from civil war. The Vietnamese were in power, of course, and the atmosphere extremely tense. I never made it to Siem Reap and the temples at Angkor, but I saw a lot. More than I bargained for."

The boy came back with the cigarettes. Yvette thanked him and told him to keep the change.

Following the verbal exchange, Emily exclaimed, "I think I understood everything you said!"

"*Félicitations, ma chère.* It is a complex language. All those pesky tones."

"What do you mean—more than you bargained for?"

"The occupation sat heavily on the people. Always there is the deep distrust between the cultures, Viet and Khmer, even now, with the signed peace agreement. It is only a small piece of paper after all, *non?*" She took a drag of her newly lit cigarette. "It was terrible to see so many displaced people trying to make their way home, to locate the missing family. Many had perished or died, murdered by the Khmer Rouge. The roads were bombed, a disaster, so traveling was impossible. I remained in the city, my heart breaking every day, witnessing such disruption. I had come to find *my* roots only to find a *country* uprooted—no roots any longer. I was sad, of course, but also *furieuse,* angry. I don't know what I'd expected, but it wasn't what I found. My culture, destroyed before I could embrace it."

Yvette's sorrowful face, flickering in the candle's dancing light, appeared more Khmer than French. Emily empathized with her, a fellow comrade in loss. "How horrible to discover your mother's homeland ruined. To not be able to find the past you searched for."

Yvette leaned her elbows on the table, still sticky from their dinner. "Everyone I met had been damaged. In the body or the mind, no matter, *tous les mêmes.* Broken body, broken heart. All looking for something lost, for relief from pain."

"You were young; how did you handle it?"

"With reflection, I didn't manage well. After a few weeks, I went home to Paris with a new resolution. I became a social worker while helping the refugees, always with the plan to return. *Et voilà!* I am here, with the UN mission. It is the immense challenge, *non?* To be here and do the work. But I found people, sympathetic people, like Johnny and Nick. And now, you." Yvette raised her glass in a toast. "Another bottle?"

Emily lifted her own empty glass as warmth that had nothing to do with the Vouvray filled her chest.

The little boys on the embankment left in search of more interesting entertainment. Night in Phnom Penh was different. During the day, busy streets charged with people moving with purpose, going from one place to another. After dark, local people retired to their homes, not risking the soldiers' threats and barbed-wire checkpoints. The homeless clustered under the few streetlights, trying to stay safe from those who might prey upon them. They spread out tattered mats with bundles of meager belongings serving as pillows. Mothers called out to barefoot children running about, catching insects drawn to the light or tugging at the sleeves of the foreigners who moved in packs from bar to bar. The city was filled with invaders, all searching for distraction. Anything was possible, for the right price.

The women drank their white wine as the city transformed into its nighttime self. *Where do the little boys sleep?* Emily pushed against the bruise-like discomfort of her leg where it fitted to her prosthesis. The familiar ache was comforting.

"Do you happen to know anything about adopting a Cambodian baby?"

Yvette regarded Emily in the unsteady light. "For whom are you asking?"

"I guess myself."

"Do you think you have been here long enough to take such a decision? To adopt a child from a place like this?"

"We can never know anything with absolute certainty." Emily ran her fingers through her curls, damp with perspiration, brushing the fine hair back from her warm face. "I know I came here for something. I feel it's there, hidden in the shadows right in front of me. Arun, the moto driver, said I had some sort of task to fulfill. At the time, I thought him crazy, but now, I'm not so sure. I *felt* his words. And seeing the portrait in Tuol Sleng—there's something here, something tied to this place I don't yet understand. Something I have to *finish*. That legless girl in the wheelchair started me thinking, forced me to face things I'd ignored. It sounds so damn condescending, but I want to take her home and give her a happier life. Or someone like her." Emily sighed.

A lamp swung from the mast of a fishing vessel chugging past, illuminating a man splashing water on his bare chest. He stopped his ablutions to stare at the Western women until he disappeared upriver. His wake caused their boat-restaurant to rise and fall, tapping against the dock with a sound like a wooden instrument. Bats darted over the darkness that was the confluence of two mighty rivers: the Tonlé Sap and the ancient artery of the Mekong. Millions upon millions of cubic feet of water flowing down from the Himalayan peaks in the north, down through Southeast Asia's battered heart, to end as the mud of the delta. With no lights on the far side, the blackness seemed to breathe. Clouds obscured a gibbous moon. The rain was coming.

Yvette covered Emily's hand with her slim fingers. "Yes, there is someone who can help you. But it will be expensive."

CHAPTER TWENTY-FOUR

MILIJANA 1977

The women in the cells closest to mine have all been taken away. One by one, they are herded out, never to return. I struggle to focus on my story, on how to appease my tormentors but still serve as a future admonition to misguided zealotry. I dig for meaning and the correct words, but they slip away like water on sand. Ultimately, I write what I hope they want to hear.

Comrades must not be distracted by false traditional concepts. Angkar is your family. Your

spouse and parent and child. The vital work of
indoctrination begins with the self . . .

Life in the diplomatic service of Democratic Kampuchea was
bizarre. Phnom Penh lay vacant, with only a few embassies
remaining, including that of Yugoslavia. We existed in a bubble, protected from the hidden truth of what was happening
in the countryside. Rainsey and I attended the occasional PR
function with the few friendly foreign diplomats left: China,
Cuba, North Korea. We huddled together, sipping warm wine,
sharing rumors. Though not officially sanctioned ourselves,
we held a unique place within Ieng Sary's international charade of legitimism. We began to realize we were some of the
last intellectuals tolerated outside of the Central Committee
leadership. Although we were of use, we knew that ephemeral
usefulness might end at the whim of a moment.

Rainsey and our daughters visited me each week. Angkar
separated us because breaking down the traditional family
unit was the first step in refiguring our new society. I stayed
in our accommodation near the palace while Rainsey shared
a cell-like room at the B1 compound with another political
affairs officer. Our daughters lived with a nurse and the few
other children left in the city. I knew it was for the good of
the revolution, but their absence was a constant splinter in my
heart.

During the visits, my husband and I put the girls to bed
and strolled alone in the overgrown garden, walking in silence,
in fear of who might be listening. We didn't see the gardener
and his little boy anymore and the plants grew wild. Orchids
dripped from trees, left untouched because they were inedible.
Hunger was rampant.

We whispered of better times. Rainsey reminded me of
our first time meeting in his Belgrade embassy office and how
poorly I made his coffee. How young and silly I had been. How

full our lives had been in Yugoslavia. And we remembered our life in Cambodia before the war, the births of our children. We shared memories like prayers. He held my hands, stroking my clenched fists smooth.

"I will love you for all my lifetimes," he said, his lips against my ear.

I touched my forehead to his. "I'm so sorry, my dearest."

CHAPTER TWENTY-FIVE

EMILY 1993

Emily dreamt about the woman from the painting. She held out her hands as if to clutch at Emily as flowers swirled like a kaleidoscope in the background. Her lovely face grimaced in frustration, lips stretched to scream, but all Emily heard was the scolding screech of a crow.

Emily woke to the noisy bird outside her window. After eating Chan's prepared breakfast of papaya and croissant, she lingered over her coffee. She enjoyed the dark, smoky taste mixed with sweet condensed milk. Yvette had left for work and the apartment was still. Minutes ticked by as Emily idly moved pastry crumbs into little piles on the tabletop. Sonny was still silent in Kampot. *Should she be worried that he hadn't been in touch? How is it possible to live in the twentieth century and be so out of contact with people?*

Choosing action over worry, she grabbed an umbrella. The weather was changing with the advent of the monsoon—it was cooler and the morning sky was often dark with a promise of thunder. She was disappointed Arun wasn't waiting in his usual spot. The first few raindrops caused her to rethink her plan; she didn't especially want to walk to the boulevard in a downpour to find a ride. She decided to risk it. She had to get out of her room and the thrashing of her mind. As she walked past the ghost hut, a sound made her look up from her balancing act on the unpaved road. Arun was in the open window.

"Arun? Is that you?"

"Madame?"

There you are, she thought with relief. Uncertain if he wanted her to join him or wait, she stepped cautiously into the muddy field. The tall grass, pushed flat by rain, formed a mat on which to walk. The rough wooden structure stood in the center. She'd been curious about it since Yvette's cryptic comment about the place being haunted.

"What are you doing in there?"

Extending his hand to help her into the entry, Arun said, "This me old house."

A plastic tarp, once pinned to cover the open window, lay in shreds on the earth floor of a simple room put together with bits of salvaged wood and tin. In the corner, an altar of sorts held a vase of drooping flowers; a small, tarnished Buddha; and a framed photo of a woman holding a baby.

"You live here?"

"Before baby, woman sick, die."

Emily was unsure what to say with their shared limited communication. Language or not, she understood the pain of loss. "I'm so sorry, Arun."

He stood as still as the Buddha figure in the corner, his dark eyes glistening. A long moment passed before he settled his hat with a shrug. "Where you go?"

"Tuol Sleng."

Getting on the back of the small motorbike, Emily put her hand on Arun's back and felt his warmth through his jacket. It began to pour. Even with the umbrella, she was soaked by the time they arrived. She had hoped to see the girl in the wheelchair, but the rain kept everyone home. Arun sheltered across the muddy lane under a mango tree as Emily tugged open the gate. The reception area was empty.

"Hello? Is the museum open today?" she called.

Leap peered around the door of the back room. "Madame! Yes, please come."

Emily was happy the older man seemed unfazed by the sight of her. She didn't want a repeat of her last visit. "Do you have time to talk?"

"Yes, yes, there is much to discuss." He came out of the room, a small girl following. "This is my granddaughter, Chivy."

Chivy had umber ringlets and she looked about five or six years old. She smiled with one missing front tooth. "What a lovely child." Emily put out her hand to shake. "Hello, Chivy!"

The girl hid behind Leap's legs, peeking out with a big smile. "H'lo," she whispered from the safety of her grandfather.

"Leap, please tell me more about the painting of the woman. You must know what a shock it was to see it like that."

"Yes, I have thought deeply on this. After meeting you, I realized I have kept my secret for too long." He sat down on the bench, pulling Chivy to his side. "But first, Madame Emily, I would like to know about you. Please, tell me how you came to be here, at Tuol Sleng? Have you lived in Phnom Penh long?"

"Not very long. I came to work for an agency supporting victims of land mines." Lifting her long skirt, she revealed her artificial leg.

Leap's eyes widened. "I hadn't noticed before. It is very real looking." Chivy squatted down to touch the plastic. "Chivy!" Leap admonished.

"No problem." Emily laughed. "See?" She knocked on the leg.

"Sak saat nas!" Chivy said with wonder.

Leap drew her back. "Yes, *chau srey*, it is a good leg."

"One of the young men who sometimes begs here was a potential candidate, but he was reluctant to have a new device. He thinks it will make people less likely to pity him."

Leap smiled sadly. "Unfortunately, he is correct. When foreigners come, I think they expect a certain type of poverty. They want to believe their donations of a few riels are enough to change a life. And Cambodian people would be suspicious of a beggar with something so expensive."

"It's hard to know how to help. What appears right to me might not be the best option here. Cambodia is so different."

Leap nodded. "It is important to try to understand. I commend you for your efforts. You are far from home."

"When a dear friend came to visit me after my accident, she reminded me that helping others would be the best way to help myself. She made an excellent case for doing work that would lift me out of my darkness. She works in Bangkok and knew about the job here with SAF. I had nothing left to lose, so deciding to move so far from home wasn't difficult." Emily looked up from her lap and met Leap's gentle eyes. It was surprising how easy it was to speak openly with the old man. "I came here without knowing why, but now I feel a strong connection to this place. And there's something mysterious about that portrait that seems to confirm it."

The rain shower stopped, and Emily shivered in the sudden eerie silence. Was she hearing echoes of her own voice speaking? The little girl smiled, and everything shifted back. She was only chilly due to her wet clothing.

"I think you have a good heart," Leap said. "I want to tell you the beginning—how I came to be here. Then perhaps you will understand."

"Please, tell me everything." She tingled with excitement at the thought of learning the mystery of the portrait she resembled so closely.

"Before the Pol Pot time, I was a cinema billboard painter. Our country had a thriving movie industry; the king himself directed and starred in many films. I painted the advertisements that promoted new films. But that all ended with the Khmer Rouge.

"They forced every man, woman, and child to leave by foot. I walked over fifty kilometers to a farm near my mother's village. Under the watchful eye of the cadre headman, we pulled and planted and starved, surviving on one cup of rice a day and tiny creatures that burrowed in the mud of the rice paddies.

"One day, soldiers came to arrest me. They brought me here and accused me of violating Angkar's moral code. I didn't know what that meant or how to answer the questions as they tortured me." He took a deep breath and reached out to touch Chivy for reassurance. "But like all the other prisoners, I eventually said whatever the interrogator wanted me to confess."

"*Chi Ta?*" the child whispered, seeing the tears on her grandfather's face.

Emily nodded in encouragement. "How horrible. I can't begin to know what it must have been like."

Leap pulled the little girl closer. "Nighttime in my cellblock consisted of fifty men lined up on the concrete floor and attached to each other with heavy shackles, so close we couldn't move, front to back, ankles bruised and seeping with unhealed sores. One night, the guard shouted at us to wake up. He unlocked the long rod that bound us. Another guard pulled me aside and whipped me to get me to hurry. I was so frightened; they had to carry me down the steps. I was certain I would be killed.

"But this time was different, and they didn't take me for interrogation. Commander Duch had received orders from the Central Committee to provide paintings and busts of Brother Number One. They wanted all comrades to know and revere their leader's features. Duch read in my confession that I was a painter, so he saved me from death and put me to work. My painting pleased the leaders. Duch gave me more food and allowed me to live in the hut where I worked. I lived without torture, though I never stopped being afraid."

Chivy slipped down from the bench and began to entertain herself with a beetle crawling on the floor near Emily's feet. As Emily reached out to touch the little girl's curls, the child gazed at her grandfather for reassurance. Leap gave her a warm smile, and she continued her play. *How sweet they are together,* Emily thought.

"One day during the rainy season of 1977 I glanced out the door, and there *she* was. A billboard from before the war flashed into my mind. A just-released foreign film and an American actress, very famous for her yellow hair. I remembered how I had to find special paint to recreate the unique color—lemon twist. I fell in love with her as I painted her image. And now she was here, my dream lady, in S21, being led like a dog across the compound toward Building A." He pointed behind them.

"Did you ever meet her?"

"No, that was unthinkable. You must remember, I was still a prisoner. But I knew the photographer. All the inmates had to be photographed when they first arrived. The Khmer Rouge leaders wanted to keep accurate records. I saved my meager food allowance and traded a bit of pork for a copy of her photograph. It was dangerous, but I was willing to take the risk. She represented the goodness of my youth and young love and all that had been taken from me by the radical communists."

"So you painted it from a small black-and-white photo?"

"Yes."

"Who was she and why was she here?"

Leap was quiet for so long, Emily wondered if he'd heard her question. "Her name was Milijana Petrova. That is all I know."

"How can I find out more about her? It's remarkable how alike we look."

"The writing of confessions was mandatory—all our names were added to a list. I searched but couldn't find anything. She isn't on the official roster. The American university is microfilming all documents salvaged from that time. Her notebook may be lost in that archive."

"Who else has seen the painting?" Though compelling, she wondered how his story could be true. A Western woman in a Cambodian interrogation center for Khmer Rouge cadre? And how did he know her name?

Leap looked across the yard, site of such grief and horror. His face was full of sorrow and regret. "No one else. Milijana was mine, alone."

"May I see it again?"

This time there were new details, unnoticed before. Milijana's nose was long, where Emily's turned up, and her eyes were more almond-shaped. Still, the overall similarity remained uncanny. She wore black homespun in contrast to her smooth, pale complexion; bright blond hair; and Dresden-blue eyes. In the manner of the artist Gustave Klimt, Leap had covered the background with the light blossoms Emily remembered from her dream.

Emily was beginning to ask about the flowers' significance when Chivy entered the grim room like a ray of sun with her laugh.

Oh my god, thought Emily, looking from the portrait to the child.

CHAPTER TWENTY-SIX

MILIJANA 1977

I count the bricks of my cell. One thousand twenty-six. I have been here at least three weeks, though time is strange—flexing and bunching back onto itself. The Guard arrives to take me for my session, sometimes twice a day. They are creative in ways to cause pain. *Vay* is a simple beating. *Tearounikam* is their word for more elaborate torture. Devices, apparatuses, all created in the vile imagination of monsters. My toes are swollen and black; gangrene is spreading. And still, they tell me to write. I begin.

New Year, 1977—The revolution of Kampuchea contributes to the common cause of the revolution in the world and the struggle of all peace- and justice-loving peoples, especially to the struggles of the peoples of the non-aligned countries and the Third World . . .

I wrote those words over a year ago and repeat them here again. Duch, the writer of notes with the red pen, directs my words. He tells me what I must confess. I don't know why a press release is part of my confession, but I do as he commands.

After our return to Cambodia, I worked daily at the Ministry of Information, drafting propaganda to spread our egalitarian global message. I was beginning to hold unspoken doubts about our leader's methods. I fought against the brainwashing all around me while writing documents to further it. We existed in a hall of mirrors, but concern for my family kept me on task as whispers floated of purges among the leadership.

Soon after the New Year, Khieu Samphan, one of the high-ranking Brothers and close to Pol Pot, informed me of his upcoming trip to Belgrade. He would lead a delegation to the Non-Aligned International Movement Summit; I was disappointed I hadn't been invited to join them. What was my purpose here, if not to help foster support from friendly nations? A few days later, my anxiety eased when I learned a Yugoslavian film crew was coming to record our revolution. I was dizzy with excitement to see people from my homeland.

When I visited the cooperative nursery where the children lived, Daevy clung to me, begging me to take her home. Rachana barely recognized me and cried for the peasant woman assigned to their care. The woman smiled as she took my baby girl from my arms. My wavering dedication to our cause became a terrible secret.

Rainsey came that night to hold me as I trembled and wept. We stood in the dim garden, out of sight of any watchers. The rising moon slowly swallowed the shadows as we comforted each other. Then a small boy, about ten years old, crept out from the darkness. It was the gardener's son, Arun.

Arun prostrated himself before us. "*Reachovong*, Royal Ones, please help me." His thin shoulders shook with suppressed sobs. "My father is dying. He said that the princess is white because she is an apsara—an angel come to earth. I beg you, *Preahneang*, don't let my father die."

I looked at Rainsey in surprise and then knelt to lift the poor child. "Where is your father now, Arun? We haven't seen him for a long time."

"They took us to a work camp not far from here. The comrade commanders tell us to dig and bring the water for irrigation, but there is no water to fill the ditches. There is no food, and the leaders are always angry. My father has *asannorok* and is very sick. He can't stand and just lies on his mat. The commander says he will kill my father if he doesn't go back to work. Please, Princess!"

I looked down at the boy's small tear-streaked face and imagined my daughters in need of aid from a stranger. "Rainsey, go to my room and get my medicine box. I may still have some aspirin for the fever." Rainsey rushed inside, then returned with a small lacquer box. With dismay, I saw that little medicine remained. And none of it would help a man dying of cholera. The gardener would die without adequate treatment. The doctors were all gone, and traditional medicines were our only option. At least I could ease his passing.

"Give your father crushed charcoal to eat, as much as he can keep down. And here, take this." I handed him the last morphine pills I had. "They will make him more comfortable."

Arun carefully wrapped the precious tablets in a bit of banana leaf and tucked them into the waistband of his ragged shorts. Bowing deeply, he said, "Thank you, Princess. I will pray to Lord Buddha that he keep your family safe, for many lifetimes." Then he slipped into the humid night, moving through pools of light and shadow.

I never heard from Arun or his father again. I sometimes wondered if they had survived.

But we were soon consumed by our own immediate worries.

CHAPTER TWENTY-SEVEN

EMILY 1993

As Emily and Yvette sat down to dinner, a man outside the gate shouted, "Hey, lovely ladies, anyone home? This goddamn guard won't let us in. We've got a bottle of real Irish whiskey!"

Laughing, Yvette called to the watchman to allow Johnny and Nick to enter. The tall, scruffy men tumbled through the door, smelling of alcohol and unwashed clothing.

"Qu'est-ce qu'il se passe, mes amis? What trouble are you making tonight?" Yvette demanded, hands on her hips. Relenting, she threw her arms around Johnny's neck and gave him a deep kiss.

"Well, what about me?" Nick advanced on Emily in a crouch, then kissed her cheeks in the French style and set the bottle down. "Where's the ice?"

Emily's face grew warm where his kisses had landed.

Yvette untangled herself and went into the kitchen. As the men sat at the table, Johnny said, "Is anyone eating these noodles?" and began to wolf them down without waiting for a reply.

"*Quel sauvage*," said Yvette, with a kiss to the top of his head as she placed a bowl of ice and some glasses on the table.

"Well, go ahead and help yourself," Emily told Nick, who was eyeing her bowl. "Apparently, you guys are really here for dinner." Yvette poured generous splashes of the golden liquor into the glasses. "*À votre santé!*"

"Cheers!" said Emily as she downed her whiskey. She was flushed and excited from more than the drink. "Good grief, save me some of that, Nick."

"Okay, okay, keep your undies on," he said, pushing the half-empty plate back to Emily with a glance that warmed her belly. "Yvette mentioned you're interested in how adoptions work here, so we thought a visit was in order. Johnny's an expert on the subject; he did a story a while back about corruption in the orphanages."

"You don't want to dig too deep in that mess," said Johnny. "Very sad. Many of the children aren't even true orphans."

"Aren't there a lot of abandoned children around due to the war?" Emily said.

"Yeah, but many of the kids still have a living parent. They're just so poor they can't afford to feed them all, so they drop them off at the pagoda or the orphanage. And then there are the recruiters."

"What's that?"

"It's fucked up, is what it is." Nick scowled. "There's big bucks in children. Sex trafficking is a pandemic here."

Johnny drained his glass. "A recruiter is someone who finds a mother or a pregnant woman and offers her payment for her child." Seeing the expression on Emily's face, he explained, "You have to understand that these women are poor in a way we can't fathom. They live out in the countryside and are extremely gullible. The recruiters come and offer a relatively large amount of cash for one of their children. They promise the kid will be educated and have a good life in the city. The women are desperate and don't know any better. Some are sick with HIV or are widows, all of whom are looked down upon in Cambodian society."

"It is heartbreaking," Yvette said as she poured more whiskey.

"Most of the little girls—boys, too—are brought here to Phnom Penh, destined for the sex trade," said Nick. "Big business, all the way up the food chain to high-level government officials. Johnny wrote an article critical of one of the ministers, and Philip had to quash it or get the newspaper shut down."

"I had no idea," said Emily. "Why isn't there some oversight on such activities, more protection in place?"

"Excellent question." Johnny reached out to Yvette and brushed her hair behind an ear. "And now there's a new angle for the bastards—international adoption—babies for sale to foreigners. These people have offices in various cities around the world. They advertise that they work with the orphanages to place Cambodian children with Western families. They offer to handle all the bureaucratic paperwork, even the visas and plane reservations, for the potential adopters. But it's all theater—they profit in pity. The orphanage directors are in on it, and the profitable business is growing. Babies and young children—just another commodity for these creeps."

Emily swirled her glass; the ice had melted. "But there must be agencies that do things the right way? That place legitimate orphans with approved homes and don't prey on these families?"

Nick turned in his chair to face Emily. "Why are *you* so curious about this?"

"It's been on my mind since I got here, especially after seeing that young girl in the wheelchair outside Tuol Sleng. I guess my American privilege is weighing on me." Emily smiled. "Don't you want to help, somehow?"

"Sure, of course. We all do. But I'm not sure I'd want to adopt a kid. Can't you just give a donation to your favorite charity like most Americans?"

"That sounds kind of disparaging."

Nick ran his hands over his close-cropped dark hair. "Apologies, Emily. I guess I've had my fill of sentimental do-gooders who want to *make a difference.* I see that help only offered in the abstract, from the safety of an armchair or an air-conditioned NGO conference room. They don't want to get close enough to smell the stink. Adopting a child would be the opposite of that. I applaud you."

Yvette reached across the table and took Emily's hands. "Don't worry, *ma chère*; we'll talk to more people. These journalists only know the darkness of people; that's how they sell the news."

"We write human interest, too, like a story about the Tuol Sleng portrait." Nick's conciliatory tone seemed intended to ensure no lingering harsh feelings remained. "We'll go back when the old man is there and I can interview the guy."

"Oh yes, *mon ami,* a painting from that place will surely have a happy ending," said Yvette. "Have you seen it? It is *bizarre*! It could be our Emily."

"I went back to the museum and spoke with Leap," Emily announced. "He told me the story of how he came to paint it. He knows the name of the woman—Milijana Petrova. He said he didn't know anything more than that, but I have my doubts."

"Why?"

"Well, for starters, his granddaughter looks a lot like the picture, too."

"Wow, an S21 love story during the Pol Pot years. What could be more romantic?" Johnny laughed.

"He said her confession might be lost in the archive somewhere."

"We'll definitely go back when Jane is around," Nick said.

"To love stories!" Johnny raised his glass in a toast.

"Speaking of *l'amour*," Yvette said, perched on his knee. "Did you bring more than whiskey, *mon amour?*"

"Why yes, my beauty, yes I did." Emily overheard the young man murmur into her ear.

"No more whispering over there," Nick said. "Yvette, have you asked Emily if she wants to be on our team for the cyclo race?"

"Cyclo race?"

Nick flicked his Zippo with a snap to light another cigarette. "It's a wild, fun thing we did last year. It was such a success, we want it to become an annual event. We'd all been drinking . . ."

"*Quelle surprise*," Yvette added.

"Five or six of us were goofing around. We decided to take cyclos instead of motos to the Heart of Darkness bar. Philip took one look at the skinny, emaciated-looking guy sitting up on his seat and declared that he, Philip, would cycle the bike to the bar on his own. The astonished driver got in the passenger's place, and the big, proper Englishman climbed up and began whooping and pedaling down the street like a crazy man. It cracked us up, so we all started racing. The cyclo guys thought we barangs were totally insane, but they sure didn't mind the huge tips they got for letting us use their bikes."

"This will be our second year doing it," Johnny added.

"How does it work?" Emily tried to visualize riding the three-wheeled bicycles that moved people and goods around the city like graceful pelicans.

"We offer the real cyclo drivers all the beer they can handle, so they'll be happy allowing us to borrow their bikes." Johnny became animated as he acted out the scene. "Then you choose your mount and pedal like crazy down to the finish line. It's a blast!"

Emily sipped her watery whiskey. She took a bigger gulp. "Are you going to participate?" she asked Yvette.

"*Mon dieu, non!* It is a debacle! White men commandeering the boulevard. I hate it. Colonialism at its worst—using the brown people's streets like a private playground for such foolishness."

Johnny put his arm around Yvette. "Oh, please, don't be so stern. Say you'll be my fair maid. I'll wear your colors upon my sleeve."

"*Tais-toi, idiot!*" She ruffled his hair. "You don't understand how it appears."

"I used to run," Emily mused, "but I don't know about maneuvering a cyclo."

She looked down at her mismatched feet, remembering a race up Missoula's Mount Sentinel. The crumbling trail of sharp switchbacks rising up the mountain's flank, the high hill reminding her of a crouching lion with its summer coat of tawny grass. And then, the relief of breath, reaching the end, jumping to stand in victory on the summit of the heavy concrete M, a tribute to the University of Montana. Watching Steven follow just behind, smiling at her despite his defeat. She doubted she'd ever want to climb that particular mountain again.

"I don't think I could do it. And I agree with Yvette—this seems really tone-deaf to the situation here."

"It's just a bit of silliness, letting off steam," Johnny protested.

"When is it?"

"Soon, the first day of Pchum Ben—Festival of the Dead."

CHAPTER TWENTY-EIGHT

MILIJANA 1977

Monsoon rain is comforting, though I shiver in the nighttime coolness. I listen to its musical poetry as I count minutes. The waiting is the most difficult, the poignant anticipation of pain. My new bruises cover the old—black, purple, yellow, green, like a painter's palette. I strive to write the correct words, but I realize there are no right words for the man with the red pen. What am I supposed to be confessing? I shelter in the memory of my family.

The morning after seeing young Arun in the garden, we shared an early meal. Rainsey, Daevy, Rachana, and I, all together for the first time in weeks. The girls chattered on about their friends at the children's compound and Comrade Nurse, who cared for them. I mourned our past life, but purposely set aside my misgivings, as it was for the good of the cause. The revolution demanded the breakdown of the traditional family structure to rebuild society in a new and better form. My intellectual self knew this, but my heart did not.

My dear husband was somber and quiet, so I did my best to cheer him, being silly and making faces with our daughters as we ate our meager breakfast of watery *bobor* porridge. Daevy asked for croissants with papaya, and I explained that we couldn't eat like we used to. Regardless of the food, we were together as a family. I hoped things would become more normal with time.

But I was wrong.

The first clue was the car taking my husband back to the B1 ministry. Instead of the usual driver, one of the "old ones," the uneducated peasants from the countryside, sat in the driver's seat. He wore the familiar black pajama uniform of the jungle fighters and spoke in a dialect I couldn't understand. Rainsey got into the front of the battered Peugeot and waved through the window with a strained smile as they drove away.

CHAPTER TWENTY-NINE

EMILY 1993

The whiskey was gone and the air in the apartment was stuffy with cigarette smoke. Nick paced outside on the patio, and Yvette lay curled like a cat on Johnny's lap. Emily slumped in the musty armchair, imagining Yvette purring as the pale young man stroked her long hair.

"Is the Gecko still open?" Nick came into the room and tipped the empty bottle upside down. "I think we need more supplies."

Rousing herself with a languorous stretch, Yvette said, "Johnny and I are staying in tonight, right, *mon chéri*?"

"Oh yes, we're staying in tonight." He grinned as he lifted her in his arms and carried her into her bedroom, kicking the door shut behind them.

"How about you, pretty lady?" Nick stood over Emily. "Want to go out with a drunk journalist?"

Holding out her hand, she allowed him to pull her up. She put a hand on his chest to steady herself. He was wearing a Sex Pistols T-shirt. "Sure, let's go."

Noisy patrons packed the Gecko Club. Cigarette smoke swirled around Emily's face as she walked into the establishment. Nick waved at colleagues like a visiting celebrity while Jules blew him a kiss from across the room. Nick pointed at a table in the corner occupied by the man Yvette had called Colonel Kurtz. He had white buzz-cut hair and wore the ubiquitous dark-green fatigues with a white polo stretched tight across his bulging muscles.

"Nick, old buddy, take a seat! Who is your lovely friend?"

"This is Emily Mclean. She works with Sovannarith at SAF. Emily, meet Lieutenant Colonel Mitch Ryder, with the United States Army Special Forces. When he's not at Fort Bragg, he's here teaching the locals how to be better killers."

"Now don't go giving the lady the wrong impression. You know I'm only here as an observer!"

"Yeah, right." Nick laughed.

"*Enchanté, mademoiselle.*" Mitch stood to kiss Emily's hand. "It's a pleasure to meet you. Have you been in-country long?"

"A bit. It's hard to keep track of time here. I'm still getting my bearings."

"If there's any way I can be of service, just let me know. Take this." He pulled a business card from his pocket with a flourish.

"Easy, soldier, stand down," said Nick. "Emily, I'm going to get us some drinks. Are you okay alone for a moment with this old shark?"

Emily had to bite her lip to keep from laughing at the two alpha males puffing out their chests. "I think I can manage." She turned to Mitch. "So you know Sonny?"

"Sure—a shame about his wife. How do *you* know him?"

"I guess he's my boss. Back home, a friend told me about SAF and their efforts with land mine victims. I was ready for a change, and here I am."

"Interesting choice for a change of pace. Did you know there's still a war going on here?"

"Honestly, I didn't give it much thought. Cambodia doesn't make the headline news in Montana very often, and I was in a hurry to get here before I changed my mind."

"Well, I meant what I said." The old soldier's face became earnest. "It's not difficult to get in over your head in a place like this." He settled back in his chair and crossed his arms the way young men do to show off their biceps. Even his fingers had muscles.

"Okay, thanks."

Emily knew she would never ask a man like Lieutenant Colonel Mitch Ryder for help. She'd grown up with men like him. Cowboys who brandished their rodeo scars like badges of courage and considered women fragile flowers, easily crushed. Thankfully, Nick soon returned with his favorite Stolichnaya vodka. A fortysomething brunette with shoulder-length hair stood behind him. She wore jeans and an embroidered '60s-style yellow blouse.

"Emily, look who I found: Jane Bigalow, the woman who is running the university archive project at Tuol Sleng. Maybe she can help us find out more about your mystery woman. I told her about our run-in with Madame Phang."

The woman squeezed into a place at the small table. "I hear you have a question about an inmate at S21?" She had a quiet voice and sparkling, intelligent brown eyes. She reminded Emily of a favorite high school English teacher.

"Yes." Emily leaned forward as she spoke over the buzz of the room. "There's a guide at Tuol Sleng who was formerly a painter, and he showed us a portrait of a woman named Milijana Petrova, executed in 1977. He had it hidden away in a closet."

"Strange. I'm familiar with several Americans and Europeans interned there, but they were all men. Petrova— that's a Russian name?"

Mitch drummed his fingers. "The KR captured and executed a couple of Western women, but none were taken there. It was for higher-ranking cadre only."

Nick poured vodka into glasses for the women. Jane took a sip and grimaced. "That's correct. The archive has the confessions of many Cambodian women, but I haven't seen any of a Russian."

Emily took a deep breath before diving in. She knew she would sound crazy. "The weird thing is she looks startlingly like me." Scanning the table, she wasn't surprised their faces all showed varying degrees of disbelief.

"Who showed you the picture?"

"His name is Leap. He speaks English."

"Of course I know Leap!" Jane looked happy to make the familiar connection. "I'll follow up with him at the museum tomorrow. I'll also remind Madame Phang to be a little friendlier to visitors."

"The dragon-lady gatekeeper." Nick smirked.

"Yes, she's a bit forbidding, but she does an excellent job of overseeing the local staff who do the actual work of processing and microfilming the documents. We must keep close tabs on the material. People have been stealing souvenirs for a long time." Jane fired a sharp glance at Nick. "After liberation, when people began to return to the city, they pilfered most of the files for cooking fires or toilet paper. At the start of the project, a colleague went house to house in the neighborhood trying to retrieve lost and dispersed material. We salvaged a lot, but it's certainly not complete. It's possible a confession might randomly appear, but a painting is another matter entirely."

Emily poured herself some of the vodka. She was growing accustomed to drinking it straight. Reaching over, she helped herself to one of Nick's 555-brand cigarettes. *Slippery slope.* She smiled. "Wouldn't Milijana have to have been some sort of big shot with the communist leaders to be incarcerated there?"

"Superb question," Mitch said. "But according to Ieng Sary, the KR weren't communists; they were revolutionaries who didn't belong with the other ideological groups. They considered themselves separate, better than the other red regimes of the region. They hated the Vietnamese and their backers, the Soviets. 'When a nation is filled with strife, then do patriots flourish.'"

Nick shook his head. "Really? Quoting Lao Tzu already?"

"'Be still like a mountain and flow like a mighty river,'" the warrior-philosopher quoted as he topped up his glass.

"Who is Ieng Sary?" Emily asked.

Nick grabbed back the bottle. "An old friend of Pol Pot from their Paris days, he was a senior founder and their foreign minister. The old fart is still alive, and the international community hopes the work Jane's doing at the Tuol Sleng archive will add evidence to any future crimes-against-humanity trial."

"But, to your question, Emily," said Jane. "You're right—the poor woman would have had to be involved in the leadership to end up at S21. She could have been caught up in the 1977–78 purges. Not surprising, as she was a foreigner. Come and visit me again at my office; early mornings are best. In the meantime, I'll see what I can learn."

Emily sat back in her chair as the conversation shifted to the upcoming election. She wondered why a European woman would travel so far from home to join a radical group that brutally suppressed and killed its own people.

CHAPTER THIRTY

MILIJANA 1977

I was a young woman when I first became enthralled by communism. It was not an unfamiliar concept; I lived in Yugoslavia, after all. Not precisely communist, but close. My parents made the ideology even more attractive with their rabid hatred of the Bolsheviks, who had destroyed their comfortable Russian heritage of overstuffed furniture, gleaming samovars, and violins propped in the corner. I realize now it was a game for me, a way to set myself apart from my stifling family and be more than a pretty girl. A way to be taken seriously during the 1950s, when women had limited roles. Meeting those ardent Cambodians in the left-bank café illuminated a different path. Falling in love with Rainsey cemented my commitment to Cambodia and the Khmer Rouge cause. We became dedicated to freeing that troubled, ancient place from her imperialist burden. But I had only exchanged a velvet-lined family prison for the gulag.

I sit in my cell and whisper through the rough brick wall to the woman who cries out for her husband to come save her. "Be still, sweet sister. He will come soon," I lie as we hear the sound of the approaching guard rattling his keys.

Which one will he take?

CHAPTER THIRTY-ONE

EMILY 1993

Emily sat by the river, watching the crowd pass by. It had been another long day doing little other than recovering from the previous night's drinking. But her analytical mind churned. As an attorney, she had toiled long hours and striven for success. Success—what an arbitrary concept. The view home on Lake Washington, a new Lexus, beautiful clothes from Nordstrom. All irrelevant here. Cambodia held her upside down and gave her a solid shake. Who knew you could travel so far only to find yourself?

The riverside promenade was always busy, especially in the evening—people out for a stroll as the heat of the day loosened its grip. Young couples walked arm in arm. Teenagers were everywhere, laughing and joking and trying to capture the attention of the others. Mothers called out to their children not to stray too far. Emily watched a little girl run to hug her mother. She might be on the other side of the world, but people remained the same. They loved and were loved in return. She found comfort in that sameness as she slapped at the twilight mosquitos. The transition from day to night was sudden, only a moment of purple sky before the velvet blackness came down and the streetlights began to buzz. A pregnant woman sat nearby, licking a dripping ice-cream cone. Her husband gently wiped her lips with his handkerchief after she finished. Then he put his hand on her swollen belly as if claiming the life there.

Emily and Steven had never considered adoption, assuming she would get pregnant quickly. He turned a spare bedroom into a nursery, painting a scene from *Goodnight Moon* on the wall. Sitting in the rocking chair his mother had shipped from New York, he would watch Emily with shining eyes.

As months and then years passed, she was secretly relieved and dove into more work, fabricating the career she thought she wanted. When she realized she'd missed a second period, she didn't tell her husband for several days. When she eventually did, he held her in an embrace that felt altogether different from what they'd shared until then. Together, they discovered a new way to cherish one another.

Emily grew to love the idea of a small seed growing within her. Would the child have Steven's lanky grace? Or her mother's dimpled chin? She often cradled the promise blossoming there. Week after week they waited, and then the ultrasound revealed the hidden secret, a little girl nestled in the folds of Emily's innermost self. Looking into Steven's eyes with the cold gel on her stomach, she reached out to touch his face, then put her fingers to her mouth, tasting his tears.

But all tears taste of the same salt. She pushed herself up from the promenade bench—Arun waited across the street. The tropical dark had arrived; she was hungry and in need of a cool shower. Even the nighttime rain was hot.

"Madame go home?"

"Yes, please, Arun."

Arriving back at the house, Emily slipped off the seat as the watchman opened the gate. "Madame?" Arun said. "You come temple? Pchum Ben time."

Emily took a moment to process his words. Pchum Ben? Thankfully, the landlady appeared from the back of the house. "Madame Thida, would you please help me understand what he's asking?" Though not fluent in English, the woman spoke more than Arun.

Thida always looked down her nose at Arun, barely hiding her disdain for the low-class driver. She was a terrible snob. "Mean kha ey nung?"

Arun took off his hat as he explained in Khmer.

"He want take you pagoda for pray. Time for remembering dead ancestor comes soon. Fête des morts, tu connais?"

Emily remembered the conversation with Nick and Yvette about the macabre holiday. "Is it customary to go to the pagoda?"

"*Mais oui,*" Thida replied in her imperial tone. "We give favorite food to ghost and pray to monk keep dead happy. This man take you, pray for family, father."

"I'd be honored to go with you, Arun. Is there anything specific I should do?"

"You wear white and Arun make special food you offer to monk." Looking a bit less annoyed, she added, "You go pagoda,

M-lee. Buddha give good luck to you. Make merit for next life. Driver say he come early morning, Saturday."

As Arun rode away, the woman took Emily's hand and turned it over to smooth her palm. Looking closely at the lines there, she smiled. "But you lucky lady already!" And with a deep laugh, she sailed back to her small kingdom in the rear like a deposed queen.

Emily wondered who the landlady had been during the war years. Definitely someone accustomed to commanding others, maybe even a big-shot cadre leader. *How did you survive?* was the unspoken question for people of a certain age.

She found Yvette curled in one of the armchairs. "Hey, are you okay?"

Yvette groaned. After one of her slow cat stretches, she said, "There's mail for you, and please, stop talking so loudly!"

"Guess no party tonight." Emily laughed. She picked up an ornate envelope from the dining table. Breaking open the red wax seal, she found an invitation to the Official Second Annual Phnom Penh Cyclo Races on Saturday.

"Yvette, I'm officially invited to the race, but they know I'm not going."

The French woman propped herself up. "Of course, *bien sûr,* you are invited. They hope you will change your mind. Now, *s'il te plaît,* bring me a glass of water and my cigarettes? I can't bear to move."

Next to the invitation was a smaller envelope. It contained a note from Sonny stating he'd returned from Kampot and wanted her to come to the office as soon as possible. "It's about time!" She wanted to finally *do* something.

Yvette lit one of her fragrant Gauloises cigarettes and began to blow perfect smoke rings. Emily watched as they floated up to the ceiling, dissipating in the slight breeze from the air conditioner.

"Yvette, will you take me to the orphanage you mentioned?"

"Sure. We can go tomorrow if you like. Shall we meet for lunch and go after?"

The following morning, Emily went to the SAF office. It had been just a week since dinner with Sonny, but it seemed much longer. Time was elastic in Cambodia, stretching and bunching like a rubber band. The boy in shorts still swept the red earth, and Boupha's pesky dogs were barking.

"Emily," Sonny said from the veranda of the villa. "Apologies for the sudden departure."

"I was sorry to hear about your relative."

"He was old. Frankly, it's surprising he lived as long as he did. He survived a lot. What have you been doing while I was away?"

"Yvette has been generous with her time, and I met a few journalists."

"Oh?" Sonny's tone turned chilly. "Be careful around those men; they'll do anything for a story." He moved toward the office, unlocked the door, and switched on the groaning air conditioner.

"Did your aunt return with you?"

"No, she stayed behind to celebrate Pchum Ben. She is superstitious and a strong believer in appeasing the ghosts. I don't believe in that, and I didn't want to leave you alone too long without direction. We must finalize several applications."

The baked, stuffy air made the office an oven. She imagined tiny mold spores from the air conditioner spewing across the room. Sonny tugged hard on the cabinet drawer and pulled out two files, which he put on the desk.

"I saw Sam outside of Tuol Sleng," Emily offered. "He was friendly but still not interested in following up with us." Emily refrained from mentioning the portrait, unsure of Sonny's mercurial mood.

"Forget about him. I met several suitable candidates while I was down south. As you know, I prefer to focus on rural Khmer. This man," he said, holding up one of the files, "is perfect. He is a farmer who, as a boy, lost both his legs during the American bombing. He can harvest pepper, picking the berries from the vines with a rudimentary cart he wheels along the path." He held up the other file. "This woman owns a fruit stand in the market, selling mangosteens and papaya. Her hands were blown off while clearing a field. She picked up an unexploded bomb, thinking it a rock. They are strong candidates. Both survivors of the American legacy."

American legacy? "Aren't they in the south? Will it be a problem managing their cases from here?"

"Not anymore. With you here in Phnom Penh, I'll have more flexibility to be away from the office." He slid the files toward her across the desk.

Emily opened the first folder to find the now-familiar application cover page with a small photograph of an older man clipped to the upper right corner. The man squinted at the camera in the photo. His mouth twisted open, revealing bare gums. The questionnaire was already completed in Khmer. She couldn't decipher any of it. The second file showed a stern, middle-aged woman, her head wrapped in a krama scarf. She held her arms across her chest, the missing hands obvious.

"I hope we can help these people. But, Sonny, how can I support you without speaking the language if you work so far away?"

"I have a new contract for you." A frown creased his forehead. "Which is what I want to discuss."

"A new contract?" Emily spun inside. How could he arbitrarily remake her signed agreement?

"I've had time to reflect upon strategies to ensure the success of SAF and my mission. When I first agreed to Kenneth's plan to bring you on board, I didn't understand how it would play out. It was a good idea, but the reality has been different than expected. I'm not sure how much longer Kenneth will finance SAF."

Emily watched circles of perspiration spread under Sonny's armpits as he spoke. He'd always appeared crisp and polished, but now there was something almost feral about him. She noticed other details, like his ragged fingernails and tiny scabs where he'd shaved poorly. She dragged herself back to his words.

"I'd decided to send you back to America. But now I think I'll use you for fund-raising here, within the country. I'm sure there are grants and other options you will explore. People and organizations with money trust someone like you more than me."

Emily's focus snapped back as she understood his meaning. "Sonny, I came to help people like *me*. I accepted the position with the understanding that's what I would be doing. If you're talking about fund-raising, wouldn't that be more successful back in the States? I don't have much experience raising money, and certainly not doing it here." She worked to keep her tone calm and businesslike.

He bristled as he spoke, glaring at the empty space above her head. "It's about legitimacy, you see. Kenneth thought your background as an attorney would help me. But he was wrong. Like all the others, he has no clue what we need."

"What are you talking about?" She was unsure if his anger was directed at her or something bigger.

"Someone like you could never understand. I don't need anything from you other than your white face."

His words hit her like a slap. "My race? What does that mean?"

"No local agency is taken seriously without Western credibility." He bolted up, chair knocking against the wall. "We brown-faced people don't know what's best for our own interests. Or can't be trusted with your goddamn guilty-conscience dollars."

Emily swept her eyes around the pitiful excuse for an office: the ridiculous air conditioner, the rusty file cabinet, the ancient desktop computer that she still hadn't seen function. Coming to Cambodia to help others like herself was a way to reconcile her own tragedy as she worked her way out of anguish. Did it matter exactly what she did day-to-day if the result remained the same—helping people with similar challenges? So what if she wasn't interviewing applicants? She could secure funding sources and use her skills to draft contracts, ensuring favorable outcomes on behalf of SAF. But where did Sonny's animosity come from? If she had been back home, she would have walked out the door.

But nothing waited at home except nightmares and pity. She came to help others, instead discovering a way to help herself. Her disability wasn't a liability here, and it didn't define her. Cambodia welcomed her as she was. But she couldn't stay without a work visa.

"Are you firing me?" she asked.

"No." Sonny was calmer now, his breathing smooth.

"Well, what's happening?"

Sonny took his chair. "I am broken Kampuchea and you are the West, come to save me yet again."

"I have no idea what you mean." The hair on the back of her neck prickled. Was the air conditioner kicking in? She would find another job if this new arrangement didn't work out.

But for now, she would have to bite her tongue.

CHAPTER THIRTY-TWO

MILIJANA 1977

I am brought back to my cell and dropped like a bag of garbage. Why do they continue with this charade? They know I will write whatever they want. As I lie curled on my side, I explore a sensation of relief. The beating has stopped for this moment. In that circle of respite, I separate myself from the pain. I summon a memory of music. Simple yet powerful piano notes move through my mind like a soft caress. I extend my arms to hold my husband, my daughters. I stroke their hair. I scratch a flower with four petals, one for each of us, into the moldy and stained yellow paint of the wall. I scratch another and another. I am here. Do you see me?

CHAPTER THIRTY-THREE

EMILY 1993

Yvette's human rights division was located in an office in one of the many government-owned buildings leased by the United Nations. Emily stood on the crumbling sidewalk before the building's mildew-streaked façade, probably new in the 1960s. She speculated the structure had once been a bank. A guard with a machine gun slung across his chest eyed her warily. She couldn't tell which country he was from, as the flag insignia on his sleeve was too small to identify.

"I'm here for Mademoiselle Morceau?" With a brusque gesture, he indicated she could pass.

A young woman, dressed in traditional Khmer sampot and blouse, sat at a desk adrift in the echoing lobby. "Votre nom, madame?" she inquired politely.

"Je suis ici pour Yvette Morceau. Je m'appelle Emily Mclean."

"Of course—you are Yvette's friend." The receptionist welcomed her in English. "She is up the stairway to the left."

An open staircase loomed before her. Her leg throbbed in anticipation. With a small sigh, she started up. At the top, she went into a room flooded with light. Several people of varying ethnicities sat laughing and chatting in front of desktop computers. A man tossed a wadded-up piece of paper across the room. "Yes!" he cried in delight as it landed in a basket. It was the first modern-looking office Emily had seen since her arrival. She felt the vibrancy of people enjoying their work.

Yvette stood near the rear, head lowered to hear a colleague speak. After a moment, she lifted her head and saw Emily in the doorway. "Emily!" she called. "Bonjour! Come meet the gang."

Emily entered the spacious, airy room. High windows faced the boulevard below. A dozen individual desks topped with computers lined the walls. A huge shared worktable dominated the far end of the room. Massive air-conditioning units thrummed with white noise. A hand-painted banner covered the wall above the worktable. English, French, and Khmer script proclaimed: "Life and liberty! Freedom from slavery and torture! Freedom of opinion! Freedom from bureaucrats!" Civil administration was the same everywhere. She smiled, reminded of her former corporate life in Seattle.

Yvette introduced Emily to an Australian doctor, a judge from New Zealand, a Kenyan physicist, and a Swiss attorney. She was impressed by the international coterie of young professionals, all under forty, who had put their careers on hold to come to Cambodia to educate and inspire fundamental human rights. Even though they bore the daily burden of dealing with the aftermath of atrocities and proximity to abuse, they seemed happy to be sharing such important work. Emily felt at ease with the group as they laughed and joked.

"What inspiring people," Emily said as she and Yvette walked back down the stairs on the way to lunch. "It's good to know that the UN isn't only police and military."

"*Bien sûr!* I'm very proud to be a part of all this. We are helping a country rebuild its broken justice system. Though the United Nations bureaucracy is so arcane and cumbersome, it is worse even than la France, where I must fill out a form to have a thought." She laughed. "Now, where shall we go to eat?"

"You're the local expert. I'll follow you, my friend," said Emily.

"*D'accord,*" Yvette said, putting her arm around Emily's waist as they walked to the street. "I know a good place not far from here, near the Central Market. *Allons-y!*" On the sidewalk, the city swarmed around them. As Yvette pointed out where the upcoming cyclo race would start, a procession of monks in dark-vermilion robes slipped silently past, a snapshot of serenity along the otherwise raucous boulevard. These were the scenes that made Cambodia so compelling, timeless images trapped in amber for eternity.

After pasta Bolognese and copious red wine, Emily wasn't sure if she could stay awake. Two strong espressos later, she rallied. The orphanage was in a villa surrounded by trees, located in the Chroy Changvar district. Like many of the neglected neoclassical homes, it appeared to be melting in the tropical climate. An open-sided shed topped by a tin roof stood to the right. Excited children of all ages mobbed them as they got down from the cruiser. With a start, Emily realized they were beside the ruins of a cathedral, now a bombed-out shell where a few remaining bits of shattered stained glass reflected the afternoon light. Emily shivered in the heat. Broken glass. Thankfully, the nightmare hadn't haunted her for weeks.

A nun in full black habit approached them. The starched white of her veil made her face look tiny. *"Bonjour, mesdames,"* she said, and then switched to English. "How may I help you?" Yvette explained that they wanted to learn about the adoption process for foreigners. The nun's attention swiveled to Emily. Her open and friendly expression became speculative, the delicate eyebrows of her lined face drawing together. She regarded Emily from head to toe and seemed to come to a conclusion. She clapped her hands, bringing the children to order, then barked a sharp command.

"She's telling them to prepare for a performance," Yvette translated.

Older children jumped to attention and corralled the little ones, arranging themselves into two lines from tallest to smallest. The nun held up her hand for silence. Then the little ones launched into a song that was vaguely familiar. They stood in the bare red dirt of the yard and repeatedly sang a refrain, completely out of tune, obviously not understanding a word.

"Is that supposed to be 'Frère Jacques'?" Emily whispered to Yvette.

"Mon dieu, you might be right!"

Song complete, a teenage girl dressed in a simple sampot and T-shirt, black hair pulled back into a ponytail, invited the guests to sit. The nun inserted a cassette into a small box, and the atonal, dissonant sound of Khmer music filled the space. Rain began to pound on the tin roof in a percussive accompaniment. They were in a bubble, separated from the world by the curtain of water.

With her audience seated, the teenager put her palms together in a sampeah and began a sinuous stretch of her arms and hands in a traditional dance. She moved slowly and deliberately, her fingers and toes bent into impossible contortions. She defied gravity with strength and grace as she balanced on one foot. The restless children were mesmerized. An apsara had come to life.

"She's magnificent," Yvette remarked. "It's a pity she's not at the Royal Dance Academy. Only a few dancers survived and are teaching again. The loss of culture is sad."

The girl finished and stepped to the side of the room. With a bark from the nun, she moved to Emily and put out her hand. "Tip, madame?" Her eyes were lowered and her cheeks pink with embarrassment.

Emily reached into her bag to pull out some notes, her eyes wet with tears. What does one pay for beauty? Yvette asked where she had learned to dance so beautifully. In a soft murmur, the girl explained that her grandmother had been a royal dancer for the court. And then the Khmer Rouge took her yeay away. She danced as a prayer to her memory.

The nun bustled over, grabbing the money before she invited them into the house. "My name is Sister Mary Agnes. We will talk now."

Emily and Yvette walked up the villa's run-down steps into a once-grand foyer. Black cobwebs dangled from high ceilings; the tiles were cracked and stained with bat droppings. Remnants of a staircase swept in a graceful curve to the upper level. Rattan armchairs surrounded a table. Several plastic stools lined the wall.

One of the older children brought bottles of lukewarm soda with straws. The older woman sighed as she took a long sip; her woolen habit must have been stifling in the heat. She lifted the tunic a few inches and revealed her ankles. She was wearing expensive red leather slippers.

"As you can see, there is little money for my charges. We depend on the generosity of the government and foreigners like you. Do you have Cambodian blood?" She turned to Yvette.

"Yes, my mother is Khmer, but I was born in France."

"And you, are you Australian?" She stared at Emily.

"No, I'm from the United States."

The woman's mouth pursed like she'd smelled something foul. "Oh, indeed? Few come from there." Her eyes lingered on Emily's prosthesis.

Emily added, "I moved here several weeks ago with an agency aiding victims of land mines." Sister Mary Agnes looked doubtful. It was impossible to gauge her age. She might have been fifty or seventy.

Yvette put down her empty bottle. "I work with UNTAC in the human rights division. Emily and I share an apartment. She is considering adopting a child. Can you explain how your orphanage functions? The process?"

The woman ignored Yvette and directed her questioning at Emily. "Do you have a husband?"

"No, I'm a widow."

"How did you lose your leg?"

"Is that relevant?" The intrusive interrogation bordered on rudeness.

Sister Mary Agnes sat back in her chair and straightened her tunic, smoothing the black wool's wrinkles. "I was a novice and had just taken my first vows when the conflict began. I am Cambodian, but of Vietnamese descent, so had to escape across the border during the war. After the liberation, I returned to find our dear church as it is now. The Khmer Rouge hated all religion, so they threw grenades into the building. Fortunately, they were fearful of the ghosts residing in the cemetery behind us, so they left the villa intact.

"Many Catholics lived in Cambodia before Pol Pot's time. But it took another fifteen years after the war ended for the government to recognize Christianity again. You can see why there are so few of us. We are in great need, and our mission to spread the love of Christ is powerful."

"When did the church become an orphanage?" Emily said.

"We prefer to call ourselves a residential care facility. *Orphanage* sounds so out-of-date, don't you agree?" She called for the girl to bring more drinks. "Do you attend Mass regularly?"

Emily remembered uncomfortable conversations about religion at school. Her parents had fled their home to escape sectarian violence and raised Emily with the freedom to choose her spiritual path privately. She resented proselytizing of any kind.

"My mother was born a Catholic in Northern Ireland. I know something of religious suppression, if that's what you're getting at, Sister?"

Sensing the tension, Yvette jumped into the conversation. "How many orphans reside here?"

The nun shifted her laser focus. "Eighteen. Another twenty or so come every day for the classes and a meal. We feed their minds and bodies, and their souls, of course."

"Have many been successfully placed for adoption?" Emily shook off her irritation. The woman was providing a critical humanitarian service, regardless of her zealotry.

"Well, none thus far. Most have parents, but they can't afford to feed them, or they think the child will get a better education with me than in their village. They bring them to me."

"How are you funded?" Yvette said.

"I receive donations from overseas Catholic charities, especially from Australia, which is why I asked if you were from there," she said to Emily. "Primarily, we survive on tips from visitors. Did you enjoy the singing and Sophea's dancing? The United Nations work here is bringing us many guests. Also, overseas people are beginning to come, now that the war is almost over. Western tourists, in particular, want to see the poor, disadvantaged children."

Emily couldn't tell if she was being cynical or not. Did the kids perform for their keep? She glanced around in the decrepit room. Where did the money go?

"What if I wanted to adopt?"

"I suppose we could consider. Many of the mothers would do anything for their child to go to the West. There would be many forms. It would be costly, of course. Do you want a boy or a girl? How old?"

"I hadn't thought about it." The audacity of the situation was unnerving yet strangely exciting. Emily could pick a child, like she could shop for a dress, and give her a chance at a better life. She wondered if this feeling was what the recruiters Johnny told her about experienced. The girl who'd danced with such beauty now sat on a stool against the wall as if waiting for a summons. Emily's life without Steven and their baby lay before her like a flat and featureless Montana highway.

"Just how expensive?"

Once again, Sister Mary Agnes looked at Emily with her x-ray vision as if she could see her bank account balance. "Twenty thousand US dollars. And I will help to get the approval from the government officials." Negotiation complete, she stood abruptly and said, "Follow me." Returning to the building where they had watched the children, she clapped her hands and told them to line up from oldest to youngest.

"Which one you want?"

CHAPTER THIRTY-FOUR

MILIJANA 1977

The Guard's stale breath surrounds me. He holds my arms from behind and jerks them up. Pain shoots through my shoulders. He laughs and then whispers in my ear that my husband is gone. Dead. Dead. Dead. Planted in the ground as fertilizer for rice.

It can't be true; I still feel him in my heart. They lie to cause pain.

As I begin to faint, the Interrogator throws a bucket of filthy water on my head. He shouts, "When did you first contact your CIA handler? Tell me everything about your trip with the foreigners!"

I would laugh if I could. Why would the American CIA have infiltrated a film crew from communist Yugoslavia? I remember the fateful journey that changed everything and brought me to this wretched place. I write to give my tormentors what they want.

Documentary filmmakers Dragan Pavić, Mira Jovanović, and Jusuf Imširović arrived at Pochentong airport on January 13th, 1977. Many high-ranking cadres were on hand to greet them. The honored guests accompanied Khieu Samphan during his triumphant return to Phnom Penh after the Non-Aligned International Movement Summit in Belgrade, Yugoslavia. They brought their camera and audio equipment in large black cases to film our people's revolution ...

I stood directly behind Pol Pot and Ieng Sary that day as they welcomed the delegation at the airport; my role was interpreter and liaison. Delighted to be speaking my mother tongue, I greeted them in the Yugoslav manner of three kisses and strong hugs. But Ieng Sary pulled me aside and hissed in Khmer that I must only speak French. He was fearful of what we might say without the watchers' knowledge.

We drove straight to the hostel where the foreign guests were to stay. The next morning, we met with our comrade leaders at Central Committee headquarters. Everyone sat around a low table with a white linen cloth. The stuffed armchairs had antimacassars on the arms and backs. I wondered who had crocheted the delicate pieces as coffee was served by two silent, unsmiling girls in green uniforms. They told me to stand behind Khieu Samphan's chair. He spoke at length about the film's importance—it must show the world the truth about our people's revolution. Dragan, the director of the project, nodded yes over and over and then met my eyes with a questioning look.

I think back over all that happened during those final days. What did I do wrong? What fatal error did I commit? In the end, it was sweet, young Mira who would lead me astray.

Not a CIA spy, she was something much more dangerous.

CHAPTER THIRTY-FIVE

EMILY 1993

"I need a white blouse!" Emily shouted. "Something to wear to the pagoda!"

Yvette poked her head out of her room with a sleepy face. "Do you realize it's not yet light out?"

"I'm sorry to wake you, but I completely forgot that I agreed to visit Arun's pagoda with him this morning. He wants me to help him feed his father's ghost, and we begin at dawn."

"You know I can't function without my coffee. Let me think a moment." Yvette wrapped her kimono tightly around her waist before rummaging through her closet. "I always thought that seems so creepy, feeding the ghosts of one's ancestors

. . . voilà!" She spun around, holding up a lace top suitable for Emily's grandmother. "This should fit you. I keep it on hand for these types of occasions."

"Gee, thanks."

It was still dark, with a glimmer of pearl in the east. Arun waited, a woven bamboo basket under his arm. His face fell when he saw she was empty-handed. "No food for husband, baby?"

She imagined the ghosts slurping pasta Bolognese and washing it down with a hearty Chianti. "I'm sorry, Arun. I forgot."

Arun passed the basket to Emily and set his floppy canvas hat on his head. "No problem. I bring plenty *cha ma sur* noodle for share and *bay ben* for *prett*."

Emily maneuvered onto the back of the small motorbike. She enjoyed that exhilarating moment when she lifted her legs and they shot forward. "Where are we going?"

"We go old home."

Curious what he meant—Whose old home?—Emily relaxed as they snaked their way through the increasing early traffic. She loved observing the scenery slipping past. Small charcoal fires burned under blackened caldrons as sidewalk food sellers prepared breakfast. Though it was still dark, it seemed everyone was on their way to feed the ghosts. She was surprised when they came to a stop not far from the terra-cotta–red National Museum where she had met Nick. Arun parked his moto and took the basket. They joined a stream of people passing through a large gate in the yellow stucco wall. Emily was glad she'd dressed appropriately in Yvette's white blouse and a long black skirt.

The vast complex of the Royal Palace consisted of four smaller compounds within the larger. Gilded *prasat* spires glinted in the sunrise. Marble pavilions of imposing Khmer design dotted the landscape, lit from below, like a scene from a fairy tale.

"This is beautiful."

"We first feed prett," Arun said.

Wat Preah Keo Morakot, or the Silver Pagoda, was located in the southern portion of the complex. Soaring Italian marble columns rose up, delicate fingers cradling the whitewashed building in their palm. The gabled corners of the traditional Khmer roof curled up, creating an impression of weightlessness. As Emily walked up the steps, she could just make out the window shutters, filigreed with a gold leaf design, mirroring the roof's upward lift. She felt like the building could float up into the heavens where the morning star shone.

To the side of the structure, people tossed small balls of rice to the floor. Arun set his basket down and pulled out a small plate of the bay ben. He handed her one of the sticky objects covered with sesame seeds.

With a smile of encouragement from a nearby young woman, Emily cast it onto the growing mound, thinking how strange it was to throw food on the ground.

"Now we pray," said Arun.

As she entered the pagoda, her mouth dropped open. Illuminated by spotlights, vividly painted panels depicting images from the *Reamker*, the Cambodian version of the *Ramayana*, dressed the walls and ceiling. Stately pillars decorated with intricate motifs lined the length of the long, narrow space. Floor coverings protected the namesake solid-silver tiles. Bigger-than-life Buddha statues, fronted by hundreds of flickering candles, greeted her from the other end. A golden cabinet housing a Buddha figure made of precious green Lalique crystal dominated the center of the room. Dozens of people in positions of prayer and meditation knelt on carpets before a line of seated monks.

Arun disappeared and returned with a plastic chair so she could sit, placing it in a perfect position for her to observe, yet not be in the way. He set the basket near her feet and took careful steps through the crowd to an open spot near the Buddha. He knelt and touched his forehead to the ground three times. Sitting back on his knees, he prayed with hands clasped before his heart.

As Emily basked in the hypnotic sensation created by the monks' chanting and the fragrant smell of incense, a plump white-haired older man, sitting cross-legged nearby, coughed softly. "Excusez-moi, madame."

"Yes?" Emily whispered, not wanting to disturb the proceedings.

"Is this your first time to pray for Pchum Ben?"

"Yes, it is."

"Welcome. We happy you here." His gesture included the elegant woman sitting next to him.

"I'm honored to be a part of respecting one's ancestors. There's really nothing similar in the States, except Memorial Day, but that's for soldiers."

"Ah, American." He had the polite but cautious tone Emily recognized. "You live Cambodia long time?"

"Not long. Would you please explain what's going to happen next?"

"Of course." He moved a bit closer. "This my wife, Botum. She university teacher—talk English better me."

The elegant woman smiled. She was small and delicate, with an ivory complexion. Her hair was twisted in a stylish chignon and streaked with white threads like the woven silver embroidery of her sampot. "The monks have been awake for many hours, praying for our ancestors," she said. "They are now calling the dead. We, the living, gather to celebrate them. Traditionally, we give food to the monks to gain merit for our lost ones, who might have bad karma." Laughing, she added,

"Also for the good of our own. We can never have enough good karma."

"That's fascinating." Emily shifted in the chair to relieve the prickly heat tormenting her.

Botum noticed her artificial leg with soft eyes. "You have some prayers, as well?"

Emily looked down at her feet. "Yes, I suppose I do."

"After this service is complete, we will go to a pavilion nearby. The monks will sit, and we will serve them breakfast. There will be plenty of food, and you must join my husband, Chea, and me. We would like to share with you my special chicken curry and coconut rice."

"That sounds delicious." As Emily looked up to locate Arun, she noticed the silhouette of a Western man seated like the locals on the floor. There was something familiar about him. She wondered who he was and how she knew him. After she'd located Arun, she searched again for the man, but he'd disappeared. She shivered.

"My landlady told me that this celebration is to feed hungry ghosts so that they leave us in peace?"

"Yes, that is true." The old man leaned forward. "Hell open this fifteen day. Devil release his ghosts. Must very careful."

Playfully slapping Chea, Botum said, "Many of our people are superstitious. We believe the spirits, *pralung,* are lost souls who sinned greatly during their earthly lives. We pity them, as they are sad and lonely. They are cursed with tiny mouths, so it is difficult for them to eat. But this is a traditional, old-fashioned belief. I am a student of Western philosophy, so my perspective is different from most."

"Yes, my wife very wise."

Emily leaned forward. "What does throwing rice balls on the ground represent?"

"Ah, Bay Ben." Botum assumed a lecturing tone. "The formal rituals of this ceremony may symbolize the relationship between the individual and the greater society. Each grain of Bay Ben rice is rolled into a ball, which is then eventually added to a larger mound, representing how our Khmer society relies on the separate to connect and bind to the whole. We quite literally put back together all the unique lost and scattered souls with the forming of the rice balls."

"But it's not eaten?"

"No, this food is for prett to eat. Those ghosts with no family to feed them. They carry heavy sins and need our compassion. We feed them while it is still dark, as they roam during the nighttime. Later we will make other offerings of food and gifts to the monks who will pray for our dead ancestors."

"It's interesting how so many religions around the world utilize food as a symbol of shared values; and the act of eating brings people together."

"Yes, exactly," said Botum.

"But what about the ghosts?" Emily asked. "How does the supernatural element fit in?"

The woman squirmed a bit. "The Western and Eastern mentalities are vastly different. We have a violent and painful past to reconcile."

"Violent histories are not unique to Cambodia."

"No, of course not. But our society is still closely tied to the earth, which is ruled by capricious spirits. *Neak Ta*, our guardian animist spirits, were here before Buddhism and will likely be hereafter. When I pray, my dead mother visits me. I prepared her favorite dish for sharing today. Who do you see when you pray?"

Wet pavement with glittering glass passed through Emily's mind. "I don't see anybody."

"How lonely for you." The woman's eyes shone.

A deep and sonorous bell began to ring nearby, indicating the service was complete. Arun was making his way through the crowd. The older couple clasped Emily's hands and reminded her to come to share some of their food, a dead mother's favorite recipe. As Emily turned to greet Arun, the man she'd glimpsed earlier appeared behind his shoulder.

It was her dead husband, Steven.

CHAPTER THIRTY-SIX

MILIJANA 1977

The monsoon is in full force. I saw a woman prisoner from my cellblock dig through the mud for worms to eat. I stumble over my rotting toes as they take me to the same room every day now, forcing me to sit at the little desk and write my story. The Interrogator stands close by as I write, smothered by his rank odor. If I stop, he whips me with a thin metal rod. I write anything that comes to mind, just to be writing. Can torture become routine?

The Interrogator and the red-inked notes always told me what to say. But today is different. I'm given a new script.

They have found my secret and will dig it out of me like worms in red mud.

CHAPTER THIRTY-SEVEN

EMILY 1993

Emily gasped and took a step back, almost crushing the bamboo basket. The Silver Pagoda hall was awash with people trying to leave to set up food for the monks. Her heart pounded out of her chest. She reached her hand toward the man, wondering if it would pass through him. Had Arun summoned his ghost? The outer door opened again, and the bright morning light banished all shadows and ghosts.

It was not Steven.

The man's coloring and build were similar, but he was much younger. Noticing Emily's ashen face, he asked, with a Scandinavian accent, if she was okay. Taking a deep breath and assuring him she was, she looked around for Arun. Her heart rate began to ease down to normal levels.

"Arun, I want to go."

"Yes. First feed monk." Taking the battered basket, he led Emily outside. "We go there." He pointed to a raised marble pavilion where people were opening food containers and spooning out fragrant dishes before a seated line of twelve saffron-robed monks. Two women were spreading colorful woven mats so everyone could sit and share in the feast. A little girl skipped past, only to trip and fall and then jump back up, smiling like a jack-in-the-box.

Botum and her husband waved an invitation. Reaching the open-sided building steps, Emily realized she wouldn't be able to sit on the mats like everyone else, so she sat on the uppermost step. There would always be that moment of accommodation, she thought ruefully. Observing her predicament, the couple moved closer.

"Please, join us," the woman said, with a nod including Arun.

The mood was festive, people talking and calling out to friends and family. As if at a happy family reunion, friends moved easily from group to group. It was not at all the somber atmosphere she expected at a celebration of the dead.

Though educated and urbane, Botum spoke about ghosts and spirits as if discussing the weather as she dished chicken curry into a plastic bowl. Emily imagined the pavilion to be crowded with the dead, like invisible moths floating and darting among the living.

"Oh, *cha ma sur*!" Botum exclaimed when Arun pulled out a bowl of stir-fried glass noodles. "My favorite! This is very traditional to eat. Like your turkey and mashed potatoes at Thanksgiving. The thin noodle is small enough to fit through the pinhole mouth of the hungry *pralung* spirit."

Emily took a small bite of Botum's curry. "Delicious, thank you!"

"Most happy to meet you. You will bring us luck, I'm sure."

Emily smiled. "I've never considered myself particularly lucky, but I'm happy to give you some if I can."

"You strong spirit," said Botum's husband.

The older woman smiled tenderly at the old man. "We both lost our spouses and children during the Pol Pot era, so we come today to pray for them."

"I'm so sorry."

"Don't be sad for us. We found new luck. We found each other and started new lives. We are newlyweds." She smiled sweetly. "Most people here lost family during that time, but Cambodian people are, by nature, happy and optimistic. Many children are being born now. Love does conquer all."

"That's good to hear. Most of the people I know are involved with the UN or working with people in need. It's great to hear something happy."

Arun reached over and placed some noodles in her bowl. It was the first time she had seen him smile. "Do you think you could help me talk about something with my driver, Arun?"

"Of course." Botum dished more curry into Emily's bowl beside the noodles.

"Arun told me something astonishing. He says he recognizes me from a previous time."

"Well, reincarnation is commonly accepted here."

"I think this is different. Arun said he knew *me* and that I came to Cambodia for a specific purpose. A *task*."

Arun began to speak in rapid Khmer as Botum watched his face closely. "*Ou preah chuoy,*" she muttered when he stopped. "He has a curious story about you." She exchanged looks with her husband. "He brought you here today so his father's ghost will see he is helping you. I think Arun might be a medium, *kru bormei* in the Khmer language. There are more and more of these people after the ravages of the Khmer Rouge era; I believe they play a therapeutic role in the restructuring of our society. He means no harm to you."

Looking at Arun, Emily asked, "What am I supposed to do? What's the task?"

"Madame know soon."

Emily turned back to Botum, who only shrugged. "Don't worry—he only wants to help you."

As they stood to leave, the older woman drew Emily into her arms for a warm embrace. "I will pray for you, my daughter."

The walk back through the Royal Palace compound to the gate in the bright morning light was dreamlike. Emily floated past the golden prasat spires and marble pavilions crowned with upturned crimson eaves. The pummeling adrenaline of the earlier fright had subsided, leaving her still tingling. Were ghosts real? It didn't seem to matter. Passing people smiled and nodded, full of holiday good humor.

Emily glanced sideways at Arun. "Did you feed your father's ghost?"

"Yes."

"How does that happen? Do you actually see him and hear him?" Emily pressed.

"Yes."

Emily had no idea how to ask what she wanted to know. "Did he mention me? Is he happy now?"

"Yes."

Uncertain he was understanding, Emily switched topics. "Do you live far away?"

"There." He waved his hand in the general direction of the river.

"Alone?" She remembered his wife and baby had died. It seemed rude to ask if he saw their ghosts in the same way as his father's. Why would innocents be in hell, too?

After a moment, he said, "Yes."

CHAPTER THIRTY-EIGHT

MILIJANA 1977

I'm crammed into a child's small seat. There are new stains on the tiled floor. I'm not the only one they bring here. The Interrogator stands over me; he holds a narrow metal rod, casually slapping it into the meat of his palm with hypnotic percussion. The threat always present. *Write!* he shouts. He wants every detail of the trip with the filmmakers. I begin with the itinerary.

Phnom Penh, Takeo, Kampot, return to Phnom Penh . . .

I worked closely with the Central Committee to find suitable locations for filming. Interviews with village cadre leaders had to be approved in advance. Others, more trusted than I, made the local arrangements. Accommodations, transportation, food. There could be no surprises. We toiled for weeks in preparation. After the Yugoslavs arrived, a new face appeared in our meetings—Vannak, a political affairs officer from Son Sen's office. Always silent, he missed nothing, like a spider in the corner of every room.

Dragan was the charismatic director and leader of the group. A big, hearty man, his curious gray eyes twinkled constantly with mirth. Jusuf, the cinematographer, was the opposite—small-boned and thin, but strong enough to heft the heavy cameras. Mira, the sound operator, was a beauty with chestnut hair and hazel eyes, and along to keep Dragan happy. I had thought her unsuitable for the project but revised my opinion of her after watching her hold the boom mic steady for hours in the hot sun. January is the dry season, and the unfamiliar heat proved a burden for them, but they laughed and didn't complain. They were always good-natured, in the manner of my homeland. Vannak ensured I was never alone with them and discouraged me from speaking my native language.

That first day, we drove around the uninhabited city looking for backgrounds. The cameraman filmed through the window of the car. I hadn't been outside my small compound for months, and the sight of all the empty streets chilled my heart. Block after block of abandoned buildings, vines smothering the desolation. We stopped the car to film a Catholic church that had been blown to ruin by KR grenades.

"Banks and churches were routinely destroyed as evidence of moral decadence," I explained.

"What does this mean? Where are the people?" the director whispered in Serbian.

"Fearing American bombs, our leaders evacuated the cities to ensure the safety of our citizens," I replied, aware of the political affairs officer listening nearby. "By returning to the countryside as a nation of workers and peasants, we freed ourselves from the shackles of corrupt capitalism." As I quoted my own propaganda, Vannak nodded in approval.

Did the leaders want me to spy on my countrymen as Vannak spied on me?

Like the pineapple, Angkar has many eyes.

CHAPTER THIRTY-NINE

EMILY 1993

Emily smiled at Nick propped against the wall, looking like the Marlboro Man advertisement from her youth. "Howdy, stranger. You lost?"

"Not this Boy Scout," he said, kissing her cheeks.

"Shall we go in?" He hadn't shaved and his beard was a bit rough. Emily's skin tingled from the contact.

Le Papillion was the restaurant where UN chiefs went to power lunch. A high-end establishment, it had a notice at the entrance prohibiting weapons. Located on the busy street fronting the massive art deco Central Market, it had a classic Parisian bistro vibe. Varied customers in suits and uniforms from all around the globe made deals and agreements determining the future of Cambodia. Emily was the only Western woman in the place.

This city is one fancy men's club, she thought. The few international women to be seen around town stood out like shiny coins. Yvette, Jules, Jane—Emily knew how the men scrutinized them with squinting eyes, like lions watching gazelles. The Cambodian women involved with the mission floated unobtrusively on the sidelines, masking their real opinions.

The maître d' was a thin Frenchman with a pencil mustache who led them across a checkered floor to their table near the back. After pulling out Emily's chair, he snapped his fingers for the young waiter standing at attention nearby. He hustled back to the front to greet a group of VIPs orbiting the UNTAC chief, Yasushi Akashi.

"Wasn't he in the film *Casablanca*?" Emily whispered.

Nick laughed and told the server to bring them bottled water and some good champagne. In answer to Emily's expression, he said, "We're celebrating the race."

"The cyclo race? Congratulations, Nick—what an achievement for the journalists." After her experience at the pagoda, the event seemed like the antics of adolescents.

"Now, don't be judgmental. It was a good time for everyone. Mitch almost beat me, but someone lobbed a pineapple at him and he stopped to harangue the poor kid."

"Threw something? That doesn't sound like *everyone* having fun."

"It happens sometimes, not often. At least he didn't have a grenade."

Emily thanked the waiter as he ceremoniously wrapped a bottle of Veuve Clicquot in a linen napkin and poured the wheat-colored liquid into a crystal glass. Small, crisp bubbles filled her flute and tickled her nose. She tilted her head back, the champagne sliding down her throat, until a shock passed through her like electricity, from another time and another bottle of the same wine. She put the almost-full glass down and took a deep breath.

"You okay?" Nick asked.

"It's delicious." She blushed as he watched her lick her lips. "I also had an interesting morning. Arun took me to the Pchum Ben commencement ceremony at the Silver Pagoda. I met an older couple, survivors, who lost everything—their families and their homes. But now they have a chance for a new life together. Their optimism and love for each other were inspiring. But, just for a moment, in the gloom, I thought I saw a ghost." Her playful tone fell flat. "I learned Arun is a medium who channels spirits, and I thought he'd summoned Steven." She tried to keep her voice steady. "Do you believe in ghosts?"

Nick topped up their glasses. "Honestly, Emily, I don't know. I see a lot of weird shit stumbling around out there. Creatures, human and otherwise, make strange noises in the night. I don't *not* believe. *Was* it your husband?"

Emily rolled her head, loosening her tight neck. The wine had blindsided her. Outside the window, a one-armed man shouted at a departing patron who refused to give him money. *Where are all the body parts buried?* She trembled.

"No, it wasn't Steven. It was some young Dutch guy, terrified I was having a heart attack."

"Are you sorry?" His warm tone and slight southern drawl brought her back to the table. "Your cornflower-blue eyes are looking distinctly more sapphire."

She put her chin in her palms. *Go away, go away,* she admonished the ghosts in her head. "Hey, Nick. Where's your rock-and-roll T-shirt today?"

With a self-conscious pat on his Hawaiian shirt, he said, "I dressed up for you."

Emily laughed so loudly, Akashi glanced over from his table with an indulgent smile. Like quicksilver, her mood shifted, and now she was the one looking at Nick's lips, feeling warmth where he had kissed her face. Yvette's words rang in her ears—*Nick is a sexy man, but beware.* She smiled to herself. It was time for a little recklessness.

"Nick, did you take a shower before coming here?"

"You mean after the race? Well, of course! Do I still stink?"

"Would you consider another one after lunch?"

His eyes darkened. "Do we have to wait to eat?"

Emily stood in Nick's bedroom, illuminated by horizontal bands of sunlight filtering through wooden shutters. The ceiling fan turned, barely budging the thick air. Muffled street noise came from far away. She loosened the straps of her dress, allowing it to flutter to the floor. She stood naked except for her panties and prosthesis.

"Can we please skip the shower?" he groaned.

She sat next to him on the bed and leaned down to detach her device. Blood pounded in her ears and it was difficult to draw a breath. No one, other than the prosthetist, physical therapists, and her mother, had seen her without it. She knew that people everywhere lived and loved with bodies reshaped by tragedy, but still, she was apprehensive for her new self to be seen, to be touched.

Nick sensed her hesitancy and remained still, not reaching for her. The plastic-and-titanium prosthesis tumbled over. Her heart continued to thrum as she lay back on the pillow. She searched the swirling fan for clues.

"Emily," Nick murmured. "Look at me."

She kept her eyes on the ceiling. "I'm not sure I can do this."

Nick smoothed her hair, taming the humid curls. "We don't have to do anything." His breath tickled her burning face. With delicate fingers, he turned her face toward his. Small wrinkles from the sun fanned out around his greenish eyes and deepened as he smiled. "Hello, beauty."

The feel of his touch on her face pulsed and spread until, with a sob, she reached out to him. Her desire to be held was greater than her fear of it.

Hours later, they finally showered. Hungry again, Nick shouted down for his landlord to send up skewers of grilled pork from the vendor across the street. He helped Emily hop to the settee, where she sat with her legs up, surrounded by cushions. When the food came, enveloped in a greasy newspaper, he rummaged in the refrigerator for some beer. They ate with their hands, tearing the tender charred meat off bamboo sticks with their teeth. Once they had eaten their fill, the conversation turned more serious.

"Why do you do what you do?" Emily licked her fingers. "Why do you take such dangerous risks—traipsing through land mine fields and interviewing Khmer Rouge jungle hold-outs for a story?"

"It's who I am," Nick said, popping open another can of beer.

"How does a boy from the bayous of Louisiana become you? Tell me the story."

He put the detritus of their meal into the kitchen sink and settled himself on the other end of the settee. "Like lots of us in the States, I heard about the crisis in Southeast Asia from Walter Cronkite on the CBS evening news. One night, he said the correspondents covering the Vietnam War risked their lives to serve up the truth for the viewing public's dinnertime entertainment, and something clicked. I'd just graduated from high school, so had managed to avoid the draft, but I worried I might miss something important. A teacher had shown me some photographs by the war photojournalist Tim Page, and they motivated me in a way the thought of college did not. I borrowed money from my freaked-out parents and purchased a one-way ticket to Bangkok. The rest, as they say, is history."

It explains a lot, she thought, *years dedicated to conflict and strife would give any correspondent a hard shell and a severe drinking problem.*

"You see, Emily, I love chasing the secret waiting to be told. And this place, victimized by geopolitical war games for decades, has more secrets than anywhere on earth. I worked as a stringer for different publications, like the *Bangkok Post* and the *Far Eastern Economic Review,* so I'd already been sneaking across the Cambodian border for years. When I heard through the grapevine that Philip Jones was starting a weekly in Phnom Penh, I showed up on the office doorstep, just in time for the UNTAC extravaganza."

Emily sighed as he reached for her left foot and began to gently knead her toes. "What *truth,* as Cronkite called it, are you searching for?" she asked. "What is it you want to achieve?"

"Achieve?" Nick barked a short laugh. "That word sounds like an altruistic bottom line lurking somewhere. Whether I interview a young woman in a paddy field, asking how she's going to vote, or some corrupt motherfucker from the army, or even Pol Pot himself, hiding in a cave, there's no difference. I'm focused on the story, nothing else in the world at that moment. And this election is a big fucking deal. I want to know how it'll play out. What about you, Emily? What do you want to *achieve*? Are you one of those sentimental liberals who come to *help* an abstraction but are scared shitless of the reality they find?"

She felt his gaze on the scarred stump below her right knee as intense anger coursed through her. "I came because I had to."

"The other night you talked about adopting a kid. Aren't you just looking for an unusual souvenir of your time in Asia?"

"Wow, you can be a real jerk!"

"No shit." Nick moved closer. "I'm only challenging you. You're a remarkable woman, and I haven't met anyone like you before. I want to believe you're who you seem to be. I've spent the last hour telling you about myself and you listen and nod and don't say much. But just your presence is the goddamn statement. No bullshit about that leg. I look at you and want to pick you up and protect you and yet at the same time I want to run away and hide."

Emily hurled one of the small embroidered pillows at his head. No one had ever spoken to her in such a manner. Peeled open, she simultaneously hated him and wanted to fuck him again.

She woke to the sound of birds. It was still early, gray light filling the room. Nick's face was beside her, softened by sleep. She rose slowly, trying not to wake him, and tugged on the silicone sheath, careful to smooth out any bunching. With a click, she pinned on her titanium leg. As she reached the door, she looked back at his sleepy eyes, now open and brimming with want.

She glowed down the three flights of stairs.

CHAPTER FORTY

SONNY 1993

His white shirt, damp with perspiration, was no longer crisp. Sonny stood in line for his mail, picking at his cuticles. One bled freely and started to drip. Noting the expression of the man behind him, he put the finger into his mouth.

A secure postal system was one of the many civil infrastructure casualties yet to return to normal after years of war. An innovative former tailor had remodeled his business to offer a safe, centralized location for the random nongovernmental agencies that needed reliable mail delivery. Repurposed shelving, previously containing bolts of fabric, became mailboxes. A working landline with a fax machine justified the high rent.

After a long delay, the line moved forward as a tall, sweaty Swede stepped away from the counter, mumbling in frustration at the young shop assistant. *How can they come here without even speaking the language?* Sonny fumed to himself. When it was finally his turn, he greeted the shop assistant in Khmer, and the woman smiled widely in relief.

"These Westerners should learn our customs," he said as she climbed a small ladder to reach his mail. "They should go back to where they came from."

"Yes, they can be rude," she agreed. She handed him his mail and pushed a ledger toward him so he could sign a receipt. She reminded him of his final overdue rental payment notice.

"I'll have the money next week," he lied.

After rushing from the hot, narrow space, Sonny stood on the sidewalk, clutching the envelopes. The paper was already starting to degrade in the humidity. His mother's letter, postmarked Long Beach, California, wondered when he would come to his senses and return. Lisa's mother had sent her monthly postcard of the Santa Monica Pier, the message smeared. And there was another fax from Kenneth, dated yesterday morning. The SAF executive director wanted to know why Sonny wasn't returning his messages. Where was he?

Where am I? Sonny pondered, looking up to the bruised sky as the rain began to pour like a faucet had been turned on. He held out the flimsy fax paper like an offering, and the ink bled into his hands.

CHAPTER FORTY-ONE

MILIJANA 1977

I fainted today while waiting in line for a bowl of the dirty water they call breakfast. A kind prisoner named Leap hoisted me up so Touy wouldn't kick me where I lay. There is goodness, even here.

I continue my confession.

The Yugoslav film crew and I began our journey south on Highway 2 in army trucks, generously donated to our cause by the Chinese Communist Party. It was exciting to be out in the countryside, observing the results of our revolution.

The Cambodians squeezed into the front while Dragan, Jusuf, Mira, and I sat on wooden benches lining the open back. Two teenage soldiers crouched with us, their machine guns slung across their thin chests. Were they there to protect us or keep us confined to the truck? It was the dry season, so we didn't worry about rain, but the merciless dust became a burden. It permeated everything; we wrapped krama scarves across our faces, leaving only narrow slits for our eyes. The cameraman worried about the equipment as the gritty red plume trailed us.

We followed a strict itinerary, only stopping at approved places. Dragan asked to film a young boy on his water buffalo, but Vannak said no, as it wasn't on the list. The men relieved themselves along the roadway, watching carefully for mines. Mira and I squatted behind the truck, with no privacy in the flat landscape.

Our first stop was Krong Doun Kaev, the capital of Takeo Province. The town was less than three hours from Phnom Penh in peacetime, but we made slow time navigating around craters in the heavily bombed highway. The area was famous for silk weaving, but as that expensive fabric was now considered a luxury, the Central Committee leadership had mandated that the region produce only rice. I thought of my beautiful hand-woven *sampot chorabap* with the fine golden threads sitting in a drawer back in Belgrade, and I wondered if I would see it again.

Ancient canals and waterways cut into the earth thousands of years ago crisscrossed the low-lying area. Now, our leaders had decreed an equally impressive engineering project. Vast acres of land would be irrigated and cultivated to feed the nation.

We drove through a massive worksite as we neared a sprawling lake adjacent to the bombed town's ruins. All the way to the horizon, people in black homespun and conical bamboo hats labored in the sun. With hoes and baskets and bare hands, they moved the dry earth from one place to another, like a charcoal drawing of purgatory. I'd expected scenes of collective work, but this was different. On such a monumental scale, it was devoid of humanity. From toddlers to grandparents, everyone worked, thousands of people swarming like ants.

Block after block of bombed and ruined buildings greeted us as we drove through the town, victim of the United States' vast campaign to defeat the neighboring Vietnamese communists. People lived in the minimal shelter offered by bare rafters and half-standing walls; the landscape was a postapocalyptic world.

Our wheezing truck came to a shuddering stop in a flat area dotted with newly constructed wooden huts, built on stilts in the traditional way. Drooping banana trees fronted each structure, all dying from lack of water. The houses appeared to be uninhabited. The heat was dizzying.

"*Somsuakom! Bienvenue!*" shouted the cadre village leader, waiting to welcome our delegation. Ten other comrades in brand-new black uniforms with neatly tied red-checked krama stood in a semicircle around him. The few women among them wore the mandatory chin-length bob haircut and appeared interchangeable.

Vannak, our watcher, had been carsick the entire journey. He walked up to the cadre leader and gripped his hand with both of his own. Speaking French for the foreigners' benefit, he explained he needed to lie down and asked if I could take over the official greetings. Then he turned his head and vomited into the banana tree. I stepped forward and began introductions.

We spent two days filming and interviewing the workers there, in the place our cameraman labeled a Potemkin village. We slept in one of the huts, the Cambodians in another. Mira and I slept behind a cloth hung from the thatched roof, separate from Dragan and Jusuf. We climbed up the steep ladder and lay on the bare bamboo floor, using our luggage as pillows. Mosquitos were rampant, so we bunched together under the flimsy mosquito netting.

"Is this how they live?" Mira whispered in my ear during the night.

"I believe so."

My years living in Cambodia before the war had been happy. I became a true princess when I married Rainsey and we moved from grim Belgrade to exotic Phnom Penh. We lived a royal fairy-tale life in our palaces and villas, with servants catering to our every need. I too easily set aside my youthful egalitarian principles while we ate confit de canard and drank vintage champagne in the garden.

When the civil war pitted the fervent jungle communists against the corrupt heart of Lon Nol's leadership, we'd fled back to safe Belgrade to protect our family. But news of the battle revived my sleeping Marxist aspirations, and when the Khmer Rouge were triumphant, I had insisted we return again.

Now here I was, in a dusty village from a Kafka novel, guarded by snarling children with automatic weapons, unsure of the safety of my family. What else had I misunderstood? The Brothers had distorted my revolution into a grotesque perversion of our ideology.

In need of the latrine, I tiptoed across the creaking floor and down the ladder. Tumbling starlight filled the moonless night; the landscape was illuminated with a silver glow. But rather than delight, I felt only oppression. The swirling galaxy weighed down upon my flawed attempt at humanity. I wondered where my daughters slept under those same stars.

In the morning, we washed in the open lean-to shed. We shared a small plastic bucket and splashed water over our bodies. For modesty, we kept our cotton sarongs on, letting them dry in the heat. For breakfast, we were fed *bobor* rice porridge that had been cooked in an enormous aluminum pot hung over a charcoal brazier. The cook watched every bite we took, either from fear we wouldn't like it, or her own hunger. Dragan and Jusuf began to clean dust from the equipment as the young soldiers observed in wide-mouthed amazement. They had never seen a camera or a microphone before. The cadre leader from the previous day came to tell us the agenda.

"But can't I choose what to film?" the director asked me in our language.

"Only speak French!" asserted Vannak, recovered from his sickness.

After breakfast, a group of young women filed up the path, all identically dressed in the standard uniform. I translated as Dragan interviewed the eldest girl. Jusuf and Mira hoisted the camera and sound boom.

"What is your name, and where is your home?"

"My name is Chanthavey." The girl spoke with a defiant sneer, as if we barangs might doubt her words.

She was sixteen years old and came from a village to the south. She was proud she'd left her parents and three siblings behind to come to be a leader in the local commune. She led the nightly youth sessions with unflagging enthusiasm, particularly the singing of revolutionary songs. She preferred the Khmer Rouge way of communal eating and working compared to her life under her father's control. Like teenagers around the world, she resented her parents' authority. I was reminded of myself at her age. When asked if she didn't miss her mother, she shrugged her shoulders and said Angkar was her family now.

We filmed the girls singing the same songs my compatriots and I had sung on the plane from Belgrade to Phnom Penh. Music of the revolution and ancient folktales of the land. Their faces shone with almost religious zeal as they lifted their eyes and fists into the air. I imagined my daughters dressed like these village girls, filled with ideological fervor. But is that what it was? Did these illiterate young peasant women understand philosophical concepts like capitalism or egalitarianism? I thought not; they just wanted some small bit of power and significance in their narrow lives. Wasn't that what had brought me back to Cambodia, too? As a young woman, I had received years of education, the best Europe could offer, and here I was, chasing a dream in the Cambodian dust.

Much to the film crew's disappointment, I chose not to join in the singing.

A bullock cart arrived to transport us to the earthworks project site. The juxtaposition of the modern equipment with the medieval-looking carriage was fascinating to Jusuf, who photographed the hand-carved wheels and moaning beasts from every angle. He was less excited when he stood upon a high levy and gaped at the thousands of people toiling in the hot sun. The white sky arced over us, endless yet paradoxically claustrophobic.

"*Bože moj*," he murmured. "My god."

Dragan asked to interview the engineers responsible for such a massive effort. The cadre leader smiled and indicated two teenagers.

"Where did you go to engineering school?" Dragan asked.

"We have no training." I translated the boy's proud words. "We are from the village over there." He gestured vaguely to the east.

Noting our confused expressions, the leader explained that the Central Committee had determined that Kampuchea's future lay with her youth. These peasant farmers would know best how to irrigate the new fields. I had written a lot about our youth's power and potential, but I hadn't expected to find it taken so literally. The young peasants knew about planting rice; they were not hydraulic engineers.

"Those canals won't function properly." Jusuf eyed the angle of the rough-hewn ditches closely through his viewfinder. "Unless water runs uphill . . ."

We left the next day, joining Highway 3 south to the seaport of Kampot. Mira sat close to me, her stomach upset by the unfamiliar food and a worried expression marring her sweet face.

CHAPTER FORTY-TWO

EMILY 1993

Ravenous after the night of lovemaking, Emily stopped at a sidewalk café outside Nick's apartment for a *jambon-beurre* sandwich and coffee flavored with sweetened condensed milk. An immense weight had been lifted from her heart. She'd left her ponderous shame behind on Nick's bedroom floor.

The restaurant was a simple setup, with one small umbrella-covered table. Sleepy families took their children to school by motorbike and cyclo as the city awakened. Her eyes followed a young mother with two little girls in blue-and-white uniforms perched snugly in front and behind on a scooter. All three laughed, faces bright with joy. Their love followed them down the boulevard, and Emily fought the urge to chase them and ask their secret.

"Madame?"

"Arun?" How did he know where to find her?

"Madame no home. Arun look friend house."

Annoyed by his assumption but relieved she didn't have to find transportation, she asked him to join her for breakfast. "Would you like some coffee?"

He placed a plastic chair a respectful distance from the table and sat. "*Cafe muoy,*" he told the hovering café owner.

"I want to thank you again for taking me to the pagoda."

"Father ghost happy, now he know you okay."

She searched the man's face for any hint of dissimulation, but there was only honesty in his eyes. "Well, I'm happy he's happy, I guess." Thinking of ghosts, Leap's portrait crossed her mind. Could there be a link between Arun's conviction that he knew her from another time and the woman in the painting? "Does the name Milijana Petrova mean anything to you?"

Shrugging no, he continued sipping his coffee.

But he might not know her name, she realized. "There's a picture I want to show you in Tuol Sleng."

Arun's face hardened. "Sorry, madame. I no go that place."

"Why not? You take me there all the time."

"Bad place during Pchum Ben time. Many ghost make trouble. No go inside."

Dammit! There had to be some sort of connection. But for the moment, she needed to get home for some real sleep. She blushed, thinking about why she felt so exhausted. She would find Jane Bigalow another time.

The buzzing of a trapped fly woke Emily from a glorious nap. The noise was quick and angry when the insect threw itself against the window, and then more leisurely as it explored other ways of escape. She sat up and pulled a yellow legal note-pad onto her lap, considering methods of extermination.

Emily was a skillful list maker. They were indispensable in her career as an attorney and helped her make important decisions in difficult cases. With them, she could identify pros and cons, weighing the options in a clear and unemotional manner. She was a visual person and preferred concepts written out, easy to read and evaluate.

Her current list was titled "Adoption." There were two columns—*yes* and *no*. Faces of the children from the orphanage and the little girl with no legs twinkled in her mind. She grew suspicious that her *no* column was much shorter than the *yes*, when the fly landed on the page halfway between them, offering no apparent opinion on the matter.

"You're no help." She waved the pest away.

Steven had always been a reliable sounding board for considering tough decisions. But he was gone. Maybe Arun could summon one of his ghosts. The idea of calling her mother crossed her mind, but it would be difficult to explain to Rose how much her daughter had changed in recent weeks. Emily didn't recognize herself anymore, even in the bathroom mirror. Her face was darker from the sun, giving her an edgier look, the planes of her face casting new shadows. Her eyes shone with confidence, the faded blue now brighter.

Emily liked her new appearance, thinking she would enjoy meeting herself in a bar somewhere, perhaps Singapore or Berlin. She would sit with herself and have long conversations about history and art while nibbling tapas and sipping frosty vodka martinis. In that fantasy, her missing pieces were not so much replaced as re-imagined.

Setting aside the "Adoption" list, she started a new one: "What I Need To Do Right Now." Remembering Milijana's flattering chin-length bob from the portrait, she wondered if Yvette could recommend a hairstylist experienced in cutting curly hair. She wrote *haircut* at the top of the page. With sudden inspiration, she jotted down *bank account, US Embassy, ministry, work reference.* The fly landed on her paper again and began to rub its tiny legs together as it frantically waved its antennae. She added *nun with red shoes* to the list.

"Yvette! What's a good local bank to open a checking account?"

Poking her head into the room, Yvette said, "Perhaps the National Bank of Cambodia? Why are you asking?"

"Well, I imagine to be approved for adoption by the Catholic orphanage, I'll need proof of income."

Yvette leaned against the door. "You could show statements from your US account, but having a local one couldn't hurt. *Mais mon dieu,* Emily, have you taken the decision to adopt?"

Emily swung her legs over the edge of the bed, waving her list. "Not one hundred percent, but I'm fairly certain that's what I want to do."

"Would you return to the States with the child?"

"I want to stay for a while," Emily said. "See how I like it."

Life in Phnom Penh was unlike anything Emily had experienced. The color of her skin and eyes and hair marked her as different in a manner that had nothing to do with weakness or disability. People didn't have pity in their eyes when they looked at her; they had desire or jealousy or sometimes even hatred. But what they didn't have was the superficial, claustrophobic, false compassion toward the disabled that she hated more than anything. Life in Cambodia had no set limits.

With that thought, she realized she hadn't returned to the SAF office since the day Sonny informed her of her new purpose with the agency. Emily would need his approval to make her chosen life possible. She added *play nice* to the list.

Out in the garden, banana trees danced in the breeze. The afternoon rain gathered, the sky darkening with mile-high clouds over the countryside. It would pour soon, the gutters rushing and overflowing, the streets becoming minor waterways that washed away the dirt.

CHAPTER FORTY-THREE
MILIJANA 1977

I scratch on the wall with a bit of broken tile. I hope to cover my cell with flowers, the billowing, blossoming plum trees from my youth in Serbia. Like fragrant snow, drifting across hillsides, the petals a promise of spring. Each flower a declaration of love, an act of defiance. I remember another flower . . .

"What is that?" Mira had pointed at the white trumpet-shaped blossoms of a clambering vine that softened the sharp edges of a burned-out tank.

"Datura," I replied. "It's lovely but poisonous."

The drive from Takeo to the seaside port of Kampot took the entire day. The battered highway was almost unnavigable in places. On several occasions, we got out and helped push the truck out of deep potholes. The relentless red dust continued, stinging our eyes like chili powder, so we poured warm water on our faces from dented army canteens. We moved under the vast cobalt vault of the sky as it grew white with enervating heat. Tall sugar palms stood like lonely lookouts protecting the flat landscape. The misty, cool Elephant Mountains were a mysterious smudge on the western horizon. Those distant hills brought back sweet memories of happy years, before the civil war's conflagration drove us away. During the hot season, we had often visited Bokor Hill Station, which was originally built in the 1920s for French colonialists needing respite from the heat. I was no better than those oppressors I'd hated. How quickly I'd folded into the velvet embrace of privilege.

Perhaps it was that guilt that had fueled my passion to dive into the maelstrom, to return to Cambodia and join the Khmer Rouge, to risk everything. The empty countryside passed as we navigated the ruin left by war. Worry for my family overtook me. I hadn't seen Rainsey for weeks.

Bouncing in the back of the Chinese army truck, I distracted myself by entertaining my countrymen with Khmer folktales about the scenery: "The King and the Buffalo Boy" and "Why the Oxen Have No Front Teeth." I described the local Cambodians' irrational fear of ghosts. I recalled recipes for delicious meals flavored with the famous white pepper of the region. Soon, tears of laughter made tracks down our dusty faces, causing us to laugh even harder. The soldiers stared at us as if we were insane. And perhaps we were, in the middle of that vast plain where we would always stand out as strangers.

At each small huddle of stilted wooden houses we passed, villagers stood mute, following us with angry eyes. Only the youngest children would smile and wave, sometimes running in the wake of our dust. The adults were statues, watching our white faces pass like the ghosts I had joked about.

"Are they afraid of the soldiers, or us?"

"I don't know," was my honest reply to Dragan's subdued question. "They might be ethnically Vietnamese, at war with the Khmer Rouge, and we are close to the border."

Before the war, Kampot was a curious mix of charming and commercial. Set along the Preaek Tuek Chhu River, which empties into the Gulf of Siam a few kilometers away, the town had been a vital hub since before the time of French rule. It was important for its proximity to the seaport—it was the land of salt and pepper, both valuable condiments of the spice trade.

The trucks stopped before an abandoned hotel. A drunken portico leaned out over the semicircular drive. The delicate ornamental details of the original building had been softened and smoothed with time and weather. Bullet spray had left bits of crumbling white plaster marring the smooth surface of the mustard-yellow walls. I was conflicted. I felt proud of what those holes represented, but the beautiful old structure's ruin deeply saddened me.

I jumped from the back of the truck down to the empty boulevard. It had been a long time since my last visit, and I didn't recognize much of what I was seeing. Usual two-story concrete shophouses with iron shutters and balconies lined the way, but most had sustained heavy damage in the conflict. The battle for the strategic provincial capital had been a turning point for the Khmer Rouge against government forces.

We lugged our bags and equipment into the foyer and stood speechless, staring at the bygone grandeur that had been stripped bare and stained by war. I walked close to the wall and gasped as I realized what I was seeing—a head-high line of discolorations indicating where soldiers had been lined up and shot. Black pools of old, dried blood obliterated the tilework of the floor. I choked down my shock, thinking I might faint. The sound of buzzing flies filled my ears.

Jusuf's voice trembled. "May I film here?"

Vannak only shrugged in reply, not understanding the horror of the story before us. "An important battle was fought here," he said. "Our soldiers were very brave, very strong."

Mira stood in the entry, her hazel eyes filled with tears. Our two guards pointed and laughed at the horrible sight. Dragan, the leader of this wretched project, stalked the space, growling like a caged tiger.

Vannak showed us two rooms, one for the men and one for us women. The once-lovely bedrooms were barren; all useful copper wiring and fixtures had been torn out of the walls, leaving deep scars in the plaster. We opened the tall shutters for some air, and light poured into the dim room to reveal mattresses, lumpy with kapok tree cotton. I walked over to the young woman and put my arms around her in an attempt to comfort us both.

"I'm sorry," I whispered. "I didn't know it would be like this."

Now, from my prison cell, I wonder if that was the moment when I accepted that our grand experiment was a failure. I see the babylike faces of those two young guards with their machine guns slung behind their backs, sitting cross-legged in the dirt and staring at us as if we weren't real.

Teenagers make the best killers.

CHAPTER FORTY-FOUR

EMILY 1993

Before returning to SAF and facing Sonny, Emily stopped by the museum, curious whether Jane had learned anything more about the mysterious Milijana Petrova. Leap and Debbie weren't there, but the men from her previous visit slouched in the same spot on the bench.

"*Soksaby!*" She waved.

"*Saysabok!*" one of the guides called back.

Cornell University had a long history of Southeast Asian studies programs. At the end of the Cambodian civil war, several prominent academics returned to the country for research purposes. With dismay, they discovered a looted National

Library as well as other damaged and destroyed cultural sites. The university initiated a project to salvage lost books and documents. The program started with the National Library, but with the discovery of the S21 archive, it had expanded to include Tuol Sleng.

Emily walked down the former lycée corridor and entered the classroom turned prison cell turned office. Once again, the formidable Madame Phang, elegant and fresh, greeted her. Her red lipstick was impeccable.

"Bonjour, madame," Emily said. "Is Jane here today?"

Without a word, the woman stood and rapped on the wall behind her desk. A door opened a crack and Jane slipped out. "Emily, hello! I hoped you'd visit. We're changing the film in the machine. It'll only take a sec, and then I can give you the grand tour. Have you met Madame Phang?"

"Yes, I have."

Madame Phang's face transformed into a welcoming smile under the gaze of her American boss. "Yes, we meet, before."

A man peeked out of the doorway. "We finish now."

"Perfect timing," said Jane. "Would you like to see where the action is?"

They entered a cool, dark room, all the windows covered with heavy fabric to protect against the sun's damaging effects. In the corner, an asthmatic air conditioner fought to combat the tropical heat and humidity. Weak bulbs hung from the ceiling, providing limited illumination. Rows of open shelving held dozens of boxes. A behemoth device dominated a table to her left.

"This is the camera," Jane explained. "It takes high-resolution microfiche. The results are sent back to Cornell for processing and posterity. Copies are given to the Cambodian government as well. These people"—Jane indicated the two men and one woman standing nearby—"do the actual work of organizing, storing, and filming the documents. They create multiple reels of images a day. Each document—some of them consisting of many pages—is recorded, then placed in a specially made insect-resistant, nonacidic box, which is kept on the shelf."

"This is quite a process. Where did you find all these papers?"

"We were able to recover a lot from homes in the neighborhood, we estimate about a third of what existed here before."

A booklet lay open on the table, next to be filmed. The page showed a crude drawing of what appeared to be a car battery with a windup handle. "I thought you were saving the confessions from the inmates. What is this?" Emily said.

"A how-to manual for torture. You're correct—many of the papers are individual confessions, but there are also propaganda pamphlets and instruction booklets like that one. There's even a collection of recipes to keep someone alive with a minimum of calories. Morning glory soup was a favorite. It's a ubiquitous green plant. Tasty if stir-fried with garlic and chilies, but boiled alone in a vat of water, per the recipe, it sounds bland."

Emily's stomach clenched at the thought of a human being subsisting on such food. "An interrogation-center cookbook? Wow. Do you have much more to do?"

"Difficult to say. We keep finding new caches of important items. Like that box of loose negatives in the corner. They photographed all the inmates when they processed them. There are hundreds, probably thousands, of faces."

Emily picked up a bit of brittle and discolored black cellulose. Holding it up to the dim light, she could just make out the face of a young man, his eyes so wide with terror, the whites glowed. Even old and damaged, the negative radiated tremendous fear. She was looking at a dead man. She gingerly replaced the negative in the box. "That's intense." She rubbed her hand on her skirt, her thumb and forefinger smudged with mold.

Jane nodded. "I met a photographer who said he'd like to help restore the negatives before they're ruined. He offered to raise money to do the work. I hope it happens because my university funding only covers the paper documents. I'm waiting for approval from the Ministry of Culture."

"You know, the guide I told you about, Leap, said that he has a photo of the woman in the painting. He told me about the photographing of prisoners. Maybe the original of her is in here somewhere."

Jane pushed her foot against the chaotic box. "It will be quite a feat to organize all this. The cross-referencing alone will be a nightmare."

"What do you mean, cross-referencing?"

"All the inmates were entered on a list and given an identification number. Similar to what the Nazis did in the concentration camps, though these poor folks didn't live long enough for any tattooing."

"Did you happen to find Milijana Petrova on the list?"

"Madame Phang and I both searched. But we didn't find any hint of her." Jane led Emily out of the stuffy room, allowing her staff to resume their duties.

Emily sat with a dejected slump. "How do I learn more about her? Did you talk to Leap?"

"No Europe woman here. Leap old crazy man. He make trouble." Madame Phang didn't seem to think much of the guide. Or Emily, for that matter.

Humidity caused Emily's hair to frizz and her blouse was dark with sweat. She feared the elegant Cambodian woman considered her some sort of backpacking tourist and didn't take her request seriously. She appealed to Jane. "Have you even seen the painting?"

"Not yet, but I will, I promise. Leap hasn't been at the museum for several days. Another guide said he returned to his village. He took the keys to the closet with him. Don't worry. We'll find out more as soon as he comes back."

Emily wiped her face in frustration. *Why are huge things possible, like choosing a child, yet little things, such as a key, so difficult?* Nothing followed familiar logic. As the image of the frightened youth from the negative came into focus in her mind, a sound tiptoed along the periphery of her hearing. A woman wept nearby. Below Emily's feet, iron-colored bands stained the floor as if someone had mopped the cracked tiles in a hurry.

"What was this room used for?"

"Interrogation of children."

CHAPTER FORTY-FIVE

MILIJANA 1977

I am back from my meal of the day. The cook remarked on my luck that there was meat in the soup, but I doubt her words. The gray gristle was something a dog would refuse. My stomach roils, and I lie curled up in an attempt to keep the foul food down. There is a pungent smell, and I remember another time and a similar odor . . .

I waited on the Kampot hotel's veranda as the driver repaired a broken part. Vannak circled the vehicle like an angry crow, kicking the tires while swearing under his breath. While I tried not to laugh aloud at his behavior, an older woman crept up beside me, her back so bent I couldn't see her face.

"*Ma princesse*," her quiet voice rasped. I looked down at her with surprise. Royal titles had been abolished under the regime. "*Un cadeau pour vous.*" Ensuring no one watched, she reached under her faded black shirt and brought out a beautiful ripe durian. The distinctive smell drifted up and filled me with delight.

"*Merci beaucoup, grandmere,*" I said, thanking her for the gift. I wrapped the spiky fruit in my scarf and tucked it into my bag. It would be a marvelous treat for later. After a deep sampeah, she shuffled away in the dust.

With the fan belt replaced, we clambered up into the truck, on our way to visit salt fields about two kilometers outside of Kampot. For centuries, people have "mined" salt by directing seawater onto prepared clay fields, leaving it to evaporate until the crystals formed. As we arrived, we saw female workers in black pajama uniforms with kramas wrapped around their heads raking the salt into small piles that sparkled in the morning sun.

Vannak had arranged for us to interview three of the women. As Jusuf and Mira set up the equipment, Dragan eyed them through his hands, screening possible shots. They stood with downcast eyes and giggling smiles. I marveled at these tough, strong women, filled with playful camaraderie, their skin almost black from the relentless sun.

"Show the barang," Vannak barked. The younger ones didn't grasp his meaning, but the older one bent down and put salt into her basket using her bare hands. She then hoisted it up on her head with a triumphant grin, revealing two remaining blackened teeth.

Putting the camera to his shoulder, Jusuf panned the scene, ending with a close-up of the woman balancing the basket on her head. Her skin was twisted with deep scars.

"Bong srey," I said, using the familiar term of address for older sister. "What happened to your hands?"

She stared at me like I was simple. *"Ambel samout!"* She laughed. Over time, the caustic sea salt burned the skin.

As Dragan pointed where Jusuf should film, Vannak began to recite memorized numbers about annual output, percentage of gross national product, and other proud statistics related to the industry, adding that Kampuchea was unique in world society because it had no class divisions. The workers walked away, balancing baskets of glittering crystals on their heads, chattering and laughing about the strange foreigners with eyes the color of seawater. For millennia, women like these had toiled in the sun, burning their limbs and then going home to cook their family's dinner.

We climbed back into the truck and drove to a factory that repurposed Coca-Cola bottles, collected from all over the country, into vials.

"I didn't know Kampuchea produces medicine," I commented to Vannak. "Are those for insulin?"

"It is for our traditional Khmer remedies," he said with authority. "It is best for our people. Not like the foreign poison."

I thought of the black, sticky, tarlike substance one of our maids took daily. I shuddered to think about all the people with chronic health issues, diabetes, heart conditions, or even cancer, treated with the concoction of wild honey, tree bark, and chili peppers. With a jolt, I remembered the gardener and his little son, Arun. Were they still alive?

The factory sat in a concrete-block building on the outskirts of town. The low ceiling trapped the intense heat like an oven. All the workers were boys, some as young as six or seven. They placed the bottles on a massive table and then, with heavy hammers, broke the glass into smaller bits. They wore no eye protection or gloves as they moved the shards into cauldrons situated over blazing-hot, furnacelike fires. The result was poured, like liquid sun, into rough molds. Many of the boys had untreated burns and cuts. Would they be given the folk medicine?

The film crew dutifully documented the process. Translating for Dragan, I asked one child, chosen in advance by Vannak, if he liked his job.

"*Bah*. Yes, I get food to eat and am proud to serve Angkar."

"Where do you live?"

"We sleep in the back."

"Will you show us?"

With Vannak's nod of approval, the little boy took my hand and led us to thatched huts in the rear. "Why are you all so white?" he murmured so the others wouldn't hear. "Are you ghosts?"

"No, we're not ghosts." I smiled. "We come from a different country where everyone is lighter in color." But as I spoke, I questioned my words. We *were* like ghosts here. Observing, disrupting, but not helping. Like the colonists who arrived to pillage the region, all the while noting the curious and quaint local customs. I clenched my fists, recalling that I had done just that as we drove south.

With pride, the child showed us the place where the workers slept on a splintered bamboo floor, ten to a small room, sleeping mats rolled in the corner. They ate outside or in an open-sided hut and had no individual belongings except a tin spoon. But it was home. They received evening lessons in party dogma and heard speeches blasted over an old radio when the electricity worked. Self-criticism sessions were held each week and denouncing others was encouraged, even for the smallest offenses.

"They give us one cup of rice every day," he said. "If we tell our leader someone has done something incorrect, we get an extra ration." In a quiet voice, he added, "But we are still hungry. Sometimes my brothers and I go to the river to hunt for snakes or frogs, but don't tell him!" he said, pointing at the factory director responsible for the workers. "He doesn't like it if we leave the compound."

"I won't say anything," I promised, my heart aching for this child. He was about the same age as my eldest daughter and his only play was digging in the muck for food to fill his empty belly.

We stopped near the river for our alfresco lunch. A concrete platform stood on a small rise where, in former days, people could sit and enjoy the view. Kampot was cooler than Phnom Penh and had a fresh breeze. Tall kapok trees ringed the area, their hanging pods bursting with white fluff.

"This fills our mattresses," I told Mira as I pried one open, scattering its contents in the air.

We spread bamboo mats and rested in the midday warmth. Towering heat clouds massed on the horizon, teasing us with their promise of rain, but the monsoon was still several weeks away. The water stretched brown and wide, with small swirling currents and ripples on the placid surface. A plaintive koel bird called out as it danced on a tree branch, swiveling its ruby eye in hopes of catching a wayward bit of food. A young woman bustled about, preparing our lunch over a charcoal fire. Keeping her eyes lowered, she served us clay cups of cooled boiled water and aluminum dishes of rice topped with stringy chicken. Jusuf joked that every part had been used, including the feathers, as he plucked a long, sharp toenail from his bowl.

For dessert, I revealed the durian the old woman had given me. It was an acquired taste, so I was curious how my countrymen would react to the infamous fruit. The cook sliced the thorny orb open with a quick chop of her machete, revealing pungent buttery flesh. A distinct odor wafted around us.

"What is that horrible stench?" Mira cried, holding her nose.

Dragan and Jusuf were intrigued but refused the offer to hold the fruit. With a chuckle, the woman scooped out the pods and put them on a bamboo-leaf plate.

"It's a unique flavor," I said. "Like onions and caramel combined."

"But it smells like shit!" Mira exclaimed. "How do you endure the odor?"

Passing around the plate, everyone good-naturedly took a sniff. Jusuf claimed it reminded him of almonds, and Dragan found the bouquet to be of smelly socks. But after a small bite, he devoured an entire piece and asked for more.

We all laughed when Mira said, "I'll never kiss you again."

I noticed Vannak glaring at us. "What's the matter, comrade? Do you also hate the smell?"

"That is a symbol of bourgeois tendencies," he said. "It is no longer allowed."

"What do you mean?"

Jumping to his feet, the man stomped on the glistening pods, smashing them to jelly with his combat boots. "The durian farmers grew rich selling this decadence, so we destroyed all the orchards—the same for the pepper plantations. Only rice and corn will be grown to feed the people. This fruit is unlawful." He glowered with indignation. "Where did you get it?"

How could any food be illegal in a country where people starved? I feared for the old bent-back woman. "It was only a gift, comrade." As I stared into Vannak's black eyes, I feared for our revolution, conceived in purity and executed in hate. I hung my head in shame and worried about what tomorrow would bring.

Now, in my cell, my stomach continues to spasm with sharp cramps from the spoiled soup. The memory of the durian's smell is the same as the terrible odor from my metal box of a toilet.

Mira was right. Durian did stink of shit.

CHAPTER FORTY-SIX

EMILY 1993

The SAF compound remained the same as when Emily had first arrived. It was cooler now, but the monsoon humidity made a sauna of every breath. Hearing the air conditioner in the office, she high-stepped through the red mud of the yard. Sonny sat behind his desk, papers and file folders scattered across the floor.

"Where have you been?" His eyes were bloodshot.

"It's Pchum Ben, Sonny. Isn't it a national holiday?"

"Yes, I suppose you're right. My people, assuaging the memories of a past no one wants."

Taking care to not step on any of the scattered documents, Emily took a chair. "I went to the Silver Pagoda and fed the hungry ghosts."

"The superstitions of my culture astound me. But the opportunity to reconcile one's past guilt is important."

With a nod, Emily said, "It might be like the Catholic custom of confession. I especially like that one can appease an angry relative with food."

"An angry dead relative. We have so many of them." Sonny rubbed at his inflamed eyes. He stood and called out the door for the boy to bring cold water.

Emily decided to cut straight to the point. "Sonny, I want to clarify my role with SAF. We left things a little uncertain. I'm making big decisions about my future, and I need to be certain that you will honor my two-year contract. I'm considering living in Cambodia permanently, perhaps adopting a child. I must know that you will support me with any documents I might need."

Sonny's red eyes scrunched together. "Adoption? A Khmer child?"

Emily leaned in. "Yes, Sonny. I want to adopt a Cambodian child and make my home here."

Sonny rose and threw open the door. He pushed aside the boy, who had just arrived with a tray of glasses and cold water. The astonished child fell back on his bottom, the glasses and bottle scattering in the mud. Sonny stormed up the veranda steps and into the house, slamming the door behind him.

"Well, that plan sure pissed him off," Emily said aloud, helping the boy to his feet.

CHAPTER FORTY-SEVEN

SONNY 1993

From the window, Sonny watched Emily leave the compound on the back of the motorbike. He was alone in the crumbling villa with only the little boy for company. He preferred to be alone. His mother, far away in California, was working in her salon, painting her wealthy white customers' nails. Smiling and laughing and bowing to their callowness, saving money to buy an expensive new-model car. His sister, at the mall, would be doing her best to be as white as her simpering friends. Boupha wouldn't return to Phnom Penh until all the family ghosts were safely back in hell. Blood sloshed in his head as he restrained himself from putting his fist through the glass. Was he already dead, too?

CHAPTER FORTY-EIGHT
MILIJANA 1977

My stomach has finally settled. Nothing remains inside my body to retch or shit. I am a floating void, empty of everything except memories.

For our final night before we returned to Phnom Penh, I convinced Vannak to allow us to visit Kampon Som, a small town with the most beautiful white sand beaches in Cambodia, perhaps all of Southeast Asia. We arrived a few hours before dusk and walked straight to the turquoise water. Mira clapped her hands, then lifted her skirt and waded out into the gentle surf. Our soldier guards finally proved themselves useful by requisitioning hammocks from some villagers nearby that we slung between coconut palms.

We persuaded a woman, walking past on the sand, to sell us her basket of fish for our dinner. With a bit more persuasion, she brought us a cooking pot and some rice. I promised the uneasy Vannak that our leaders would approve of the unscheduled stop, as it would show the Yugoslavs the beauty of our country.

"Beauty is useless in a revolution," he said.

"But, comrade, don't we want them to present to the world our wonder?"

Somewhat mollified, he said the blame was on me if our leaders disapproved. We all needed a respite from the intensity of the trip. I wanted to show my new friends the bioluminescent plankton of Koh Rong, a picturesque island nearby. From a previous visit, I remembered the spectacular vista of stars frothing in the ocean's waves.

After a delicious meal of steamed sea bass flavored with lemongrass and galangal, we sat around a fire and watched the moonrise. Several village children took turns providing us with dried palm leaves to throw on the flames. In the relaxed atmosphere, Jusuf pulled out a packet of Gauloises cigarettes and, to the soldiers' delight, passed them around. With a sampeah, each boy took one back to his hammock. Grumbling about the barang bourgeois influence, Vannak declined the offer and retreated to crouch on a rock outside the campfire's circle of light.

Released from our strict teacher, we stripped down to our underclothes and jumped into the warm, glowing waves. Weightless, I floated on my back, cradled by Mother Ocean, with bright stars above and below, ancient radiance captured just for me.

I thought of my family and wondered where they were at that moment. Did they see the same night sky? Our firstborn,

Daevy, a testament to our love. Baby Rachana, only two years old and chattering nonsense, so sweet with her immense eyes and fawn ringlets. My heart constricted as I thought of my husband's love-filled mahogany eyes, his pillow-soft lips and smooth skin. Tears slipped down my cheeks to join with the salt of the sea. The corridor of memory stretched in my mind. What had brought me to this moment?

Jacques, my first love from Paris, warming his paint-splattered hands on my youth. My parents, a product of their own lost and useless society. Did they all offer signposts leading along the highway of communist ideals? Had I been so hungry for respect and a small bit of power that I might risk everything? I didn't know.

I walked out of the waves to sit beside Mira on the powdery sand. We towel-dried our bodies and wrapped our hair with our krama scarves.

"Will we get to meet your family before we leave?" she asked in our forbidden Yugoslav language.

"I don't know," I said. "For the good of the party, we must stay apart."

She leaned back, elbows supporting her. "*Bože moj.* Milijana, listen to yourself! How can you live like this?"

"What do you mean?"

"This isn't communist ideology. This is something evil, very dangerous and wrong." She pointed to the luminous waters. "How can such horror exist in such a beautiful place? Why don't you return home to Belgrade with us?"

"Leave? But, Mira, this *is* my home. My family is here."

"You're blind, my friend. This place is hell."

The men slept; Jusuf and one of the boy soldiers joining the sawing cicada choir with their snores. From the corner of my eye, a shadow moved, something malignant, and I shuddered. But it was only Vannak, awake and watching, perched on his stone like a gargoyle.

That night, I dreamt of a weeping woman surrounded by broken glass and blood. Paralyzed in the manner of nightmares, I called to her with the harsh cry of a crow.

CHAPTER FORTY-NINE

EMILY 1993

Jane invited Emily to observe the special Ben Thom commemoration ceremony at Tuol Sleng. It was the last day of the two-week Pchum Ben celebration. In a final bid for better karma and a chance to say farewell to any lost and hungry ghosts, people flocked to the temples and pagodas with gifts of flowers and food for the monks. Tradition said that the gates to hell would close again until next year.

Nick was away, following a story up north near Siem Reap. Yvette was also out of town, interviewing prisoners at a facility in the old capital of Oudong, about forty kilometers northwest of Phnom Penh. When Emily arrived at the museum, a group of people was milling about the reception area. Guide Debbie gave a little squeal of delight and grabbed Emily's hand to pull her into the back room where the ceremony would take place. The open, spacious room had pale-blue walls. Three monks in bright-orange robes seated on the floor against the far side chanted prayers. Several dozen people sat before them in formal white blouses or shirts, the women in traditional sampots and the men in dark trousers. The room grew crowded as more people arrived and squeezed into spots on the cement floor. The mood was somber yet welcoming as people shifted to accommodate the newcomers. Debbie indicated an open area near the corner where Emily could sit. Observing the other women, Emily lowered herself to sit mermaidlike on the floor. No one looked twice as she arranged her different legs. The young woman helped an older man find a place and then returned to kneel nearby. Jane arrived and shimmied down.

"Thank you for inviting me," Emily whispered.

"You're welcome," Jane said. "I thought you might find it interesting."

"Will Leap be here today?"

"I think he's still away in his village. He should be back soon, though. People often return to their familial homes for the duration of the holiday."

Disappointed she wouldn't see him, Emily leaned back and allowed the monk's murmuration to wash over her. People joined in the chanting prayers, and the reverberation became almost tangible, expanding and contracting. She closed her eyes and drifted from the room, imagining herself with a bird's-eye view from above, looking down at the people below. Once again, as in past visits, she heard the intimation of weeping just on the edge of her consciousness.

Jane leaned over and said, "Everyone here lost loved ones when this place was a prison. They're praying that the spirits will find peace after the pain they experienced."

Many of the people, both men and women, openly wept. Emily closed her eyes again. The murmur of the weeping woman grew louder, more distinct. But the sound wasn't in the room. Goose bumps rose on her arms as she recognized the voice.

❈ ❈ ❈

It was raining, the November night of Emily's car accident. She and Steven had left the Group Health Women's Care clinic arm in arm. The ultrasound had been positive, the fetus healthy, with a strong heartbeat. After several weeks of worry due to Emily's age and occasional high blood pressure, the doctor's prognosis of a standard delivery left them ecstatic. Emily had come to share Steven's excitement at starting a family and becoming a parent. But, as she hadn't experienced any of the usual early pregnancy symptoms, like nausea or fatigue, the concept didn't become real until the moment she saw the rapid firefly twinkling of her baby's heartbeat. A magical Morse code of love.

"Where shall we go to celebrate?" Steven bent to kiss her for the umpteenth time.

"I don't know, the Virginia Inn?" Emily said, laughing and pushing his face away.

"The VI it is!" Steven said, and then shouted, "I'm going to be a father!" causing nearby pedestrians to glance at the handsome couple and smile.

They'd sat in the cozy window seat of the downtown Seattle bar and shared a plate of freshly shucked oysters and a bottle of Veuve Clicquot, Emily's favorite champagne. Steven greeted each new customer with the happy news. Smiling at her crazy, wonderful husband, Emily took her time, sipping at the champagne while Steven speculated that their baby would be the most amazing child ever born. He poured himself another glass.

"It's almost gone. You better have a little more." Steven's lips tickled her ear. "It won't hurt Little Peanut—all the French ladies drink champagne during their pregnancies, and they've created some important babies, like Napoleon and Coco Chanel!"

"You're a nut, yourself," Emily said.

She insisted on driving. Steven slipped into the passenger side, making a halfhearted attempt to fasten his seat belt. He leaned against the watery window and started to snore.

Impatient to be home, Emily didn't slow down as she ran through the yellow light at 85th Street, assuming the Metro bus looming on her left would stop to pick up the drenched people waiting at the bus stop. But the out-of-service vehicle, wheels spinning on the wet pavement, couldn't stop in time. Emily's last thought was wondering who was using their horn. Nobody honked in polite Seattle.

She regained consciousness in the eerie silence that follows an accident. The rain had stopped. Turning her head, she saw glinting glass thrown across the asphalt, saw its galaxy of stars. She called out for Steven as pain crashed down.

When Emily read the police report weeks later, she learned that their little Honda had been crushed like an aluminum can. Steven died instantly from blunt force trauma. He had been thrown through the windshield, as he hadn't fully latched his seat belt. The bus's momentum had shoved Emily's belly into the steering wheel and peeled open her door, tearing off her trapped foot.

❄ ❄ ❄

Nestled in the room of strangers, the endless weeping of that rainy, dark night came back to her. She recognized her own weeping voice, the imprint of vibration in her chest, her throat. Opening her eyes, she saw the image of a baby, outlined in gold, resting weightless in her lap. Wrapping her arms around the apparition, she joined with the others in the survivor's lament of guilt and grief.

CHAPTER FIFTY

MILIJANA 1977

I'm surrounded by garden. Plum blossoms cover the walls. Even the brick partitions erected to divide the former classroom into tiny cells have petals scraped with a concrete chip. There is nothing left of me to share. The Interrogator, the Guard, the Watcher, my trinity of jailers. I am squeezed dry. A fourth will come soon, the man with the red pen. The Executioner.

My captors have book after book filled with my words. My attempt to tell my story, my truth. Naive, I wanted to change the world, but I only helped with its destruction.

I write.

Dragan, Mira, Jusuf, comrade Vannak, and I arrived back in Phnom Penh on International Workers' Day, May 1st, 1977. Our film project was a triumph. We were excited to edit the footage and share our vision of a new society . . .

Two days after our return from the trip south, we gathered in the meeting hall with Central Committee members to brief them on our success. Jusuf had worked night and day developing the footage. As before, Comrade leaders in starched uniforms sat on musty stuffed armchairs with delicate crocheted doilies behind their heads. Silent girls placed porcelain cups of coffee on the table. The lights were dimmed and the projector fluttered, revealing images from the countryside.

Comrade villagers with nervous grins revealed white teeth in sun-darkened faces. Hundreds of skeletal people in black pajamas hefted heavy buckets of dirt up and down a mountainside. Women smiled and staggered under baskets of caustic salt. Children stared with hatred at the camera.

Dragan spoke eloquently of his plan to edit the footage into a ten-minute piece to be aired on Yugoslavian television and shared with other friendly countries. Jusuf's black eyes moved from face to face of the watchers, looking for a grain of understanding. Mira watched only me with wide, frightened eyes. I sat behind Pol Pot, who clapped his hands in delight, immune to the tragedy unfolding on the screen.

The projector stopped, and at the moment before the lights came on, I heard a deep, whimpering sigh. Was it me? Then the room was bright again, and our Comrade leaders, the Brothers, with their beaming wives, stood to congratulate the crew, shaking hands and slapping backs. Champagne was opened with a clumsy flourish, and I poured memories of a different time into smudged glasses. Son Sen glared at me in a way that froze my blood. Something was terribly wrong. He snapped his fingers and Vannak nodded.

As we moved into the adjoining room for the gala dinner, Vannak pulled me aside and instructed me to follow him. I wasn't allowed to say goodbye to my countrymen. A car waited outside with a driver standing at attention. I recognized the man who had taken Rainsey.

But what joy! My little girls, Daevy and Rachana, were nestled in the back seat. We hugged and wept. Frozen-faced Vannak sat in the front as we drove through desolate streets, the city barren of life except for foraging dogs.

"Where are we going, comrade?"

"You will know soon enough."

My happiness deflated as we continued past my quarters in the Royal Palace compound. Soldiers lined the boulevards— useless sentries guarding the silence. We stopped in the center of abandoned Monivong Boulevard. Two of the soldiers approached the vehicle and opened the car doors. They yanked us from the car, tied blindfolds harshly around our heads, and then shoved us back into the vehicle. Now that I could no longer see, my senses became attuned to the smell of the driver's unwashed clothing and the car's eventual turn onto a bumpy lane. My daughters wept in fear as I held them close. We came to another halt and were told to remove the blindfolds. They wrested my girls from my arms. A yellow-lettered red sign above us proclaimed: Fortify the Spirit of the Revolution! Be on your guard against the strategy and tactics of the enemy so as to defend the country, the people, and the party!

It's now been six weeks since we passed through that iron gate into hell. My flowers keep me company as I wait for the Executioner. I lie on my side. No tears remain. It is my fault my family may be dead. It was my weakness, my ego, my pretentious effort to re-create a better society that brought us to this beautiful country of horror. What a foolish girl I was, now drowning in hubris. The sights, the screams—repeating in my mind as these masters of torture intended. I pray they will come soon to kill me.

My prayers are rusty—a relic of my childhood when I wished for a pretty new dress or the attention of a particular boy. Dragi Bože, molim te izbavi me iz ovog pakla. Please, dear God, save me from this hell.

I am distracted by the sweet, earthy fragrance of the rain outside my putrid cell. I listen to its soothing sound. It cares not upon what it falls. No judgment, no concerns. It descends from above, a singular purpose ruled only by gravity. My terror wanes. In its place, a new sensation grows, spreading, opening like a lotus bud, grown from muck and mud. Memories of death and pain recede. I see vivid bougainvillea against an azure sky. I feel my husband's tender caress, the whisper of my daughter's breath on my cheek as she wishes me good morning.

Beauty, the greatest ideology, is stronger than any terror-fueled philosophy devised by man. May I be forgiven?

Why did I do this?

Why else?

For love, of course.

CHAPTER FIFTY-ONE

EMILY 1993

After the celebration, Emily found Arun waiting under the mango tree. "Madame happy now?"

"Why do you ask?"

"Madame find lost baby, yes? Now no alone."

The group of amputees stood nearby, holding out their hands to the people leaving the museum, hoping to benefit from their good nature and desire for acts of merit. They didn't swarm her anymore—she was one of them now. The little girl in the wheelchair smiled and waved hello from across the muddy lane.

Yes, she thought. *Something* has *changed*. "I don't know, Arun. You might be right. Let's go home."

Two unfamiliar black-and-white cars were parked in front of the house, blocking the way. A man in a tan uniform with fancy epaulets and medals on his chest leaned against one vehicle. Another, less senior, was dressed in green fatigues with a peaked cap; both men smoked and carried heavy black pistols on their belts. Thida peered out from behind the closed gate, the watchman beside her. A man sitting in the back of the second car ducked down. It was Sonny.

"Are you Emily Mclean?" the senior officer asked in accented English.

"Yes, I am. What's going on?" Emily's heart pounded. "Is there some sort of problem?" She knew the horror stories about the Cambodian police. Basic human rights were rare and bribery common. Was this a shakedown because she was a foreigner? But why was Sonny in the car? A terrible realization washed over her.

"You charge with steal Khmer babies," the officer said. "Very serious offense in Cambodia. You go prison long time."

"Are you kidding? I'm here working for an NGO. I have nothing to do with trafficking. Ask him." She pointed to Sonny, sitting low in the back seat of the police car. "He's my employer."

"He one make charge. You go prison now, wait trial for talk. Now give passport."

Flabbergasted, Emily took her passport out of her bag and held it out to the man. He grabbed it and stuffed it into his uniform pocket. She wondered if she should offer money. "Thida," she said, "please contact Yvette through her office. She's out of town, but someone can reach her. She'll know how to figure this out."

Yvette was the first person that came to mind. Emily didn't know anyone at the US embassy. The wondrous feeling she'd experienced during the ceremony of the dead at Tuol Sleng was gone, shocked away by the absurdity of the situation. What was Sonny doing? Why would he accuse her like this?

"Arun, maybe you can try, too? She told me she would be near Oudong. Will you find her?"

At the first sight of the police, Arun had shaded his face with his hat. He looked up and locked eyes with Emily. "Yes," he said with a nod. Turning his motorbike around, he headed down the lane, driving so fast that red mud splattered his back from the wheels.

Emily panicked as he drove away. She was alone, with no idea what was happening. Nick was inaccessible, wandering the northern jungle in search of a firefight. Her landlady was making herself as unnoticeable as possible behind the gate. Sonny was hunkered down, avoiding eye contact. The guns clipped to the policemen's belts were matte black and absorbed the light.

Prey Sar prison, located on the outskirts of the city, was overcrowded with inmates incarcerated for drug offenses, prostitution, or black-market trading. But in reality, poverty was their primary crime. Jammed into bare cells, they slept on concrete floors. They were fed meals of rice and soup twice a day. Relatives were encouraged to provide food purchased from the prison canteen at inflated prices. Prisoners without family supplemented their diets with crickets, worms, rats, and the occasional snake.

The two police cars arrived at a wooden barricade protected by a guard with a machine gun. He saluted, peered into the car at Emily, and then waved his arm for the barricade to be opened. After driving a short distance, the car stopped again before a multilevel concrete building, streaked with the ubiquitous mold, with narrow slits for windows. Her teeth chattered with fear as she was pulled from the back seat into a compound surrounded by walls topped with razor wire.

"Allez!" barked the officer. "Move!"

Emily was photographed. Her visa information was entered into a massive ledger by a sneering clerk who spent a long time looking at her passport photograph. Two female guards took her into another room, where she was stripped naked. They pointed at a matching orange top and pants. They spoke Khmer but Emily couldn't understand a word. The tone was different from what she had heard in markets and restaurants. Their voices sounded rougher and somehow dangerous; the consonants were sharper and more explosive. They shouted when Emily was slow to follow directions. Curious about the prosthesis, they touched it often, laughing as she stumbled to pull on the pants.

Emily kept her face neutral, not wanting to give them the pleasure of seeing her shame. She tried to keep her thoughts blank, to not let fearful images wash her away in a tsunami of anxiety.

They led her by the arms to another part of the facility and thrust her into a bare cell crammed with dozens of female inmates. The women clustered on the floor, leaning against one another like furniture. After slamming the heavy iron door shut, a guard turned the key and left. Emily stood with her back against the door, scanning the faces of her fellow prisoners. They were of many different races, including several Caucasians.

"Êtes-vous français?" one woman asked Emily.

"No. Does anyone here speak English?" The cell was silent, everyone watching the evening's entertainment of a new inmate.

"I do," called an older woman from the corner. She had limp reddish hair and an Australian accent. "What did they get you for?"

"I don't know what's happening," said Emily, voice thick with rage. "An officer was waiting for me when I got home. He arrested me for trafficking, which is the craziest thing. I work for an NGO." She slid down to a small spot near the Aussie woman. "My insane employer brought the charges. I'm an attorney, for Christ's sake. This is all a mistake!"

"Welcome to Cambodia, love. What's your name?"

"Emily Mclean."

"My name's Martha Johns. Pleased to meet you."

"How long have you been here?"

"It's been a while now. I think almost three weeks. I've yet to be heard by the magistrate."

Stunned, Emily stared. "So you haven't even had a hearing about your case?"

"Nope. We're all here waiting to see the judge."

Emily scanned the packed room. The inmates appeared to be from all over the world; as the conversations resumed she could discern multiple languages. "Is everyone in this cell a foreigner?"

"Yeah, they keep us separate from the Cambodians. Supposedly we get better treatment. I'd hate to see how the poor Khmer girls manage."

Emily tried to recall everything Yvette had mentioned about the jails and prison system and her heart sank even further. She hoped Thida would reach Yvette. But why had her landlady been so timid? Thida didn't seem afraid of anyone. Why was she nervous now? Arun was her best chance. Arun would have to find Yvette.

The concrete floor was uncomfortable as Emily squirmed to adjust her aching leg. She turned to Martha. "Why are you in Cambodia?"

"I connect unwanted Cambodian children with Australian families who will give them a better life."

Emily recalled the conversation with Johnny and Nick about people who went to villages and paid women to give up their babies. Martha looked like any other middle-aged woman, only a bit worse for wear, given her situation. Could she really be one of those traffickers that deceive villagers into selling their children for the sex market?

"Why were you arrested?"

The Australian woman sneered. "I didn't pay off the right contact with the right bribe. These people change up the rules, and it's impossible to keep track of who is the big guy with the power. Since the UN arrived, it's gotten worse."

"Why do you do it, then?"

"Why do anything, love? For the money! Why do you do it?"

"But I didn't *do it*! I was accused, but it's a lie."

"Sure, sure," Martha cackled. "It's always a lie." Looking at Emily's prosthesis, she added, "But you've sure got a grand cover story with that bum leg. No one would ever think you were doing anything nefarious. Until now!" Martha laughed at her own joke and poked Emily in the ribs.

Emily turned away. She felt a familiar sense of helplessness, which she hated more than anything. The door to her past swung open. She had spent weeks in the hospital with no control over her body or future. She'd wanted nothing else but to be dead; her will had been destroyed. But she had crawled back from that.

She struggled to stand, her residual leg flaring in pain, then limped to the front of the cell. Two guards were playing cards at a small table at the end of the corridor. "Hello?" she called. "I want to phone my embassy."

"Fuck off," the guard said in perfect English. "You sit. You wait."

Several of the women grinned at her and shook their heads as she slid down to the bare concrete floor.

Fear settled back in her belly.

CHAPTER FIFTY-TWO

LEAP 1977

Touy lead Milijana through the muddy S21 compound, and Leap's heart splintered at the sight of her. Though a shadow of her former self, she was still beautiful. The stolen photograph burned in his pocket. He edged closer, unsure what he, a lowly prisoner, could do to help.

Two little girls stood waiting, their faces streaked with tears. It was impossible to determine their ages; starvation made fragile ghosts of us all. Sela, the female guard in charge of minding the prison children, gripped their hands, holding them back. The elder girl began to cry; they must be her daughters. The youngest only blinked, not understanding. Guard

Touy kept his hand on Milijana's shoulder as she wailed in despair and stretched her arms toward the girls.

"Your confession is no good," he shouted into her ear.

"No, please, no!" She dropped to the ground, clutching his legs. "Mon dieu, save my daughters."

"You know very well, there is no god here," Commander Duch said as he came out from his office.

With a wave of his hand, he signaled to a third guard, standing at attention, who picked up the older girl. She seemed to float, weightless, in his hands. Turning to a terra-cotta water vessel nearby, he plunged her headfirst into the water.

"Stop! Take me!" wept Milijana.

The guard held her under the water until she went limp. After pulling her body out, he threw her down like a rag doll and turned next to the younger girl.

"This is what happens to traitors who conspire with the CIA," Duch spat, standing over Milijana. "Comrade Vannak witnessed your collusion with the Yugoslav spy."

Touy yanked Milijana up to stand with her arm twisted into an impossible position behind her back, her shrill shriek of pain that of an animal. Leap stood with his useless painter's hands in fists at his sides as the horror washed over him like black paint. All the terrible things he had seen merged into that moment. The other guard hoisted the other child, swinging her through the air by the ankles, around and around until, with a monstrous wet smack, he crushed her tiny skull against a palm tree.

Milijana wrenched away from the guard's grasp and threw herself to the ground, burrowing her face into the mud, crawling into the earth. Touy lifted her like a sack of rice and carried her to a waiting black truck filled with blindfolded prisoners. Her once-golden hair was now red with the dirt of Kampuchea. She was tossed in with the other captives, all destined to die in a field of open graves at Choeung Ek. Nameless bones tangled together for eternity.

Leap raced to the spot where the children lay. He told the guard he would dispose of the bodies. The guard shrugged and walked away. Leap dropped to his knees and gathered their delicate forms into his arms. A whisper of a moan.

The youngest girl was still alive.

PART THREE

CHAPTER FIFTY-THREE
EMILY 1993

Emily passed a sleepless night in the prison cell. The dirty blue walls created a sense of being underwater, and she was drowning in the heat. Martha, curled into a ball, snored nearby. Women lay scattered and clumped together on the grimy cement floor. A cacophony of shrill insects and droning frogs thrummed outside the window. Their thunderous noise was only interrupted by the slap of a woman fending off a mosquito. Emily's leg ached, but she didn't want to remove her prosthesis in such a filthy place.

She had come to Cambodia to be free and now she was sitting on the floor in a jail cell. She had wanted change and a blank slate. And she'd found it—the potential for a new beginning, where her *disability* didn't define her and her *ability* did.

Now, Sonny was jeopardizing everything. She wondered how much longer she could stay in Phnom Penh. She knew the charges couldn't be substantiated and she would be released eventually. But would the authorities put her on the first plane out, deporting her back to her former life? How much influence with the court did Sonny really have? Martha groaned in her sleep, a minor-key accompaniment to Emily's tormented thoughts.

The deafening clamor stopped just before dawn, and, in the silence, Emily dozed. But at some unknown signal, the trilling resumed, and she jerked awake. As the blue light in the room began to brighten, the guards came, taking them in shifts to use the toilets. Martha held Emily's hands to help her balance over the disgusting latrine.

On the way back from the toilet, one of the female officers pointed at Emily and called, "Barang come!"

Following the stocky woman, Emily entered a room with a few tables and chairs positioned about for visitors. Yvette sat in the far corner. Emily had never been so happy to see someone.

"Oh my god, Yvette, you're here!"

"Emily! *Ça va, ma chère?* Are you all right? They wouldn't let me come until this morning."

"How did you know I was here?"

"Arun. He found me in Oudong and I came right then. We drove back through the night. I have no idea how he tracked me down. What is happening? Why are you here?"

Emily sat with her elbows on her knees, face in her hands. Her bright-blond hair was dark and limp from sweat. "That crazy son of a bitch, Sonny, accused me of trafficking babies. The police were waiting for me at the house. Thida hid behind the goddamn gate while Sonny cowered in their car."

"*Bordel de merde.* I hired a lawyer on your behalf last night. He is speaking with the prison director now and trying to clean up this mess."

"What's happening?" Emily slumped. "This is insane."

"*Non, mon amie,* this is Cambodia. There is always the solution."

After a breakfast of gritty rice and morning glory soup, the same scowling guard came for Emily. "Go now," she said, standing so close that Emily smelled her musky scent. "You one lucky lady."

Emily waved goodbye to Martha and followed the guard to the changing room. Once again the guards mockingly exhorted her to move faster. After putting on her own clothing, she went to the room with the ledger. The same clerk waited at his desk and shoved a book toward her, pointing to a column of beautiful, but illegible, Khmer script marked in red. It went against her training to put her signature on something she didn't understand, but she would sign anything to be free.

"Where is my passport?"

The clerk only shrugged his shoulders in a dismissive gesture.

The sunlight when she walked outside was blinding, so she raised her hands to shade her eyes. A small crowd of people milled around, waiting to visit their loved ones. Food vendors were doing a brisk business selling small banana-leaf packets of rice and dried fish. She almost ran down the steps to get away from the prison.

"Emily! Over here."

"Yvette." Emily's voice cracked.

With glistening eyes, the Frenchwoman kissed Emily on both cheeks. "I know how terrible it is in there. In my work, I often visit the jails to interview prisoners. You must be exhausted. Let's go home." She gestured at her Land Cruiser, parked near the barricade. She put her arm around Emily as they walked. Arun stood nearby, clutching his mud-splattered floppy hat.

"Arun, you found her!" said Emily.

"Madame okay?" His face was tighter than usual, the edges of his cheekbones so sharp they might crack. He looked to Yvette for confirmation.

"I hope so, for now at least. Thank you both so much. I would still be in there without you."

"*C'est un miracle.* Now let's take you home—you need a long shower and some rest."

"Yvette, they didn't return my passport."

"I think they will keep it until your court date. When you meet with the attorney later this week, he will explain the situation. You are lucky they freed you until the trial."

"The guard just told me that. I appreciate your help, Yvette, but I don't feel very lucky at the moment." Emily hobbled toward the vehicle, anxious to shower away the filth of the prison cell. She was done being afraid. Her anger quickened her step.

CHAPTER FIFTY-FOUR

LEAP 1977

The youngest child lived.

Her left eyeball was distended grotesquely, as the horrible blow had crushed the side of her head. She moaned when he gathered her and the body of her older sister in his arms—both as light as starving birds. With care, Leap put them like dolls on his bamboo cot. The elder girl was dead, drowned in the cistern. But the small one was twitching. *A seizure?* Leap clasped her tiny body to his heart until she calmed and swept the curls back from her heart-shaped face. He had to find help and there was only one option.

Because of his work as a painter, Leap was able to move about the compound and the guards mainly ignored him. His one trusted friend in the prison was a teenage medic who happened to be from his home village. That night, like a ghost, he slipped through the shadows to the room where the young man slept.

"Comrade little brother." Leap touched the boy's shoulder. "Come with me. I have an emergency."

Rubbing his eyes, the boy nodded and followed Leap on silent feet. He gasped at the sight of the two little girls.

"Please help her!"

The medic stooped over the child and turned her head to reveal her injury. "I can't do anything. She will die soon. You must take them from here now and bury them. This is too dangerous."

Tears ran down Leap's cheeks as he wiped at the girl's battered face with the corner of his tunic. "But I must do something for her."

"Why do you risk so much for them? Who are they to you?"

Leap held the girl closer. "I don't know who they are, but I heard whispers. I saw the mother and recognized her from my life before these dark days. They did this to these poor children before her very eyes and then took her to die. She was an apsara, an angel. And they killed her—like they kill all the angels."

"*Bong proh*, older brother, I don't understand you. I will put the dead one in the ground. But the living one can't stay here." He hoisted the small body over his shoulder and vanished out the door of the hut.

Leap settled the damaged child on his lap. She moaned, "Papa?"

He had to save at least her.

CHAPTER FIFTY-FIVE

EMILY 1993

A passing urchin sold Emily a wilted jasmine bracelet. She held it to her nose and inhaled the evocative blend of sweet flowers and decay. The Gecko Club was almost empty in the early afternoon, but she still chose an outside table for more privacy. The waiter brought her a week-old *New York Times* to peruse while she waited. She felt relieved to see Nick arrive, parking his Willys jeep under the twisted frangipani tree. He wore his standard grubby fatigues and rock-and-roll T-shirt.

"Hello, pretty woman," he called, dodging a cyclo loaded with car tires.

Emily pulled him into a deep hug, overwhelmed by sudden emotion. Embarrassed by her fragility, she swallowed a sob. "Nick, where have you been?"

"I told you I was going north. Hey, what's the matter?"

"They put me in Prey Sar prison."

Nick lifted her chin. "Are you kidding?"

Gaining control of herself, she shoved away from his chest. "It was Sonny. He accused me of trafficking children." She wiped at her eyes.

"That's nuts! Why would he do that?" Nick's hands clenched the back of a bistro chair, almost bending the metal. An older woman passing by on the sidewalk glanced up at the vehemence of his tone. The moto drivers waiting near the entrance all turned their way.

"Sit down. Everyone's watching us." It started to rain, and they moved to a table under the striped awning of the restaurant. "Yvette pulled some strings to get me released. She's meeting with a lawyer today to see if he'll represent me. She should be here soon." Emily patted at a chair so he'd sit down. "I'm all right, now. I have to figure out what to do next." She cradled his face in her palms.

Nick traced the damp streaks on her face. "If you say so. But if you want me to shoot him, just tell me."

He kissed her in the honey-like way she loved. She knew he was serious.

He looked up. "Hey, here's Johnny!"

The young journalist slipped off the back of a moto and stood on the sidewalk like he was on the deck of a heaving boat. "All work and no play makes Jack a dull boy." He gave the driver some riels and stumbled to a chair. He laid his head on the table. "Whew, long night."

Nick laughed. "Looks like it's still going."

Emily poured Johnny a glass of bottled water. "Here, drink this; it might help."

"I might need something stronger. Where is Jules?"

Conjured by Johnny's magic, the British bar owner appeared through the door. "Well, susaday, my favorite journo dearies. And Emily, too. Been lost and wandering the jungle, have we?"

"We found some bad guys, but no bang bang to report," said Nick. "There'll be something in the *Post* for tomorrow."

"Glad you're both back unscathed. I see Johnny's been celebrating. Do you all want the Sunday roast lamb to nosh on? It was my gran's special recipe."

"I'll pass," Johnny whimpered, his pale face a distinct shade of puce.

"And the usual Russian?"

Johnny raised a finger. "Oh yes, *spasibo*, fast as you can!"

Jules returned with a bottle of vodka so cold that condensation puddled the table. A waiter in a white shirt and black pants followed her, balancing a tray with plates, glasses, and a heaping dish of meat and potatoes. For the first time since the prison, Emily began to soften the stiffness from her spine. She took a bite of the succulent lamb then pushed her plate away.

"Have some of this medicine," Nick said, pouring a generous measure of the vodka into her glass. "Yvette will be here soon and we'll know more, right?"

Emily's chest tightened. Nick's eyes appeared bruised from lack of sleep. Where had he been the last week? She hadn't even asked. His fatigues were stained with an oil-like substance and he had the acrid odor of dried sweat. Johnny was in a similar state, or worse off for whatever he had taken to recover from the adrenaline of the jungle. They put themselves at risk for the story, searching for violence, shining light wherever darkness crouched.

"Bonjour, mes amis." Yvette arrived, her long black hair twisted up in a chignon. Her face was pinched. "You're all here.

Mon dieu, what a day it has been." She kissed Johnny on the top of his head. "Ça va, mon cher? Et tu vivant?"

Johnny roused himself with a weak smile. "I'm much better, now."

"Is that Jules's *grandmere*'s roast lamb? Oh, I'm hungry!" Yvette squeezed into Johnny's chair and grabbed his untouched fork.

"Have a drink, mademoiselle, and tell us all about it." Nick poured her a glass. "Choul mouy."

"*Santé!* Emily, how are you doing? I have news. I met the attorney again this morning—he has agreed to represent you. Your hearing is set for later in the week." She took a big bite of the lamb and sighed.

Emily sat up straighter. "What did he say?"

Wiping her mouth, Yvette said, "It's difficult to prove a charge of trafficking, and the judge can be bribed to avoid the inconvenience of a useless trial. He is certain there is no way you will go back to prison." She set down her fork. "But . . . if your work permit is revoked and you are here illegally, there is a chance you could be deported."

"What's going on?" asked Johnny, finally waking up. "Trafficking? Deported?"

"Our friend has had a rough few days," said Yvette.

"Emily arrested? For trafficking what?" Johnny's voice had a curious combination of surprise and awe.

Still not quite believing her own answer, Emily said, "Children."

"They put you in jail for selling children?"

Emily nodded. "The experience was excruciating. Yvette, I can't imagine how you go into those places for your work. And those poor women; some of them have been incarcerated for weeks without even being charged. I didn't know if anyone would find me." Her throat now dry, she took a sip from her glass. "Are you certain this guy knows what he's talking about? For sure they won't take me back there?"

"Yes, I am certain. The charge was completely made up—how do you say it? Bogus?"

Johnny asked, "Who accused you?"

"Sonny. I've been thinking a lot about this, and I think he just snapped. He lost his wife in that horrible accident and now apparently SAF is losing its funding. That was his dream. I mentioned adoption and he went berserk."

Nick reached for Yvette's pack of Gauloises. "I'm still going to take care of him." He flicked his lighter open, roasting Sonny right before them.

"Good grief, Nick. Don't joke like that." Emily took a cigarette for herself. Yvette's confidence that prison was no longer a threat lifted a huge weight, and she felt she could float up into the clouds.

"Trumping up false charges is no joke in a place like this," Nick declared, his anger still simmering.

"I wonder if I triggered something lurking for a long time. Some sort of deep residual hatred of Americans? Don't get me wrong—he's a monster for what he did, but it doesn't make sense."

Johnny filled his glass. "Well, we're very easy to hate."

Emily frowned. "Don't say that! I thought people would trust me, realize that I understood their experience. I wanted to make a difference." She pushed her uneaten plate farther away. "Christ, I sound pathetic, like a cartoon. Another American coming to save the world, like we know what's best for everyone. I hate what he did, but maybe Sonny is right to be distrustful."

Yvette reached across the table for Emily's hands. "Your empathy is commendable, but, ma chère, he lied to the police and sent you to that horrible place. He must have gone to the Ministry of the Interior for them to arrest you." She picked up her fork and waved it around to emphasize her words. "There is nothing wrong with wanting to be of service. We all want to help. That's why we're here, even these filthy ones." She swept her hand to include the men. "There's nothing pathetic about that."

Nick topped up the glasses. "A toast. May we always be pathetic!"

Emily downed her drink with a grimace. "I'm a fucking attorney." She was beginning to slur her words. "Why can't I defend myself even for a mock trial?"

"Don't worry, he is good. A colleague from my office worked with him before. It will be a formality."

Emily put her head in her hands. "Fuck. Fuck. Fuck."

They finished the pack of cigarettes as they drank the bottle. The bright afternoon turned to lavender evening. The hour of the museum bats. Emily envisioned the small creatures swooping and soaring. She wanted to stay sitting in that spot forever, on the uncomfortable chair with Nick's hand grazing between her thighs.

CHAPTER FIFTY-SIX

SONNY 1993

Hunkered down behind Nick's jeep, Sonny watched Emily and her friends as they ate. The streetlight cast contorted shadows of the frangipani tree on the dark-red earth. He picked up a fallen yellow blossom and methodically tore the fleshy petals into strips. What they spent in one evening would feed a Cambodian family for a week. Maybe even a month. He ground the ruined bits of the flower under his foot.

When he'd informed Emily that he was reworking her contract and Kenneth had threatened to withdraw his financial support for SAF, he had assumed the shock would make her leave. But she didn't respond as he'd expected. She wanted to stay, like all the other do-gooders, stuffed with distorted aspirations, trying to remake his home into a carbon copy of the West.

And then she'd stated her intention to adopt a Khmer baby, and he'd almost vomited. He would not allow another child to be poisoned by the false gods of America: Hollywood and Avarice. He had risked getting the authorities involved. But there she sat, smiling and free. Hearing her laughter, he bit his cheeks to keep from screaming. He squatted and found a stick.

He began to dig a trench in the wet earth that would never be deep enough.

CHAPTER FIFTY-SEVEN

LEAP 1977

Leap formed a dangerous plan to smuggle the damaged child to his family village.

He made a nest beneath the cot and prayed that the little girl would stay quiet while he went about his usual duties. He poured a bit of water down her throat before she drifted back into unconsciousness. The wound to her skull had stopped bleeding, and the protruding eyeball retreated into its socket. In the corner of the workshop, he placed a wooden frame and cut fabric for his next painting canvas. He set the small photograph of Milijana and some additional cloth next to the girl. He vowed to paint a portrait of the girl's mother in remembrance.

At breakfast, Leap drew the attention of his friend. "Where did you bury her?"

"She's under the papaya tree in the back field. With many graves near the walls, one more won't stand out."

"Thank you, little brother," Leap said. "Now, I must ask for your help yet again."

The medic cast his eyes around the room where guards, staff, and a few authorized prisoners sat alone with hunched shoulders, slurping their breakfast noodles. "I can't help you again."

"But you will, my young friend." Leap leaned his mouth close to the boy's ear. "Or I will inform Comrade Duch that you buried the girl without permission." Leap hated to black-mail the kindhearted boy. "You must take the other girl to our village, where my mother will care for her."

The boy looked at Leap like he was mad. "And how can I do that?"

"You will find a way, I'm sure."

※ ※ ※

A year later, the war was over. Vietnamese rocket shelling had been going for days. Pol Pot's Kampuchea had cracked open like an egg against the rock of their organized advance. Guards and other staff disappeared, fading into the night. Black trucks, gorged with prisoners destined to be murdered, worked non-stop. But it took time to slaughter so many.

"Exterminate them all!" roared Duch, standing with his fists on his hips. "Leave nothing for the Viet dogs."

Machine-gun fire could be heard in the streets nearby. Guard Touy stood calmly, slicing the throat of one of the last inmates. An interrogator with wild eyes ran to throw an arm-load of paper on a fire.

Leap hid in a filthy latrine behind the canteen for hours, uncertain of whom he was most afraid—the Vietnamese or his own people. When the scuffling and muted shouts stopped, and all the Khmer Rouge cadre had run away, he walked into the center of the compound. People lay where they'd been murdered, blood soaking the dry earth.

The portrait!

Having pulled Milijana's painting from her hiding place, he rushed to the administrative office containing the confessions. He had little time. Finding the correct file cabinet, he yanked open the drawer and rummaged until he found her notebooks. As Vietnamese soldiers entered the iron gates, he slipped over the back wall and disappeared.

CHAPTER FIFTY-EIGHT

EMILY 1993

Soth Sopheap's law office was above a computer repair shop on Achar Mean Boulevard. The only daylight came from the doors leading to a terrace overlooking the busy commercial street. The diffused light illuminated an antique desk and several framed diplomas hanging proudly on the wall behind it.

Monsieur Soth cut a dapper figure in his hand-tailored blue linen suit and yellow silk tie. A handsome man of indeterminate age, he combed his hair to the side, partially covering a jagged scar. Emily did her best to follow his unusual mélange of French and English.

"*Asseyez-vous, s'il vous plaît, madame. Voulez-vous une boisson fraîche?* One cool Coca-Cola?" A young man glided into the room from the rear of the apartment and set a bottle of Coke and a straw wrapped in paper before her. "*Mon fils*, my son, Kiri."

For the first time since her arrival in Cambodia, Emily wore a professional jacket and skirt and belatedly noticed her tanned skin no longer matched the beige of her prosthesis. She unwrapped the straw and took a sip. It had been years since she'd had a Coke. It left a bitter aftertaste on her tongue.

"I didn't do anything wrong," she said, tamping down her rage like the straw in the glass bottle, worried it would over-flow on the wood of the beautiful desk.

"Bien sûr. There is no evidence for the indictment of traf-ficking. Your *accusateur* has *n'a aucun mérite*. It is possible you can bring the charges back against him. Are you interested?"

Emily shook her head in frustration. "I want this to be over."

"*D'accord*, we let that drop. *Mais je comprends vous voulez continuer à vivre au Cambodge?*"

"Yes, I want to keep living here. I will not be forced to leave."

Monsieur Soth wiped his forehead with a handkerchief. "It will be a bit difficult. The accuser will make void your work visa. But we can manage. *J'ai des amis au service de l' immigra-tion.* They may be helpful. With a donation, *vous comprenez?*"

Emily was both appalled and intrigued that the laws in Cambodia encouraged such potential for outright fraud. "Yes, monsieur, please talk to your friends. *Merci beaucoup.*"

Outside the attorney's building, the air smelled of exhaust and the copper fragrance of impending rain. An enormous poster advertised one of the dozens of hopeful political can-didates. Emily hoped that the general election would make a dent in healing the past.

A green plant emerged from a crack in the pavement near the wall. She followed the thin vine with her eyes to find the entire building façade covered with glossy leaves grown from the same fragile root.

"Madame," Arun said from his post under the awning. "My friend say me old man come back Tuol Sleng."

"Finally." Emily welcomed the distraction of the mysterious portrait. She wanted Nick to go with her. She hadn't seen him for a couple of days and hoped he was around. She leaned against Arun's narrow back as they sped across town.

After pulling herself up the steep stairs to Nick's apartment, she paused for breath. She was accustomed to the convenience of a telephone, and it felt uncomfortable to just drop in on someone unannounced. He might not be alone. She'd never asked him if he still saw other women, but Yvette had warned her of his reputation for more than journalistic talent. She shook off the thought. With a push, the unlocked door swung open.

"Hello? Anyone home?" She stepped inside.

Nick emerged from the bedroom, munching on a baguette. "Emily, I was just thinking about you. How did things go with the lawyer?"

"He makes corruption sound straightforward, so I'm cautiously optimistic about the trial. Unfortunately, the visa is another matter."

"Sit down, lovely lady."

"Nick, I came to tell you that Leap is back. I can show you the portrait now."

"Hot damn! What are we waiting for?" He grabbed her for a kiss and then dug through his pockets for his keys.

Nick plowed his jeep down Norodom Boulevard toward Tuol Sleng, swerving and dodging the traffic of refurbished Toyota sedans, overburdened cyclos, and the occasional bullock cart.

Motorbikes streamed past; a few passengers gave the foreigners a friendly wave. Emily's blond hair sparkled in the sun and always turned heads. The morning rain shower eased into the afternoon, laying heat and humidity over the city like a soggy blanket.

Sam and the girl in the wheelchair were crowded around several Japanese UN peacekeepers visiting the museum. Emily waved and Nick held her arm as she navigated the slippery mud to the gate, her slide-resistant foot almost useless in the muck. Chan would have a job, cleaning her shoes later.

Leap sat in his usual spot on the bench, with Debbie, in her bright lipstick, beside him. Chivy was wearing a pink dress and chasing a shrieking crow across the compound yard, her curls flying.

"Leap! Hello, I'm happy you're back. This is my friend Nick. He's a journalist with the *Phnom Penh Post*," Emily said. "I told him about the portrait. Would you show him?"

Nick put his hand forward to shake. Leap looked at the outstretched hand as if it were dirty. "She was a secret for so long. To share her with strangers is difficult."

Nick pulled his hand back. "I don't want to intrude in any way."

As the little girl crept closer to observe, Emily squatted down and said, "Hello, Chivy. Do you remember me? You have on a pretty dress today." The child nodded and slipped her hand into Emily's.

Leap stared at them for a long moment. "Perhaps the time has come." He walked to the back office and returned with the rusty keys as the Japanese visitors entered the compound in a chattering rush, released from the pleading bunch outside. "Welcome them," he instructed Debbie.

With his granddaughter in hand, he led Emily and Nick to Building D. "Have you been here before?" he asked Nick.

"Yes, many times."

"I created these pictures of what I witnessed during my time as a prisoner."

"Documenting the atrocities is critically important," Nick said. "You've given a great gift to the historical record. Were you a painter before?"

"Of a sort," Leap said. "I painted billboards for the cinema. Milijana was my first portrait." He unlocked the door to the closet, wrenching it open. "Here she is." His voice was soft and melancholy. "The woman I never met but who changed my life forever."

"What?" Emily was incredulous. "You never met her?" She indicated Chivy. "Then who is your granddaughter?"

"Let's take Milijana out from the darkness and into the fresh air." He carried the portrait to the corridor.

"Holy shit," Nick exclaimed, looking from the picture to Emily and back. "That's quite a resemblance!"

Leap nodded. "When I first met Mademoiselle Emily, I was indeed surprised." He pulled out a small photograph from his shirt pocket. "This is the original picture of Milijana I used as a reference."

Emily cradled the curling black-and-white picture in her palm. It showed a Caucasian woman with light hair. Her pale eyes were wide with anger. Or fear. "Did she really die here?"

"Everyone died here," Leap said. "Everyone except me and one of Milijana's daughters, who was horribly injured. I smuggled the little girl to my home village, where she lived with my mother. But she never recovered. She spent her short life without sight or sound, or speech. Yet, I saved her." Leap seemed to be convincing himself. "Her name was Rachana."

Emily and Nick exchanged puzzled glances. "So who is Chivy?"

"She is Rachana's daughter, Milijana's granddaughter."

"If you never met Milijana, how did you know their names?" Nick asked. "And how did you get the photograph?"

Leap took the photograph from Emily's hand and put it back into his pocket. "I learned from one of the guards."

"Are you the father?" asked Nick.

"No! My mother was old and unable to protect Rachana. An evil boy took advantage of the broken child. Rachana's life was simple—confined—her mind literally fractured. She passed her days sitting in the shade under my mother's wooden house. When she became pregnant she didn't understand. She was only thirteen. After the birth, she wandered into a paddy field and drowned in a few inches of water. She didn't remember how to find the air."

"That poor girl! And Chivy is her child?"

"Yes, she is my *tevoda*. She gave life and love to me. I brought her to Phnom Penh to live with me after my mother died. Now I am an old man and worried what will become of her after I am gone." He stroked Chivy's shoulder with gentle fingers.

Nick peered at the painting. "As an inmate in S21, how did you have the freedom to paint something like this?"

Leap straightened his shoulders. "I worked in secret using stolen supplies. I didn't worry about the consequences. I risked my life with every brushstroke."

"But why? Who was she to you?" Nick pressed. "Why was she a prisoner here in the first place?"

"Does it matter who she was to me?" Leap said, his face now shuttered. "And I never learned anything more about her."

Emily thought he knew more than he was telling them, but why would he have anything to hide? "Did you try to find her confession?"

"How could an inmate get those documents?"

"What about later, after you came back?" Nick insisted. "Did you ask Jane for help?"

Leap stepped back. "Why do you question me like this? There was nothing left, everything destroyed in the chaos at the end of the war. She and Madame Phang assured me there is no record of Milijana Petrova anywhere in the archive."

"You must realize how strange this is." Nick held up the portrait. "Why would a Westerner be imprisoned in an interrogation center designed specifically for Khmer Rouge cadre? And is it just a coincidence she resembles Emily?"

"That is for you to decide for your paper, I presume. Write whatever you want. I'm past caring—the secret is mine no more." He took the painting back from Nick and tucked it under his arm. Then he clasped Chivy's hand. "I have nothing more to say." He stalked across the compound without a backward glance.

Nick called after him, "Hey, Leap, why did you become a guide in the same godforsaken place where you were a prisoner?"

"Nick!" Emily tapped his arm. "You're coming on a little strong, don't you think?"

"There are some big holes in his story. I'm curious."

Emily watched Leap lock the painting in the office and then greet new visitors. She felt sympathy for the frail old man. *At least he isn't alone,* she thought, watching Chivy pick a frangipani flower to give Debbie.

"Seems harmless enough," she said. "He had an imaginary love affair with the woman and he's embarrassed to be talking about it. He risked his life for Milijana's daughter. And now he's raising her little girl. It's a wonderful story in this otherwise horrible place." She stepped onto the grass lining the walkway and picked up a fallen crow feather. "What's a *tevoda*?" she asked.

He rummaged for a pack of cigarettes. "Look around us, Emily. There's nothing harmless about this place. A *tevoda* is a kind of benevolent spirit or angel. There are temples in Angkor Wat dedicated to them."

"Nick, I saw one here."

"A ghostly spirit?" He flipped his Zippo, urging the old lighter to work. "This is the place for them."

"It was my baby."

Nick's head swiveled. "What?"

She turned the feather in the sun, watching its iridescent glimmer. "The car crash that killed my husband, and did this"— she looked down at her leg—"also killed our unborn baby girl. Her spirit came to me during the ceremony for the dead. As I sat on the floor surrounded by all those grieving people, I held her in my arms for a moment. And I felt her love."

Emily knew she would never be able to describe her profound experience in the room of mourning survivors, but she would cherish the memory forever. She thought of Milijana and was happy the woman still lived through Chivy.

"What are you talking about?" Nick moved closer and put an arm around her shoulder. "If ghosts were real, I'd be fucked."

"I know what I saw, mister." She laughed, tucking the feather behind his ear.

Noting her lighter mood, Nick joked, "Are you aware, miss, that the tropical heat can unhinge some people?"

"Well, I'm definitely unbalanced!" She kicked Nick's ankle with her muddy nonskid sneaker. "Let's go back to your place, and I'll tell you some tales about my time behind bars."

"You understand that I'm an investigative journalist and I only do in-depth, probing interviews?"

Emily whispered against his lips, "I'm counting on it."

CHAPTER FIFTY-NINE

LEAP 1993

With elbows on knees, Leap sat on a bench regarding the dingy hallway linoleum of Calmette Hospital. He'd been waiting several hours for his appointment with the doctor to review his test results. He knew the news would not be good. Cancer's tendrils had grown and spread throughout his body like a deadly morning glory vine. One year? One month? He hoped it would be quick, but he needed enough time to find a home for Chivy.

A nurse rushed past, leaving the smell of perfume in her wake. She didn't even glance at him. Leap mourned not only his situation but also that of his country, both riddled with lethal cancer. Looking at the stains on the hospital floor, he pondered Cambodia's legacy. Is it a place where tourists come to witness the visceral horror of Tuol Sleng for a small visitor fee? A storage place for crumbling relics of a lost civilization? Or a nation of masters and slaves, where people starved and tortured their own in the name of a fearful ideology?

He prayed the future would prove him wrong.

Leap stood and shuffled down the hospital corridor. No need to see the doctor.

CHAPTER SIXTY

EMILY 1993

The languid ceiling fan did little to cool their sweaty bodies. "That was nice." Emily rolled over to put her head on Nick's chest.

"That was better than nice," he said, tugging at a curl, pulling it taut, and letting it spring back. "Did they call you Shirley Temple when you were a little girl?"

She thumped his arm. "I know something that might be nicer."

"What?"

"Pizza. I've been dreaming about it for a week." She pushed up on an elbow. "After noodles and rice every day, with the occasional roast lamb, I'm dying for some pizza."

Nick grabbed a cigarette. "Don't forget about Mexican food."

"Oh my god. I hate you!"

"I'll take you to my favorite joint. Have you experienced Happy Herb yet?"

Nick entered the packed restaurant like a linebacker close to the goal, and Emily followed in his wake. She noticed Jane Bigalow waving from across the crowded space, sitting alone with a bottle of Angkor beer and a half-finished margherita pizza.

"What's going on?" Emily shouted over the buzz. "Why the massive crowd?"

"Half-price Tuesday at Happy Herb," the archival project director told them, laughing. "The best bargain in town!"

"What do you want?" Nick asked.

Emily scanned the menu painted on the concrete wall above their heads. "I'll have what she's having."

Nick pushed his way to the counter, where the harried owner took orders. His daughter delivered the cooked pizzas while his son slid uncooked pies into the hot oven—the only wood-fired one in Cambodia.

"Here, try a slice while you wait," Jane offered, putting a piece on a paper napkin that turned translucent with grease. "It tastes better than it looks."

"Is this a *happy* one?"

"I'm fairly certain that's not oregano. But don't worry, there's not enough to do any damage. What makes me *happy* is that the owner makes his own fresh mozzarella."

Emily took a tentative bite. "Delicious! Marijuana or not, I'm going to eat a whole pizza myself." She inhaled the slice.

"You've got a greasy chin," Nick said, licking her face as he set down two beers. "It's very becoming."

With a laugh, Emily turned to Jane. "We visited Tuol Sleng today and saw Leap and the mystery painting."

The director dabbed with a tissue at a drop of sauce on her blue tank top. "Oh, yeah? I want to see it, too. Did he tell you any more about it?"

"Heartbreaking. He showed us the photograph of the woman that he used to paint her portrait. Leap said the woman's youngest daughter survived, and he smuggled her out of S21 to live with his mother. She had a baby and that is the little girl he's raising."

"What a story—almost unbelievable."

"That's what I think," said Nick.

Emily sipped her beer. "Why would he lie?"

"I'm suspicious after hearing so many tragic yet improbable survival stories." Jane gave up on the sauce staining her shirt and took another slice. "And didn't you mention the picture looked like you? Maybe he's trying to trick or con you somehow?"

The owner's daughter placed an immense pizza before them. Nick rolled a piece into a burrito shape, waved it around to cool it off, and then shoved it into his mouth, all in one bite. "That's how you do it," he mumbled around the mass in his mouth. As he chewed, his eyes scanned the room. "The whole portrait situation is weird."

"The woman and I do look a lot alike. It's only a coincidence, based on Leap's story." Emily attempted to copy Nick's pizza-eating technique, but grease still dripped down her arm. "Oh, fuck, I'm a mess."

Jane tossed her a packet of tissues. "Don't worry—it's all part of the experience."

Nick pushed back from the table. "Apologies, ladies, but I see a guy who came back from Pailin today and supposedly interviewed Son Sann. KPNLAF is up to some weird shit on the border. I want to talk to him. Emily, will you be all right if I take off?"

"Go get that story, soldier!"

"Roger that, mademoiselle." He bent down to speak in her ear. "I don't want to leave you alone with Sonny skulking around causing trouble. He's probably pissed off that you're out of prison."

"I'll be fine. Jane's here."

With a touch to her cheek, he slipped away through the crowd. Jane eyed him as he sat down at a table with a shady-looking Cambodian man wearing oversize sunglasses. "Are you two a couple?"

"Oh no." Emily was unsure how to answer as she balanced another dripping piece of pizza and her beer bottle. Where they a couple? Did she want to be in a relationship? Changing the subject, she asked, "How do you keep all the acronyms straight?"

"You become accustomed, I guess. Better than saying the Khmer People's National Liberation Front all the time." Jane lowered her voice and leaned closer. "Apologies for being nosy—we're a rather intimate community here—but a rumor is circulating. Were you actually arrested?"

Emily pulled another tissue from the pack and wiped her hands. She was uneasy that Phnom Penh's gossip mill was churning. She didn't like people knowing her business. For a big city, it was a small town.

"Yes," she admitted. "I came home to find the police waiting. They arrested me and took me to Prey Sar. Sonny had accused me of human trafficking."

"Why did he think that?"

"I don't know for sure. Survivors Assistance Foundation, the NGO he founded, is in real financial trouble, so he's worked up about that. Also, I mentioned wanting to adopt a local child and he became outraged. How he concluded I was selling children is beyond me."

"Did you talk to him? Try to straighten things out?"

"I met an attorney today and he believes the trafficking charge will be dropped. But I'm worried about my status. If Sonny revokes my work visa, I could be deported."

"What will you do?"

"The lawyer will expedite an early hearing. He seems well connected and comes with glowing recommendations."

Jane pushed away from her uneaten pizza as the waitress set down more bottles of beer. "I heard about the prostitution and the narcotics coming down the Mekong from the Golden Triangle, but babies as commodities? My god, it makes me sick." She took a long drink. "Time for another beer?"

"Roger that," Emily said with a wink.

Much later, the women stumbled down the restaurant steps in search of a ride home. The usual group of panhandlers surged forward. As Emily began to hand out riel notes, a familiar voice called her name and Sam came swinging on his crutches from the shadows.

"Madame Emily! I come hospital." The others moved away, ready to pounce on the next happy diners.

"Are you sick?"

"No, Madame. I help friend, girl in chair."

"She was at Tuol Sleng earlier today."

"She die now," the young man stated. "Truck hit on street."

Cold water poured down Emily's spine. "How horrible. Can I do anything?"

"She finish now. No more trouble. Her karma very good. Next life be better for her." Sam shrugged. "We all die, no more problem then."

The music and noise from the raucous restaurant receded. Emily wrapped her arms around herself.

Who decides who gets to survive?

CHAPTER SIXTY-ONE

LEAP 1993

Leap and Chivy lived across the street from the Tuol Sleng Museum of Genocide. They shared a modest room on the ground floor of a two-story concrete house. During the night-time darkness, they ignored the lonely ghosts calling from behind the former prison wall. But each day, Leap walked through the iron gates and reopened his painful wound.

Most Cambodian homes include a spirit house, often placed outside as a rest stop for traveling souls. It also distracts mischievous spirits, keeping them from entering and causing mayhem. Leap's shrine sat inside, on a high shelf. Every day Chivy stood on a small stool and put out a fresh fruit offering such as a banana or a mango. The day Leap spoke with Emily and the journalist about the portrait, he brought the painting home and set it beside the shrine.

Chivy stood spellbound. "Is she an angel?"

"No, little one. She is your *yeay*, your grandmother."

Chivy's eyes grew enormous. She reached up to touch her own curling hair. "Like me!"

"Yes, *songsaa*. Just like you."

※ ※ ※

Six years after slipping over the S21 wall, Leap had returned to Phnom Penh. The war still simmered, nibbling at the periphery. Royalists, Vietnamese, and Khmer Rouge battled to the death in the jungles and forests, with villagers trapped between them. People flooded to the cities in droves.

Many times during the years of his exile, Leap had prayed and wept for the dead of S21. He carried his survivor's burden like a heavy coat that stooped his shoulders and bent his back. Milijana often entered his sleep. *You must go back,* she whispered. Her face lay under the surface of the water as he planted rice in the paddy fields. Her yellow hair was reflected in the color of rice chaff tossed in the air during harvest.

Driven by Milijana's memory, he left his village with nothing but her portrait slung over his shoulder in a rice sack. His heart broke to leave Rachana with his mother. *I'll come back when I can,* he told them both. *I'll send money. I'll visit each year.* He stroked Rachana's empty face, certain she could sense his love. Sweet girl.

Back at the former prison, he discovered it was now a Museum of Genocide. He painted, the images spilling out like blood from an opened vein. He kept the portrait a secret, stored away in a locked and unused closet. Milijana kept silent.

Time passed, and the number of paintings grew. Once a year he made the trek home to his family.

"Rachana was raped," his mother wept during one visit, seven years after he'd left. "The boy from the next village must have come while I slept and violated her. I didn't know until the baby came. Please forgive me, son."

Leap held the newborn girl in his arms as Milijana broke her silence and spoke to his heart. *Name her Chivy,* she whispered.

※ ※ ※

"Will my hair be like my grandmother's?" Chivy gazed up at the portrait, bringing Leap back to the present.

"You are perfect as you are, my little *tevoda*. Not all angels have yellow hair." Leap lifted her chin and looked into her gold-flecked eyes. "Now, go check if the rice is ready for dinner."

A soft cough caused Leap to look outside. Arun stood in the front garden. "May I enter?"

In his dreams, Milijana had mentioned her former gardener's son and to wait for him, though Leap hadn't known whom to expect. Of course. The driver.

"Yes, please sit." Leap motioned to the bamboo mats on the floor. "We are about to eat; will you join us?"

Chivy helped serve the rice and fried sweet potato. They all laughed as Leap ate a raw chili and had to rush to the pump in the rear for more water. As he leaned into the lever to start the flow of water, the disease in his body tightened its clasp, and he gasped in pain. There was no more time.

Leap returned to find Arun standing before the portrait, head tilted to the side. "That's my *yeay*," Chivy said. "She's an angel."

"Yes." Arun nodded. "I knew her when I was ten years old and worked in the palace garden with my father."

Chivy jumped up, clapping her hands. "Oh! What was she like?"

"She was a princess." He had a sad smile. "She helped my sick father. I also met your *mak* Rachana and your *meng* Daevy. We played together with flowers."

Bitter tears rolled down Leap's thin cheeks. Chivy reached out to touch his face. "Why are you crying, grandfather?"

"No worry, child. I am drowning in the past. The land of ghosts is calling me." He wiped his eyes with the corner of his krama. "Why are you here, Arun?"

Arun sat on the mat near the old man. "Princess Milijana gave me a message to give to you."

Leap took a quivering breath. "I've been waiting a long time."

"She first came to me many months ago, after my wife and baby died," Arun began. "We were new to the city, here from the countryside, but the capital is a hard place with no friends. When my wife became ill, we had no money for medicine. There was no princess to ask for help." Arun took a deep breath. "First my wife and then our daughter died from the fever, just like my father."

Leap fetched tea, giving the young man a moment to collect himself.

Arun blew on the hot liquid and took a small sip. "I sat in our hut, holding my dead child in my arms, and prayed for her to open her eyes, but she remained still. Eventually, I slept. I awoke in the garden where Princess Milijana had given me medicine for my father. She spoke with a soft voice I understood in my heart. *You must not be sad anymore,* she said. *Your family is here, with me.*" Tears shone in Arun's eyes. "My wife was in that garden, cradling our baby in the shade of the jacaranda tree. My father was there, too, his smiling face free of suffering. *Thank you,* I told her, *for keeping my loved ones safe.*"

"I knew she would live in heaven," Leap murmured.

"Months later, as I slept, she came again. She told me how you had saved her youngest daughter, who lived to give birth to her granddaughter." He smiled at Chivy, sitting nearby. "She is grateful but knows you can't care for her much longer. She asked me to watch for a Western woman. *You will recognize her because she will look like me,* she said. And then I saw her, the American, living in the house next door to my old home."

"Mademoiselle Emily," Leap said.

"Yes. Princess Milijana instructed me to keep the American safe because she is the key, the answer to the problem."

"The key?"

"For her." Arun looked at Chivy.

"Yes, of course," whispered Leap. "Now I understand. I painted a portrait of the future, not the past."

CHAPTER SIXTY-TWO

EMILY 1993

The courtroom was warm. Emily pondered what it would be like to live in the tropics without any air-conditioning at all. Her lawyer, Monsieur Soth, fanned himself with a folded newspaper. He'd exchanged his blue suit for one of light green. She worried he could hear the knocking of her heart. The judge's chair sat in the front of the room, with tan-colored drapes for a backdrop. *Legal beige,* she thought with a grimace.

The attorney had explained that lower-court proceedings in Cambodia were informal. The judge would rule without a jury. Due to the years of civil war, the judiciary system remained chaotic, with nepotism and corruption endemic. That morning, they'd given the magistrate's assistant a basket filled with delicacies such as chocolate, caviar, and a bottle of excellent cognac. An envelope containing five hundred dollars in crisp new notes was nestled at the bottom.

Sonny and his attorney sat at the table to her left. Sonny was disheveled, different from the smiling young man of the airport. His shoulders hunched as he chewed on his fingernails.

After a long wait, the magistrate, a portly man with dyed black hair and a loose-fitting jacket, burst through the door. His heavy cologne infiltrated the small room, creating an odiferous cloud. Taking his place, he rustled around like a hen finding a comfortable seat on an egg. His young assistant called the inquiry to order. Emily's lawyer whispered a running translation.

"The case before us is severe." The judge looked sternly from Sonny to Emily. "Human trafficking is a horrific crime. Particularly when children are involved."

From across the room, Sonny lifted his head, now paying attention. His knuckles were white where he clutched the edge of the table.

"I reviewed the facts presented to this court and have made the following ruling. Based upon a lack of any evidence, I've found Madame Emily Mclean is not guilty of the crime of trafficking—"

Sonny jumped to his feet. "She admitted to wanting to take a child out of the country!"

"*Silence!*" admonished the judge. "Or you will be sent to prison yourself. Be grateful I am not charging you with false witness, *mon garçon*. Falsely accusing someone of a crime they did not commit is a significant offense."

"*Monsieur le juge,*"—Sonny's voice cracked with emotion— "she intends to take a Khmer child to America."

THE FOREIGNER'S CONFESSION

"Enough! This case is closed. Now, should you revoke her work visa with the Department of Immigration, there is nothing I can do." He lifted his eyebrow like a wink toward Sonny's lawyer. "But the issue of trafficking is terminated. You are all excused." He rose and left the room, trailing his cologne and assistant behind him.

Sonny crossed the room in three strides. "This isn't over." He glared down at Emily, then rushed from the courtroom, pushing the exit door with so much force, it slammed against the wall. His attorney just shrugged his shoulders as he gathered his papers.

"What just happened?" Emily said.

"My competitor"—Monsieur Soth tilted his head toward the man putting documents into a satchel—"is also a friend of the judge. You are not guilty of the larger crime, but . . ."

"But what?"

"You will likely be deported."

She needed time to process what had happened. After thanking the attorney for his help in keeping her out of prison, she walked across the once-beautiful marble floor to the exit of the Phnom Penh Municipal Court, her rubber shoes squeaking. Numb, she gazed across Monireth Boulevard at the sports stadium.

"Madame go home?" asked Arun from his spot near the doorway.

"No, not yet. Can you take me someplace quiet?"

He wheeled his motorbike closer. "No problem."

Emily remembered her first time riding on the back of Arun's small moto as he threaded his way through the traffic. *What a wonderful feeling that was,* she thought—*the glorious sensation of freedom that waited within complete surrender.*

He stopped in front of a distinctive colonial villa in the lovely district adjacent to the Royal Palace, not far from the SAF office. The building had been restored to its original grandeur, and a sign at the entrance read Café No Problem. Emily dismounted and hobbled up the steps. Her leg, encased by the silicone sleeve of the prosthesis, itched painfully due to an outbreak of prickly heat.

She entered an airy room with a checkered tile floor. Teak fans circled the high ceilings. Discrete air conditioners, tucked into the eves, cooled the space. Comfortable white wicker chairs and sofas with plush cotton cushions gathered around tables. The perspiration on her face tickled as it dried. Perfect. How did Arun know about this place?

A handsome young man stood behind the mahogany bar, the antique polished to a glowing shine. "*Bienvenue, madame. Welcome. Asseyez-vous où vous voulez.*"

The only other guests—three men in light-blue uniforms—sat near the front windows. She recognized the Irish flag insignia on their shirts. They appeared to be deep in conversation, with icy drinks and bowls of peanuts before them. After ordering a gin and tonic from the bartender, Emily limped to a sofa on the far side of the room. She wanted to be alone with her thoughts.

"Put that on our tab," called the older man of the group.

"You don't need to do that." Emily wasn't in the mood for pleasantries. She hoped her astringent tone would dampen further conversation. Sipping her drink, she tried to make sense of her thoughts. Leaving the country so soon was heartrending. Despite its heat and inconveniences, chaotic, crazy Phnom Penh had lodged in her heart. The food, the architecture, the smiles and resiliency of the people—she'd only just grazed the surface. She knew there was so much she didn't yet understand about the culture, but Cambodia offered her a fresh start with no obligation to her past. She sat in a gorgeous bar that could be anyplace in the world, but it wasn't. It was in Phnom Penh, Cambodia, with all the beauty and bitter pain that encompassed it. And that poignant contradiction mirrored her own.

But it was in jeopardy. Would she be forced to go back? She imagined the brick house on Evans Avenue and the life in Montana she'd outgrown. Seattle would be even worse, an abyss, with memories of Steven everywhere. She had purposely left everything behind. All the furniture, the photographs, the mementos of a life, crushed like glass on a wet street.

Emily nodded at the bartender for another drink and then gulped it down. Would there be time to learn the meaning of Nick's hidden blue tattoos? She pictured the lost little girl in the wheelchair and a sob rose in her throat.

Across the room, the tipsy officers began to sing traditional Irish ballads. Finding the thread of their harmonies, the tunes wove into lovely melodies. Ancient songs of longing and remorse comforted Emily like a tender blanket. She remembered her father singing her to sleep with his mellow, off-key baritone, and her mother's sweet soprano as she washed the dishes. Emily put her face in her hands and let the sobs pour out.

"I realize we're terrible, but no reason to weep so," joked one of the men. "Come join us, lass. There's naught that a hearty cry while singing an old tune won't cure."

Wiping at her eyes and blowing her nose with a small cocktail napkin, Emily hiccupped. "I doubt I'm pleasant company at the moment."

"Don't be daft. Get yourself over here, and that's an order," said the older man.

Something about the men's comfortable familiarity was soothing. "Are you some sort of military choir?"

"No, we're Irish police here with UNTAC," said the larger man. "Generally speaking, men in uniforms don't sing so well. But we're Dubliners, and we like to share a song or two when the drink is flowing." He had a lovely burr of a voice. "Where are you from?"

"The United States," she said as she lowered herself into a chair at their table. She was thankful their eyes hadn't lingered on her legs as she crossed the room. "Though my parents are from Belfast."

"I knew she was Irish!" the third man cried. "No other lass is so pretty. We won't hold you at fault for the Scottish blood." He laughed. "Barkeep, another round!"

"I'm Wee Jimmy," said the massive redheaded man sitting on the low seat with his knees almost to his ears. He smiled at Emily's expression. "Aye, me mam called me that from the moment of my birth, and it stuck. The old geezer is Noel and the daft Republican is Andrew." He made an obscene gesture at the man who'd commented on Emily's Northern Irish heritage. "Take no mind of him. He's had a few, but we still love him, bad manners or no. He's got the grandest voice of us all."

"Pleasure to meet you." The bartender set out yet more drinks. "My name is Emily Mclean. Only in Cambodia is day drinking with singing Irish policemen a normal occurrence."

"Amen to that," Wee Jimmy toasted.

"How about another song?" she asked.

Noel smiled, the corners of his black eyes wrinkling. "Only if you sing one first."

Emily had never been a strong singer. Steven used to tease her if she squawked along with the car radio, putting his hands over his ears. But the Irish sang sad songs better than anyone. And what were the odds of meeting kindly drunken Irishmen as her world fell apart? She racked her brain and then tentatively began her mother's favorite ghostly ballad of love and loss, "She Moves Through the Fair."

In a thin, quavering soprano, growing stronger as she gained confidence, she sang:

> *My young love said to me*
> *My mother won't mind,*

My father won't slight,
For your lack of kind.
She stepped away
And this she did say,
It will not be long till our wedding day.
I dreamt it last night that my dead love
*   came,*
So softy she moved,
Feet made no sound.
It will not be long till our wedding day . . .

When she faltered over the lyrics of the second verse, the men joined in, blending their harmonies, all the way to the poignant end. As the last notes lingered, their faces glistened.

"Here," Wee Jimmy said, "take this." He handed her a device that looked like a giant walkie-talkie. "It's a sat phone; you can call anyone, anywhere on earth. You go, right this moment, and ring the bastard who broke your heart and tell him the Irish police will come knocking on his door."

Emily took the bulky phone and retreated to her table. She pushed the numbers from memory and waited to connect to the other side of the world.

Leap entered the restaurant as the call connected with a spinning satellite.

CHAPTER SIXTY-THREE

LEAP 1993

He held the small pile of school notebooks close to his heart as he might hold a beloved. The bindings were coming apart, the glue failing due to humidity and time. He had read every word, scoured each page, hoping to retrieve the essence of the woman for himself, to absorb her through his fingertips. Every day for years, he had lingered over certain passages. Phrases speaking of longing and love. But he learned that if he touched the text too often, her words became blurry and might pass away into nothingness, stealing her voice forever.

He questioned himself about the nature of his obsession with the yellow-haired stranger, born from painting a billboard advertisement for a barang film long ago. What was it that had seized his heart? Her exotic beauty, which reminded him of the mythical Devi his mother worshipped during Sangkran's New Year festivities? As a little boy, he imagined the seven angel sisters as pure gold, the color of Milijana's hair. Or was it the impulsive rescue of her daughter? Ultimately, it came down to the fact that she was *his*. With her confession, he alone knew her heart.

While Emily sang with the soldiers, Arun had fetched Leap, who now stood before the café, uneasy about going into such a place. The restoration of the French-colonial building and the legacy that heritage represented didn't offend him. He had met many barang working as a guide at Tuol Sleng, but this was different. He would be entering their unfamiliar world with a request, a plea for help. He glanced down at his simple trousers.

"Go," urged Arun. "Don't be afraid."

Leap smoothed his shirt with one hand while holding the notebooks with the other. Once inside the restaurant, he immediately saw Emily, her eyes cast down and a military device in her hand. A table of United Nations soldiers watched as he stood in the doorway.

"Can I help you, *chi ta*?" the Cambodian man behind the bar inquired.

"I am here to see her." Leap tipped his head at Emily, hoping the young man wouldn't ask him to leave. Or the soldiers question him. His damaged heart pounded in his chest.

Emily looked up. "Leap? What a surprise!"

Shivering in the cold air as he approached her, he recognized the alert attention of the military men. How does a uniform allow such arrogance and suspicion? Black pajamas or blue helmets, it made no difference.

"Madame Emily, I have something to give you."

"Please sit down. Would you like something to drink? I was just trying to call my mother, but I couldn't connect."

Leap sighed, sitting in the soft white chair. "No, thank you. I brought you these. I don't want to intrude, but I think you should take them now."

Emily took the small stack of books. She carefully opened the cover of the first. "Oh!" she exclaimed, the air punched from her lungs.

He nodded. "It is the missing confession. I'm sorry. I lied to you. I took everything when I fled in 1979. Including the ledger page documenting Milijana Petrova as a prisoner. I was afraid they would come looking for Rachana and me, that we wouldn't be safe from the authorities."

"Shouldn't we give these to Jane and Madame Phang at the museum?"

"I leave the decision to you, Madame Emily." He took another small book from his shirt pocket. "I want to give you this, too."

Emily opened a brand-new Cambodian passport with a black-and-white photograph of a young child.

It was Chivy.

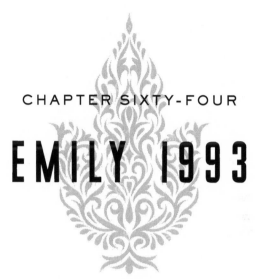

CHAPTER SIXTY-FOUR

EMILY 1993

Back at home, Emily slogged in the murk of one too many gin and tonics. She set her bag on the dining table, steadying herself against a chair. Anxiety roiled through her. Why was she hesitating? Wasn't this what she wanted?

She found her friends in the garden. A plate overflowing with cigarette butts sat next to a depleted bottle of Johnnie Walker Red.

"There you are!" Yvette said. "We waited at the Gecko for hours. How did the trial go? Are you all right?"

"I'm sorry I worried you all." She moved the makeshift ashtray to the ground and set the notebooks down. "You're never going to believe this."

Nick stood to hug her. "Where were you?"

"So what's the verdict?" Johnny pulled Yvette into his lap to free a chair.

Emily sat down unsteadily. "Shit, I'm drunk. I don't know how I managed to stay on the motorbike. Are there any cigarettes left?"

Yvette passed her a crumpled pack of Gauloises as Nick held out the flame of his Zippo. "What are those notebooks?" Johnny asked.

Emily took a deep inhale before releasing a long plume of smoke. "Milijana's Tuol Sleng confession. The woman from the portrait."

"She was real?" Nick said. "Where did you get it?"

"Leap. He had the notebooks all this time."

Yvette poured Emily a splash of the scotch. "Why did he give them to you?"

Emily winced as she swallowed the fiery liquid. "Because of her." She passed Yvette the passport.

Yvette's eyes narrowed. "What does this mean? Who is this child?"

"Leap asked me to adopt his granddaughter, Chivy." Emily was still uncertain how to process his request. "He's very sick, dying of cancer, and there's no one to take the little girl."

"Goddamn. And the books?" Nick said.

"For her to read when she's old enough. To know her grandmother."

Johnny leaned forward to grab the last cigarette. "But what happened at the trial? Are you a free woman?"

Emily's stomach tightened as she remembered the small room and Sonny's malevolent gaze. "The judge acquitted me of the trafficking charges but I face probable deportation if

Sonny revokes my work permit. I'm not sure how much time I'd have, maybe a week or two, unless I can find a way to be issued another visa."

"*Putain.*" Yvette grabbed the cigarette back. "We must do something—you can't leave us so soon!"

Above them, black rain clouds piled into a mountain. At its heart tiny forks of lightning glowed; the evening downpour was gathering. Emily shivered as the temperature dropped. "It gets stranger, my friends. Leap told me that he and Arun were *waiting* for me. Milijana told them to expect someone who looked like her."

"What?" Johnny said. "Hasn't she been dead for a long time?"

Emily ran her hands through the tangle of her curls. "Apparently, Milijana helped Arun when he was a child. They believe she's been appearing in both their dreams and giving them instructions to watch for me."

Nick stood and tossed a pebble at a crow that perched on the wall waiting for crumbs. "I knew it was a scam. Don't you think this has gone on long enough? Tell them to fuck off!"

"Spoken like an American." Yvette ground the stub of her cigarette into bits.

"I realize how bizarre this sounds. I'm an attorney, for fuck's sake. I'm trained to collect the evidence and find the truth among the bullshit." Emily took a shaky breath. "But whose truth? The longer I stay here the more I understand how much I don't know. This country has a culture of ghosts, of spirits. I've even experienced my own ghosts—Steven in dreams and my unborn daughter during the Pchum Ben ceremony. And this." She tapped her prosthesis. "I feel the ghost of this lost leg every moment. Why is it so fantastic that a dead woman told them to wait for me?"

"Why wait for *you*?" Johnny said. "What's special about you, for them?"

"Good question. Here, take a close look at this." Emily drew a small photograph from one of the notebooks. She handed it to Yvette.

"This is the photo of Milijana, no? That Leap used to paint the portrait?"

"Yes, but look closer. I thought she seemed just like me when he first showed us the painting. But when I examine her more closely, she doesn't. We share the same face shape and light hair, but that's all, really."

"Let me see." Nick grabbed the small bit of paper. "You're right. You just resemble each other. But isn't the portrait more like you?"

"There are some minor differences, but yes, the painting looks more like me than the photograph."

"How could the old guy have painted a picture of *you*, years ago?" Johnny said. "Then be waiting for you to come to Cambodia and adopt his granddaughter?"

"I have no idea." Emily sighed. "It reminds me of a double exposure, like when a photograph has two images superimposed on one another."

"It's all bullshit," said Nick. The crow gone, he continued throwing pebbles at the wall, attacking imaginary enemies.

Yvette got up from Johnny's lap to take Nick's chair. "But why can't it be true? We are so *logique*; our expectation of how things must be creates the narrow box, like the coffin. Reality bends and shifts, especially here. The reality, ha! Who are we to say what it is?"

"I do, Yvette!" Nick's face twisted with disdain. "How can these two guys show up with a half-baked tale of a dead woman who looks like Emily and then ask her to adopt a kid? It's an intricate trick to get the child out of this cesspool of a country to the West."

Yvette's lovely face grew dark with anger. "How can you be so foolish? Do you think everyone in Cambodia, or in any other so-called developing country, only dreams to live in the West? To have the televisions and the automobiles and the new Levi jeans? Some may, and it is their choice what they desire. But others, perhaps most, want only to live safely in their own homes, their own cultures, with peace and opportunity for their children."

"Gee, Nick, I thought you liked it here." Johnny attempted to lighten the mood.

"That's not the point," Nick thundered. "All I'm saying is that I don't want Emily taken advantage of."

Everyone turned to Emily for a response. "Leap and Arun aren't trying to trick me, Nick. I'm certain of it."

Yvette took Emily's hand. "What will you do about the little girl? Isn't this what you wanted?"

Emily joked, "How can I refuse a ghost?"

"Ghosts can be very motivating," Nick said sarcastically. "But this is too weird, even for ghosts."

"Nick. Come here." Emily put her arms around his neck and pulled his lips down to hers. "Thank you," she whispered, "for wanting to protect me. But this is all meaningless if I'm kicked out of the country. Let's hope Milijana's spirit can pull some strings with immigration."

Yvette picked up one of the *cahiers*. "Enough of this debate. Let's see what Milijana has to say, shall we?" The school notebook looked as if it was made of old leaves decaying on a forest floor. She started to read aloud, translating as she went.

> *Of what am I guilty, other than my own stupidity . . . ?*
> *We returned to Cambodia in 1976 . . .*
> *We wanted to bring our skills and talents to forge a new world order . . . The Guard. The Interrogator. The Watcher . . .*

Thunder rumbled in the distance as the first few drops of rain began to fall. The fear in Milijana's voice settled over them. She seemed to crouch, hidden from sight, in the shadows.

Why did I do this? Why else? For love, of course.

As Yvette spoke the final words, she set the book down. Tears filled her eyes, then spilled down.

Emily stood to stretch. Her leg itched and she was stiff. Reading the entire confession had taken a long time. The Yugoslav woman's suffering was tragic. She'd sacrificed herself and her family for her beliefs. Would she have done it all differently if she'd known about the prison cell that waited at the end?

"Did you know about all that?" Johnny asked Nick. "About the film crew?"

Nick shook his head. "No, I didn't. She was from Yugoslavia—that explains how she came to be allied with the communists."

"I wonder what happened to the footage . . ."

"Is that all you can consider?" Yvette snapped. "The news story?"

"Well, it is fascinating from a historical perspective."

"*Oh, la la.*" Yvette wagged her finger. "Where is your compassion, silly boy?"

Inside the house, fluorescent lights illuminated the main room. Chan must have turned them on. Emily remembered her first impression of the apartment—the magic contrast of the sterile, white-tiled rectangle and Yvette's opulent furnishings. It was familiar now, no longer strange. The gilt-framed landscape painted by a mediocre art student and the frayed rose carpet littered with stains.

Nick followed her in. "Are you all right?"

"I think so; I just need some rest."

"I have to leave early tomorrow for the delta; I'll be gone for a couple of days. Should I stay with you tonight?"

"No, I'm okay. I'll see you when you come back. I'll know more about what's happening then." She held him close, loving the way her face fit under his chin. "Have I ever told you that I like your T-shirts?"

That night, lying alone on her wooden bed with the air conditioner blowing, Emily struggled to sleep. The security floodlight from outside filtered through the handwoven curtains, leaving blue silhouettes across the floor. There were similar shadows in her mind.

Hearing Yvette read Milijana's confession in her dusky, accented voice had made a fairy tale out of the story. Like something from the Brothers Grimm or a haunting tale told around a campfire. But later, after turning each page of the notebooks herself, she had felt the horror seep into her system as though the ink had been poisoned. Some of the words were so blurred as to be unintelligible. Others were smeared with the rust brown of old blood.

When she had turned off the light, Sonny's malice-laden face lurked in the dark. Their shared story of trauma and loss should have brought them together, but another, more profound tragedy had broken his heart. He'd lost his soul, and Emily had become a symbol of that humiliation. She lay coiled tight in her bed, the yellow pad of lists untouched beside her.

When the prickly heat itching became unbearable, she took a tin of the powder Yvette had given her and sprinkled it liberally on the end of her leg. It burned a bit but calmed the discomfort.

She sprinkled some on the missing parts, too, just in case.

CHAPTER SIXTY-FIVE

SONNY 1993

Sonny trailed Emily on a moto. His intention was cloudy, but he trusted clarity would arrive in the perfect moment. Watching. Waiting. He didn't know if her driver had detected him, but so what if he had? There was nothing they could do about it. Cat and mouse. Meow. He grinned.

"Please, my *kmuoy proh*," his aunt had wept that morning. "You must eat something! You must get some sleep!"

She'd prepared his favorite food, but he pushed the meal aside. A bowl fell and shattered, flinging noodles across the tiled floor. When Boupha had crouched down to clean up the mess, he threw a glass full of water, narrowly missing her head.

Shards glittered in the pooling liquid. Striding from the house, he glanced in the old mirror. A stranger had smiled back.

Now he waited across the street for the American to leave the embassy. He would wait hours if needed. He felt the comforting weight of a Beretta M9 pistol tucked into the waistband of his trousers. The American army's handgun of choice.

For a price, everything was for sale at the Russian Market.

CHAPTER SIXTY-SIX

EMILY 1993

The US embassy in Phnom Penh was small, but it concealed an enormous contingent of secrets. Covered with the ubiquitous mildew of rainy season, the concrete building resembled the bunker it was. Along an iron fence, Cambodian people waited patiently under colorful umbrellas to apply for American visas. Emily showed the marine guard her passport at the gate and skipped the queue. She was grateful it had been returned promptly after the hearing. She entered a dingy foyer where a tired-looking bureaucrat behind a clear bulletproof screen asked her business.

"I'm looking for information about adoption."

"Down that hallway, second door on the left." He had a Brooklyn accent. "A consular officer will be with you soon."

Two hours later, she emerged from the building cradling a thick packet of forms and cursing bureaucrats under her breath. The line of waiting people appeared unchanged. After summoning Arun from his sheltered spot under the umbrella of a flame of the forest tree, she asked him to take her to the Cambodian Ministry of Foreign Affairs.

With her limited French, she described the reason for her visit. Again, she walked down a corridor to sit and sweat in a small room. It was a deep-blue color, an unpleasant reminder of the prison cell. The ceiling fan pushed warm air in a stifling bath as she perched on a chair in front of a battered metal desk. The wait lengthened, and the painful itch of prickly heat became unbearable. She squeezed her prosthetic to stifle the discomfort.

After long minutes, a middle-aged Cambodian man came into the room. He introduced himself as the deputy minister and proffered Emily a cigarette, which she declined. He flicked a lighter that looked like solid gold, adding smoke to the already dim space. There was an old-fashioned Parisian flair to his gestures as he smoked, holding the cigarette between his thumb and forefinger. His eyelids were heavy, giving him a sleepy appearance, though his crisp army uniform implied otherwise. *How did you survive the Khmer Rouge years?* Emily wondered.

"How may I help you, mademoiselle?" His narrow eyes opened wider as he took in the sight of his pretty visitor.

"I am interested in adopting a child."

His expression changed to the same speculative look the nun had given her. He tugged at his left earlobe. "Hmm ... you are *Américaine*, yes? Things are not so straightforward as in the West. With foreign adoption, there are many difficulties to consider."

"Unfortunately, I don't have much time," Emily interjected. "Is there a way we can expedite the process? For a fee, of course." She returned his gaze. "I don't want to be an inconvenience for you."

"You must have the letters of recommendation. The proper photographs, the medical releases, the proof of citizenship, and so on. All very complex. The list is long."

"That won't be a problem. I can provide everything you need." Emily hoped that was true. "This is the child." She handed him Chivy's passport with a hundred-dollar bill nestled inside. "I understand there will be expenses." Her palms were damp with fear. She was taking a considerable risk that the official might be offended. In a land where government officials received exceedingly low wages, she considered it a sort of informal taxation.

Corruption also existed in the US. It just cost a lot more. She had enough money to get what she wanted, and she was desperate enough to try. Hopefully, she would find a new job and be able to remain in Phnom Penh, but she didn't know what trouble Sonny might attempt.

The man opened the small booklet and deftly tucked the note into his breast pocket. "Excellent that the child has the passport. This should not be a difficult decision. Come back *avec toute la documentation*"—he winked and patted his chest—"and I can issue the papers. *Au revoir, madame.* Until we meet again, *je vous attends.*"

Chivy charmed everyone when she and Leap arrived for the dinner party that evening. Even Thida peeked from her backroom realm when she heard the lilting sounds of the little girl's voice. Emily wanted to get to know the child better, and spending time with her away from the harsh environment of Tuol Sleng seemed like a suitable start.

"Soksaby." Emily greeted Leap with a sampeah. "Hello to you, too!" She leaned down to the girl. "Please come in. Yvette and Nick are waiting."

Chivy gazed around the apartment with an open mouth as Leap took off his slippers. Emily led them to the garden, where they settled at the dining table, which had been moved from inside. In case of rain, a piece of waterproof cloth had been draped overhead. Mosquito coils made a woody fragrance.

"Sit next to me," Emily told Chivy as Chan brought out a tray with sparkling wine for the adults and a Coca-Cola for the little girl.

Blushing from the attention, she whispered, "*Sank* you."

"I am teaching her English," Leap said with pride. "The language of business and the future."

"Well, I might argue with you, *monsieur!*" laughed Yvette. "*Le français* is the language of love and diplomacy."

"But it's true, Yvette," said Nick as he filled everyone's glasses. "Everyone will speak English or Mandarin Chinese by the end of the next century."

"I'll be too old by then to care. Now pass me some of that wine, *s'il te plaît!*" Yvette grumbled.

Bored with the banter, Chivy slipped down from her perch to explore. "Would you like to look inside?" Emily asked.

She nodded and then glanced at Leap. "You may go with Madame Emily if you like."

Emily took the girl's hand and guided her into the main room. "What would you like to see first?"

Chivy stood with her nose pressed against the cabinet, putting one of her curls into her mouth in an unthinking gesture that touched Emily's heart, as she recognized her own nervous habit as a child. Chivy noticed the pastoral picture leaning against the wall and let out a small "ah." She brushed the surface with her fingertips then rushed outside to Leap, chattering in Khmer.

"The only painting she's ever seen is the portrait of her grandmother," Leap explained. "She wants to know if this is Milijana's home in heaven."

Chan surprised everyone and served a delicious meal of *samlor korkor* soup, made from catfish and pork belly and flavored with fragrant *prahok* fish paste. After eating, they continued the conversation with cigarettes and drinks of brandy and soda. Emily was quiet, observing the child's animated face turn from one speaker to the next as she tried to follow along.

They speculated about the election results, agreeing that the coalition government would take time to get established. Ultimately, all that mattered was peace. Nick asked Leap about his life, in a more deferential tone than he'd used in his previous questioning. Cautiously at first and then more freely, Leap talked about his remarkable past.

When Nick offered to write his life story, Leap said, "Perhaps one day. There are many important stories in Cambodia. But for now, we must go home. The night is late for us both. Say good night, Granddaughter."

Chivy put her hands together. "Good nigh'." Moving closer to Emily, she softly stroked her curly blond hair. *"Sak sa-at nasa."*

"Yes, child. Beautiful hair," Leap murmured.

CHAPTER SIXTY-SEVEN

SONNY 1993

Sonny spent the nighttime hours taking his weapon apart and reassembling it. He learned everything about the M9 short recoil, semiautomatic pistol. It weighed only 33.3 ounces, and the 4.9-inch barrel was small enough to keep with him always. He ran his fingertips over the crosshatch design of the black polymer surface, clicking the safety on and off.

In a rare, exhausted moment of sleep, he dreamt of his wife. She sat at the end of his bed, intact and lovely. "Lisa," he wept. "I miss you so much." But her scalp came away with a horrible sucking sound and slipped down the side of her head, leaving a red smear. Her lap filled with hair, overflowing into a tsunami of glinting, suffocating gold. He struggled, attempting to wake from the horror, but the dream clutched him tight to the bed. Lisa morphed into Emily, whose legless body balanced beside him on the pillow.

"I told you, but you didn't listen," Emily's ghastly vision mocked through bloody lips. "You were never going to change anything. You're pitiful."

Sonny skittered away to the other side of the bed, unsure if he was still dreaming. He pulled the Beretta from under his pillow and woke up to yellow sunlight burning his naked body.

He had been to the Department of Immigration, but they didn't care when he told them the American no longer worked for SAF. They agreed that her visa was invalid unless she found a new sponsor, but no one was doing anything about deporting her. He followed her as she went to the embassy, the ministries, and the doctors, amassing the documents that would let her steal the Khmer child.

His rage narrowed into focus. He dragged the old French mirror up to his bedroom and stood before it for long minutes, hand gripping the gun, arm out straight, pointing at his image, until he quivered from the strain. He lined up fifteen bullets on his bed, counting them repeatedly like a mantra.

But he would only need one.

CHAPTER SIXTY-EIGHT

EMILY 1993

It was happening! Emily had most of the forms necessary to take Chivy with her to America. She'd decided to handle the official adoption in the States; American citizenship would make things easier. Emily could then decide if she wanted to return immediately to Cambodia or go, with her daughter, to someplace new.

Chivy stayed with Leap as they made their plans. But a week after the dinner party, the child stood outside their gate, drenched and crying. A cyclo-driver friend of Leap hovered nearby. Through her sobs, the little girl explained to Yvette that her grandfather had collapsed. The friend had taken him to the hospital, but the doctor said Leap wouldn't leave alive. Would Madame M-lee and Yvette please help?

Emily wrapped the child in a towel and swept her into her arms. "Of course, sweetheart. Let's dry you off and we'll go talk to this doctor."

Leap lingered for five more days. The twining cancer strangled his lungs and made breathing difficult. He shared the ward with ten other dying men, his mosquito-covered iron cot pushed against a far wall. Family members of the other patients came and went, bringing food and lively voices, but he shunned them, preferring to be alone except for his granddaughter.

Emily and Chivy visited him every day, talking and sharing dreams for the future. In the beginning, the child said she wanted to be a famous singer like Ros Serey Sothea, but now she aspired to be a doctor. Leap shrank before their eyes, becoming as small and transparent as a ghost. He refused medication, only holding his granddaughter's hand and murmuring that that was enough.

On the evening of his final day, soft shadows swirled around his bed in the fading light. He gestured for Emily to come close and rasped into her ear, "Thank you."

"Of course, Leap," Emily said, swallowing her tears. "I will love her."

The old man's face brightened as he gazed at something just beyond her shoulder. There was a shift, like a shimmer of air. The fragrance of blossoming plum trees suffused the room. Speaking to the shadow, he said, "I kept my word, didn't I?" Then he lifted his arm as if to take someone's hand. He smiled as his heart slowed and stopped.

Emily held Chivy tightly.

Arun brought a monk to chant and pray over Leap's body, explaining it would help calm his soul during the transition from life to death and keep away any bad spirits that might impede his journey.

The funeral took place on the third day after his death at the Buddhist temple near his house. The monk who'd collected Leap's cremated remains gave Chivy a small bit of bone strung on a delicate silver chain. She squeezed it in her hand, uncertain what to do.

"Let me help you with that," said Emily, slipping the necklace over the child's head and giving her a kiss. "Now your *ta* Leap will always be near."

In the following days, life filled with promise. Emily smiled in the bathroom mirror at her healthy-looking, tanned face. Airplane tickets and passports felt like portals to a new life. She was confident that returning home to Montana wasn't failing, but a means to her own self-chosen luck. Her parents were delighted when she spoke to them over the phone about Chivy. They would accept anything so long as it provided their daughter with a ladder up and out of hopelessness.

Past sorrows lost their sharp edges but still remained. One night, Chivy came into her bed, tearful and missing her grandfather.

"Don't cry," Emily whispered, stroking Chivy's butterscotch hair. "You'll like where we're going; there are golden hills, like gentle lions to protect us." She told her about her new grandparents, Rose and Jack, who knew the risks one took for love. And about *Baka* Milijana, who would have loved her granddaughter like breath itself. Emily promised to take Chivy to Belgrade one day, to visit her yeay's birthplace. The child understood little from her words, but she fell asleep, soothed by Emily's love.

CHAPTER SIXTY-NINE

SONNY 1993

Sonny was prepared and waiting.

He'd spent the long night in an abandoned hut in the field next to the American's house. He sat cross-legged on a narrow scrap of tarp, keeping his head low so no one would see him. He wondered who lived in the dilapidated structure and why a Buddha figure still remained in the corner.

When they'd first arrived in America, his mother had encouraged him to continue with their traditional Buddhist practices, but the secular atmosphere of Long Beach, California, was too persuasive. Cambodian gang members who'd brought the civil war with them jockeyed among themselves for what small bit of power the Americans would allow them. The mall eventually replaced the pagoda as the family strove to assimilate into the alien culture. His mother and sister easily embraced the new religion of consumerism. Sonny learned to hate both the past and the present, equally.

At dawn, Sonny heard the watchman unlock the gate.

CHAPTER SEVENTY

EMILY 1993

Emily, Chivy, Nick, and Yvette ate fresh papaya with their croissants and café au lait. The early-morning sky glowed deep blue, reminding Emily of Montana. Nick had stayed the night, wanting to spend as much time together as possible before her upcoming departure. *Less than one week,* she thought, looking across the table at his still-sleepy face. She would miss more than his T-shirts. He scraped a bit of the bright-orange fruit with a spoon, carefully coated it in lime juice, and slid it onto his tongue. Her belly warmed, thinking of that tongue. She had such conflicting emotions about leaving him. She knew there was no future for her in following him into the jungle as he searched for interviews with the devil, but . . . She beamed when he met her gaze.

Chivy finished her breakfast and left to join Chan in the kitchen. Yvette's eyes were glassy as she watched the little girl. "I will miss you terribly. *Tous les deux.*"

"I don't know how long the adoption process in the US will take." Emily dipped her pastry in her coffee bowl. "But we'll come back when we can. The world is really not that big. You could visit us at Christmas, and I'll find you a cute cowboy to play with."

Nick snorted. "Johnny wouldn't like that."

"*Madame, Arun est là,*" Chan announced.

Emily had to deliver one more document to the embassy and close her bank account before leaving. "Are you sure you don't want me to drive you?" Nick asked as she leaned down to kiss him.

"No, thanks. I don't know how long I'll have to be at the embassy."

Arun waited with his motorbike just outside the gate, wearing a brand-new canvas jacket that matched his ever-present hat. As she walked out the door, Emily noticed he wasn't looking toward her, but at something down the lane behind the wall. He scowled as he put up his hand to fend something off. Emily still couldn't see what or whom he faced.

"*Chhoup! Khnom choull!*" he shouted.

Emily heard a loud pop and a red flower blossomed on Arun's new coat as he dropped to the ground. An instant later, a second crack reverberated. The watchman also fell into the dust.

Stunned, Emily was paralyzed, uncertain where to flee. Into the house? Where was Chivy? Sonny appeared around the wall, his face a rictus of hatred. He stopped before her, panting, his once-handsome face shining with sweat and tears.

"Sonny! What are you doing?"

"It's too late." He pointed the handgun at the ground. "I have failed. The poison is too deep."

"What poison?" she cried.

Nick and Yvette rushed to the doorway. The scene froze, a moment trapped forever.

"*Chhob pleam!*" Thida suddenly charged from the back, planting herself only a foot before him. "*Mahnous kamsaki!*" she hissed as she tried to wrench the gun from his hand.

Sonny lifted the handgun up to the sky, his eyes searching. His expression fell like melting wax when his gaze landed on Emily. "Yes," he wept, "I may be a coward. But this is your fault and you must bear witness."

He shoved the Beretta into his mouth and pulled the trigger. The loud noise reverberated and then stilled to a ghastly silence.

Nick jumped into motion, pushing Emily aside and kicking the pistol away from where it had fallen. It was obvious Sonny was dead, his head shattered. Emily stared beyond Sonny's body to Arun, lying in his own blood as his life drained into the ground.

"Help him!" she sobbed. But it was too late. Arun would wait for her no more. She knelt by his body and whispered, "Are you with your family in the garden, my friend?"

"*Très mauvais!* Very bad!" Thida snarled, coming to grab Arun by the ankles. "Nick, *aidez-moi avec les corps!*"

"What are you doing?"

Nick and Thida exchanged a look. "Emily, we have to bring the bodies inside the compound. We want to keep the authorities away as long as possible."

"Why?"

"Sweetheart, think about it. This is a mass-casualty crime event. And you're at the center of it. Sonny accused you of trafficking and now he's dead. They might think you shot him. You'll be detained and questioned for weeks."

Emily sank to the ground. "Why did he do this?"

Yvette took hold of the watchman's arms and began to tug. *"Putain de merde,"* she huffed. The man's body left a thick smear in the dirt.

After all the dead were hidden inside the walls, Thida marched out to the street to scare away nosy neighbors with her ferocious will. She pulled the gate closed with a crash. *"La police viendra bientôt.* Police come soon. M-lee, you go now!"

"She's right, Emily," Nick said. "You and Chivy need to leave today, this moment. There's a plane this afternoon."

"I don't understand. Sonny did the shooting." Emily's mind was numb with shock and she couldn't wrap her head around what had happened. "Why do we have to leave?"

Nick looked to Yvette. "Will they take Chivy if she stays?"

"Yes," said Yvette as she wiped her hands on her kimono, leaving a crimson stain. "I think you're right, Nick. They must leave now."

Nick strode over to Emily and pulled her up to standing. "Put a few things together, only what will fit in one bag. And all your documents."

Chivy slipped out from behind Chan's legs, where she'd been crouching. "M-lee?" she whimpered.

As she held Chivy in a tight hug, Emily's brain kicked into gear. The fog dissipated. "Okay," she said. "We'll go." Lifting up the small girl's tear-streaked face, Emily said, "Come help me pack."

CHAPTER SEVENTY-ONE
EMILY 1993

Nick swerved into the loading zone, almost ramming a Toyota sedan in his haste. Pochentong airport swarmed with curious onlookers and travelers—unchanged since Emily's arrival less than a few months ago. With the jeep still running, Nick leaped out to grab their luggage. "I'll park and come find you," he said. "Don't worry, it will be okay."

Emily twisted her head in every direction. "I hope so." She hoisted her bulging backpack across her shoulders, then picked up her case in one hand and the bag with the portrait in the other. The Air France flight to Bangkok was departing soon. "Come on, Chivy, let's hurry!"

They snaked their way through the crowded hall, straight toward immigration. An officer in a crisp white cotton uniform stood waiting.

"*Vos passeports?*" she demanded, her thick orange lipstick unsmiling. Emily unzipped her purse and pulled out two passports—one dark blue and the other iron red. The woman snatched them from her hand. Emily's prosthetic had shifted in their rush and was making a huge blister, but it didn't matter. They had to make that airplane. It had taken too long to reach the airline and change their tickets, and now they were very late. Emily was having difficulty catching her breath.

Still the woman dawdled, deliberately examining each page. Sweat ran in rivulets down Emily's sides in the sweltering heat. Chivy pushed against her legs, still trembling. Time was ticking away like a bomb as Emily remembered the gunshots and the slow-motion way Arun's body had fallen to the earth.

"Do you speak English, madame?" Emily asked the woman. "Our flight is boarding soon, and I'm worried we will miss it."

"*Vous venez tous les deux avec moi,*" the official said, retaining the passports.

Emily panted with anxiety. Would they be detained? Would they take Chivy? She followed the woman into a stifling cubicle where a senior official sat at a desk piled high with paper. She had known their visas would be closely examined, but not to this extent. She prayed that the American visa in Chivy's passport would be enough. In their haste, she'd been unable to find one of the many documents issued by the Ministry of Culture.

"Sit," the man said, motioning toward a bench against the grimy wall. "Why do you have this Khmer child?"

"I'm her guardian, sir. I will finalize her adoption after I return to the United States. I have papers explaining this from the Cambodian minister himself as well as the US ambassador." She pulled out the hastily assembled folder proving Chivy could leave Cambodia with Emily and put it, along with their newly re-issued plane tickets, on the cluttered desk.

With a sigh, the man removed his glasses and wiped them with a limp handkerchief. Picking up the folder, he began to peruse the pages. Their flight was announced as the man held each paper up to his nose to read. Screaming at the man would only make things worse. She trembled with the effort to control her temper. From the corner of her eye, Emily was aware of the other agent, who was stamping passports as she stole glances their way. With every passing second, Emily expected the police to arrive and arrest her. The final call boomed overhead. They were going to miss the plane.

Chivy pulled at Emily's shirt as Nick loomed above the orange-lipped agent. "*Saumtoh,*" he said. "Excuse me, but my friend and her daughter are late!" His voice commanded authority as he walked past the surprised woman into the cubical. His words were polite, but his intention was not. The air around him quivered. "What is the delay?"

The officer glanced up through his glasses, shrinking under Nick's presence. He squinted from Emily to the little girl and back down to the pile of documents. Barangs were always too much trouble. He stamped each passport with a vicious thud. "*Pas de problem, monsieur. Pas de problem. Allez-vous!*" The female officer planted her hands on her hips, glaring at her boss.

Nick grabbed the luggage. "Come on, the cops are here," he whispered. Trailing in his slipstream and clutching the bag with Milijana's portrait, Emily and Chivy ran to keep up. Emily noticed two uniformed police officers silhouetted in the entryway, the crowd flowing around them like rocks in a stream. As they stood in line for customs, Emily gripped Chivy's shoulder so hard the girl cringed.

"I know this guy!" said Nick jubilantly as they reached the counter. With a ferocious grin, Nick seized the startled man's hand and palmed him a hundred-dollar bill. The man peered at the money in his hand and then up at Nick. Emily was certain he would raise the alarm. One of the policemen had stopped a Western woman nearby and was demanding to see her passport.

With a sly nod, the customs official allowed them to pass directly to the Air France agent, who ignored Nick's lack of a ticket.

Bursting through the door, they ran out of the building and stood on the hot tarmac at the base of the plane's aluminum stairs. Emily slumped against Nick in relief. He bent down to Chivy and drew a hand-sewn doll with light-brown skin and yellow yarn hair out of his pants' cargo pocket. "Be a good girl, for M-lee. And for you, mademoiselle," he said to Emily, "I'm afraid I only have this." He held her in a deep embrace. "Come back to me," he growled. "I'll be waiting."

From the top of the narrow stair, she watched as the blackness of the terminal doorway swallowed him whole.

Emily began to breathe again when the airplane took off. Chivy sat mesmerized by the streaming clouds outside the window. How appropriate that *Chivy* meant "life" in Khmer. The air-conditioned cabin was chilly, so Emily tugged a thin blanket out of its plastic wrapper. She would miss the tropical warmth. Tears filled her eyes.

"M-lee, okay?"

"Yes, M-lee is better than okay."

"*Meng* Yvette come America?"

During the chaos of those last hours, Yvette had assured Emily that she and Nick would be fine. Emily wasn't abandoning them to deal with the aftermath alone. Thida had revealed that Prime Minister Hun Sen was a close friend and could make the debacle vanish. They pondered Thida's ability to take charge, speculating about her possible past. Nick had held

Emily as she wept for all the dead—the watchman, Leap, Arun, Milijana, and tragic Sonny, who had been so broken.

Emily reached to give the little girl a brief hug. "One day, sweetie." The meal service was starting. "Chivy *khlean bai?* Are you hungry?"

With a nod, the child clasped Nick's doll to her heart.

The final evening alone with Nick at his apartment, her face had rested against his shoulder. They hadn't known it would be their final night, but they made love like it was. As she stroked the small blue tattoos under his arm, she had asked, "Will you finally please tell me what it means?" In the past, he'd always changed the subject, superstitious of saying the words aloud.

"The truth? It's a little embarrassing."

"Of course."

"'If I'm dead, call my mother.'"

The attendant reached down to help with the tray tables. "Oh, my, what a pretty little girl! I would kill for those eyelashes," she said. "Is she a . . . relative?" She peered from Chivy to Emily.

"She's my daughter."

Emily looked out the porthole window. She could just discern the ruffled ocean below. She visualized the gracious boulevards and flowering trees of Phnom Penh. People bustling about, leading their lives, surviving, and rebuilding hope and life after so many years of trauma.

She imagined Yvette and Johnny tumbled together in the musty armchair. Sam and his friends stood at restaurants, relying on the pity of strangers. Tour guide Debbie touched up her makeup as she waited to show off the prurient horrors of Tuol Sleng. Botum and her new husband, Chea, expanded the circle of their love, pebbles dropped in the pond of forgiveness. And, healthy again, Leap tended his vegetables, a blond ghost by his side.

Emily hoped that such violent death wouldn't make hungry ghosts of Arun and Sonny. *Not again. Not again,* she heard Sonny saying to himself as Arun followed. She understood that Sonny considered himself a hero, fighting the effects of spoiled imperialism, gone putrid like rotten meat. But he was no better than those who came before him, unleashing their archaic savagery, destroying themselves in the process. What new future could grow out of such bloody soil? Would it only repeat?

She hoped not.

After dinner, somewhere over the immense Pacific, Emily fell into a deep and peaceful sleep. She dreamed of motorbikes scattering for shelter as the monsoon rain began to pound. Except one.

A single moto driver with a drenched, floppy white hat. Still waiting.

CHIVY 1997

I try to write something in my notebook every day. I was only a little girl when we left Cambodia. Now I'm almost ten and in the fourth grade at Paxon Elementary. Montana is called the Big Sky Country because of the wide-open spaces. I remember Cambodia as a big sky country, too. Especially in the cool season, when heaven is bright blue and puffy white clouds stack up into forever.

Mama M-lee helped me pack my suitcase carefully, with *Yeay* Milijana's painting wrapped in paper and protected with all my dresses and T-shirts stuffed around to keep her safe. We're moving back to live in Phnom Penh! M-lee got a job working at a nongovernmental agency, whatever that is, and my grandmother's portrait will be displayed in the museum where anyone who wants can look at her and read her notebooks. We get to see *Ta* Leap's other paintings, too.

I'm nervous about leaving my best friend Patricia, Grandpa Jack, and Grandma Rose, but I'm super excited to be going back to my REAL home. I don't remember a lot, but M-lee says I will when I start to taste the food and feel the humidity. *Meng* Yvette will come to visit us from Paris and *Mea* Nick will hop over from Bangkok. I have to stop writing now, cause we're about to leave!!!

☒ ☒ ☒

Wow! I have so much to write about! I LOVE Phnom Penh! It's crazy and busy and people are everywhere but it's good in a different way than our home in Montana. I like that it smells sweet and bad at the same time. M-lee says I'll go to an international school with kids from all over the world. We might even rent a house with a pool, but she says I shouldn't hold my breath. Ha ha.

I didn't know that I was an actual princess! I met the king of Cambodia, Norodom Sihanouk, yesterday when they put *Ta* Leap's picture in Tuol Sleng. He's a cousin of my *ta* Rainsey, Milijana's husband. I have more grandparents than anyone else I know. The king is short and super old and he gave me a gold pin with rubies and pearls that M-lee says is very valuable, so I can't wear it every day, only on special occasions. I'll keep it in the silver box where I keep *Ta* Leap's chain.

The party was weird. I sort of remember the museum. I can't believe that I used to live across the street from that place. Lots of people died there and I'm sure it's haunted. They hung the portrait in a room with other paintings of really horrible stuff. M-lee made me keep my eyes closed as we walked by some of them. The king gave a long speech and then people stood around. Some were crying.

It felt bad to leave my yeay Milijana alone in that scary place, but M-lee explained that the painting and her confession are important to help people understand what happened in Cambodia. Not just the terrible stuff about the stupid Khmer Rouge, but also about how—no matter what—love survives.

M-lee says she'll start reading me the notebooks soon.

She says I'm almost ready.

ACKNOWLEDGMENTS

Writing a novel is like finding your way in an unfamiliar city at night without a map or knowing how to speak the language. I want to acknowledge Thant Myint-U, who first invited me to Cambodia, and John Badgley, who took a risk and hired me to take over the Cornell University project at Tuol Sleng Museum of Genocide. I'm deeply grateful to my critique partners and writing group friends who hold me accountable each week and encourage me to work harder: Catherine, James, and Sarah. And, of course, Jillian, Carrie, and Melissa. Thank you to my respected beta readers: Meg and Sonia. Special mention goes to Sreymom Serey, who double-checked my Cambodian translations and cultural practices, and to the amazing Nicole Karidis, who taught me that putting on a prosthetic can be like pulling on a boot. Hugo House and the Women's Fiction Writers Association have been marvelous resources.

In addition to my personal experience living and working in Cambodia, I drew on the academic work of fine scholars and journalists such as Elizabeth Becker, Nate Thayer, David Chandler, William Shawcross, and François Bizot, as well as the incomparable memoir and fiction of Raddy Vatner, Haing Ngor, Chanrithy Him, Laurence Picq, and Christopher Koch. Thank you. Arkoun chraen. អរគុណច្រើន.

ABOUT THE AUTHOR

© 2021 Carlos Cruz

Author Lya Badgley was born and spent much of her childhood in Southeast Asia. She moved to the Pacific Northwest in the eighties, where she became a part of the Seattle arts and music scene. In the nineties, she returned to Asia, where she opened a restaurant in Myanmar, interviewed insurgents for Human Rights Watch, and microfilmed documents at the Tuol Sleng Museum of Genocide in Cambodia, helping to bring war criminals to justice.

She is fascinated by the culture and customs of the region, which has been a huge inspiration for her writing. Tense war zones and insurgencies form an intense backdrop in many of her stories. Political and social upheaval vividly mirror the personal and sometimes violent transformations of her strong female protagonists.

Badgley lives in Snohomish, Washington, with her Serbian husband.

 lyabadgleyauthor

lyabadgleyauthor

www.lyabadgley.com